BEST SF: 1974

BEST SF
1974

Harry Harrison
and
Brian W. Aldiss

The Bobbs-Merrill Company, Inc.
INDIANAPOLIS/NEW YORK

Published by the Bobbs-Merrill Company, Inc.
Indianapolis/New York

ISBN 0-672-52012-5
Library of Congress catalog card number 74-116158
Designed by Irving Perkins
Manufactured in the United States of America

SECOND PRINTING

ACKNOWLEDGMENTS

"After King Kong Fell," by Philip José Farmer, copyright © 1974 by Roger Elwood; reprinted by permission of the author and his agents, Scott Meredith Literary Agency, Inc. First published in *Omega*.

"When Petals Fall," by Sydney J. Van Scyoc, copyright © 1973 by Thomas N. Scortia and Chelsea Quinn Yarbro; reprinted by permission of the author and Centaur Literary Agency. First published in *Two Views of Wonder*.

"Paleontology: An Experimental Science," by Robert R. Olsen, copyright © 1974 by the Condé Nast Publications, Inc.; reprinted by permission of the author. First published in *Analog Science Fiction/Science Fact*.

"The Women Men Don't See," by James Tiptree, Jr., copyright © 1974 by Mercury Publications, Inc.; reprinted by permission of the author and his agent, Robert P. Mills, Ltd. First published in *Fantasy and Science Fiction*.

"Listen with Big Brother," by Brian W. Aldiss, copyright © 1974 by Brian W. Aldiss; reprinted by permission of the author. First published in *Punch*.

"The Rise of Airstrip One," by Clive James, copyright © 1974 by Clive James; reprinted by permission of the author. First published in *Punch*.

"Owing to Circumstances Beyond Our Control 1984 Has Been Unavoidably Detained. . . ." by Alan Coren; reprinted by permission of *Punch*. First published in *Punch*.

"Lost and Found," by Thomas Baum, copyright © 1974 by Thomas Baum; reprinted by permission of the author. First published in *Playboy*.

"The Four-Hour Fugue," by Alfred Bester, copyright © 1974 by the Condé Nast Publications, Inc.; reprinted by permission of the author and his agent, Lurton Blassingame. First published in *Analog Science Fiction/Science Fact*.

"The Scream," by Kate Wilhelm, copyright © 1974 by Damon Knight; reprinted by permission of the author. First published in *Orbit 13*.

"The Gahan Wilson Horror Movie Pocket Computer," by Gahan Wilson, copyright © 1974 by National Lampoon, Inc.; reprinted by permission of the author. First published in *National Lampoon*.

"The Executioner's Beautiful Daughter," by Angela Carter, copyright © 1974 by Angela Carter; reprinted by permission of the author and Quartet Books, Ltd. First published in *Fireworks*.

"After Weightlessness," and "A Picture by Klee," by Lawrence Sail, copyright © 1974 by Lawrence Sail; reprinted by permission of J. M. Dent & Sons. First published in *Opposite Views*.

"Backward, into Beasts Evolving," from "The Space Sonnets" by Dick Allen, copyright © 1974 by Counter/Measures; reprinted by permission of the author. First published in *Counter/Measures.*

"Science Fiction Story," by Duane Ackerson, copyright © 1974 by *SF Directions* and The Edge Press; reprinted by permission of the author. First published in *SF Directions.*

"DNA," by Duane Ackerson, copyright © 1974 by Dragonfly Press; reprinted by permission of the author. First published in *Rocket Candy.*

"Eyes of a Woman—From a Portrait by Picasso," by Lisa Conesa, copyright © 1973 by Lisa Conesa; reprinted by permission of the author. First published in *Zimri.*

"Songs of War," by Kit Reed, copyright © 1974 by Kit Reed; reprinted by permission of Brandt & Brandt. First published in *Nova 4.*

"Time Deer," by Craig Strete, copyright © 1974 by Universal Publishing Corp.; reprinted by permission of the author. First published in *Red Planet Earth* and *Worlds of If.*

"A Typical Day," by Doris Piserchia, copyright © 1974 by Universal Publishing and Distributing Corp.; reprinted by permission of the author. First published in *Galaxy.*

"Programmed Love Story," by Ian Watson, copyright © 1974 by the *Transatlantic Review*; reprinted by permission of the author. First published in *Transatlantic Review.*

Contents

BEST SF: 1974

Editorial

I T *has* been an interesting year for science fiction. Both at home and abroad. Speaking selfishly—that is, from the point of view of the editor of this annual anthology—there have been riches galore. In past years, despite the efforts of the writers and the editors of both magazines and original anthologies, I have always approached November with a feeling of quiet desperation. By that recurring point in time I would have read ninety percent of all of the short science fiction to be published in the given year. And I would, usually, have far less than ninety percent of this anthology completed. Each year I would have the depressed feeling that the science-fiction writers and/or editors had let me down. Why did I not have an overflowing file of masterful stories that would make me suffer and sweat in order to decide just which were the absolute best of the year? Why did I have to make my annual slog through the non-SF magazines, the college and literary magazines, the heretofore best-left-unread sources? Why did I have to make poor Brian Aldiss bend under the lash and read all of the latest issues of *The Serbo-Croatian Science Fiction Bazaar*? Why was I forced to chain Bruce McAllister to his desk to be sure he read every copy of *Southwest Rotarian Monthly* and *Proceedings of the Junior English Department of Biloxi University*? I did this only because you cannot publish a book with blank pages. Every year, as the calendar rolled inexorably toward January, we have found good stories, sound stories, the best stories written in this particular field of literary endeavor, and have assembled them into this anthology. Victory achieved, but always at a price.

Therefore I am most pleased to report that this has been a year of luxuries. Good stories, fine stories, have been pouring in from all sides. So much so that I have had the painful decision to make, always at the last minute of course, as to which of two stories deserves anthologizing, both of them excellent in their own right. If this goes on we must perhaps install a runners-up department, or a list of the best of the stories that could not be squeezed in, the sort of department Judith Merrill used to have when she did her *The Year's Best SF* anthology many, many years ago. Those were richer days and perhaps the richness is returning.

One unexpected richesse this year was the absolute triumph of the ladies. By chance, coincidence or karma, the first five stories obtained for this anthology were written by women. How far we have come from the dear, dead days of ur-SF when Kingsley Amis could comment, truthfully, that "science fiction is written by Americans and Britons, not by women and foreigners." Seeing that the first five across the finish line were fillies, I did hope that the year might continue this way. But the stallions did come through as well. However, I must give a hearty welcome to the ladies. Many, including my wife, accuse me of being a male-chauvinist swine at times. I suppose I am, he sighed, but I really do appreciate the individual approach and clarity of vision that women bring to SF, and I welcome their works—if not them in person—with open arms.

In addition to good short stories, this has been the year of exceptional novels as well. In his iconoclastic and individualistic summing up of the year in SF, Brian Aldiss has seen fit to dwell upon the novel and the novel alone. There was good reason for this as you will see when you read his afterword. How pleasant it is to say nice things about something in these days of inflation, shortages, and murderous hatreds.

Another high point of the year was the founding of a new science-fiction magazine, this one in Britain. *Science Fiction Monthly* leans lovingly and beautifully toward the visual aspects of science fiction, reproducing in delicious four-color tabloid size some singularly attractive SF art work. (Their fiction is something else again—you won't find any of it here—but much can be forgiven for the visual joys they are bringing us.) That this artistic superiority was recognized by the readers was evidenced by their sales. The earlier editions sold 100,000 copies each. Only outside factors such as the paper and printing shortages laid these mighty sales figures low, forcing the publisher to print far less than he had been selling. We can only wish this magazine the best of British luck, followed by the humble plea that some editorial attempt should be made to improve the quality of the fiction.

In the international scene SF booms on like a mighty barrage of cannon. Every European country now has its own SF publishers—not to mention its own SF fandom. At a convention in Birmingham, England, I met SF fans from Germany, Italy, Holland, Belgium, France, Spain, and Hungary, just to mention a few. All of them are involved with fannish activities, some of them putting on SF conventions in their own lands. I am proud to report that Brian Aldiss and I are charter subscribers to the first SF magazine to be published in Turkey, *Antares*. Not that I can read a word of Turkish, but the editor, Sezar Ergin, is kind enough to print editorials and correspondence in English. He is also introducing a Turkish term for science fiction, for the good reason that Turks find "science fiction" too foreign and hard to pronounce. The term, in case you are planning a visit to Turkey and wish to make the right kind of friends instantly, is *bilim kurgu*.

But it is the stories you want to read and I should not keep you from them any longer than necessary. Silencing myself early permits the unfilled space to be used by our managing editor, Bruce McAllister. He is most knowing about the ever-stronger connections being forged between academia and science fiction, so he can give us an illustration of the forces of Good and Evil at work this past year.

HARRY HARRISON

IT has finally happened. Just as it happened to Homer, Chaucer, Melville, and Hemingway, it has at last happened to science fiction: the field has been immortalized in the pages of Cliff Notes (*Science Fiction: An Introduction,* by L. David Allen, M.A., $1.95).

Cliff Notes? Do we need a painful reminder? With Monarch Notes, Cliff Notes are those saviors of many a high school or college undergrad career—those skeletonized instruments clutched at by students who, on the eve of final exams or term-paper deadlines, find themselves without handles on *Oedipus Rex, Romeo and Juliet, War and Peace,* and now—by God—the entire science-fiction field.

The fanfare obviously contains a Bronx cheer or two. Do we really need Cliff Notes? Cliff Notes certainly need us. Nowhere else in the world is education the industry, the business, that it is in the United States. By now there are at least 1,000 science-fiction courses taught at the college and university level (not to mention the mushrooming numbers at high schools). And 1,000 × 30 (i.e., students per class) = 30,000 buyers . . . not a market to be ignored. In jubilant response, the textbook industry has in the past two years spawned nearly 100 SF or fantasy or SF-and-fantasy or "speculative fiction" textbook-anthologies in the hope of hooking the market. The arrival of the Cliff Notes SF edition was inevitable; business, when it spots a mark, is always inevitable.

I don't usually bitch at length about inevitabilities. What is disturbing in this instance is our field's open-arm acceptance of the Cliff Notes' arrival. In the spine-chilling words of one of our leading SF writers and magazine–book reviewers, "This is the first academic work meant to explain our field which I can genuinely applaud." And one of our finest SF teachers (as well as award-winning writers) has even approved the slim Cliff Notes volume in the public pages of *Analog*. The chill can best be shared by a brief look at the species of thinking that permeates the Cliff Notes' treatment of SF: "*Rite of Passage* by Alexei Panshin seems to be largely Extrapolative Soft Science Fiction, since it takes known social institutions, governmental organizations and psychological patterns and projects them into an unusual situation. It would, however, be placed somewhat down the axis toward Speculative Hard Science Fiction, because the spaceship, the scout ships, the space suits and the faster-than-light travel are basic to the story." *Axis?* What axis? And of course space suits and FTL travel are basic to the story—to *any* SF story that happens to use them. But Speculative-Extrapolative-Soft-Hard-Science-Fact-Fiction? Does the SF field really need such simplistic, reductionistic, easy-graph, and category-wielding analyses as these—especially when such analyses will be snatched up by the masses of Cliff Notes–consuming students and substituted for a *real* reading of SF—a personal, individual, reflective, soul-osterizing, continuous *reading* of SF . . . ? (Let's be honest. We all know what Cliff Notes are used for in the Real Non-Speculative Student World. Answer: last-minute cramming, short-cut digestion.)

Do we need pablum literary criticism when we are just now beginning to hear from Academe the voices of bright, talented SF scholars who will *not* talk down to their audiences, who will be as rigorous and respectful in their SF scholarship as they are in their works on Melville and Fitzgerald, and who are not afraid to be committed—cerebrum and soul—to the SF field? The flattering army of scholars with eyes and ears on SF is at last large enough that we can see two visible groups—the Top Scholars, and the Many Others. And the Top Scholars are all producing major scholarly works on SF. At last. Weren't we a little afraid it would never happen . . . ?

No, we don't need Cliff Notes. . . . Even though they'll *always* need us. . . .

BRUCE MCALLISTER

After King Kong Fell

PHILIP JOSÉ FARMER

What a drab world this would be without Phil Farmer!
Little joys of memory pop up when we see his name,
items such as the ship that did fall off the edge of the
world in "Sail On! Sail On!" or the extremely interesting
sexual relationships in "The Lovers," not to mention the
chilling vision of the entire world losing its memory in
"Sketches Among the Ruins of My Mind." He has done
it again, here, telling us finally what really happened to
King Kong.

THE first half of the movie was grim and gray and somewhat tedious. Mr. Howller did not mind. That was, after all, realism. Those times had been grim and gray. Moreover, behind the tediousness was the promise of something vast and horrifying. The creeping pace and the measured ritualistic movements of the actors gave intimations of the workings of the gods. Unhurriedly, but with utmost confidence, the gods were directing events toward the climax.

Mr. Howller had felt that at the age of fifteen, and he felt it now while watching the show on TV at the age of fifty-five. Of course, when he first saw it in 1933, he had known what was coming. Hadn't he lived through some of the events only two years before that?

The old freighter, the *Wanderer*, was nosing blindly through the fog toward the surflike roar of the natives' drums. And then: the commercial. Mr. Howller rose and stepped into the hall and called down the steps loudly enough for Jill to hear him on the front porch. He thought, commercials could be a blessing. They give us time to get into the bathroom or the kitchen, or time to light up a cigarette and decide about continuing to watch this show or go on to that show.

And why couldn't real life have its commercials?

Wouldn't it be something to be grateful for if reality stopped in mid-course while the Big Salesman made His pitch? The car about to smash into you; the bullet on its way to your brain; the first cancer cell about to break loose; the boss reaching for the phone to call you in so he can fire you; the spermatozoon about to be launched toward the ovum; the final insult about to be hurled at the once, and perhaps still, beloved; the final drink of alcohol which would rupture the abused blood vessel; the decision which would lead to the light that would surely fail?

If only you could step out while the commercial interrupted these, think about it, talk about it, and then, returning to the set, switch it to another channel.

But that one is having technical difficulties, and the one after that is a talk show whose guest is the archangel Gabriel himself, and after some urging by the host he agrees to blow his trumpet, and . . .

Jill entered, sat down, and began to munch the cookies and drink the lemonade he had prepared for her. Jill was six and a half years old and beautiful, but then what granddaughter wasn't beautiful? Jill was also unhappy because she had just quarreled with her best friend, Amy, who had stalked off with threats never to see Jill again. Mr. Howller reminded her that this had happened before and that Amy had always come back the next day, if not sooner. To take her mind off Amy, Mr. Howller gave her a brief outline of what had happened in the movie. Jill listened without enthusiasm, but she became excited enough once the movie had resumed. And when Kong was feeling over the edge of the abyss for John Driscoll, played by Bruce Cabot, she got into her grandfather's lap. She gave a little scream and put her hands over her eyes when Kong carried Ann Redman into the jungle (Ann played by Fay Wray).

But by the time Kong lay dead on Fifth Avenue, she was rooting for him, as millions had before her. Mr. Howller squeezed her and kissed her and said, "When your mother was about your age, I took her to see this. And when it was over, she was crying, too."

Jill sniffled and let him dry the tears with his handkerchief. When the Roadrunner cartoon came on, she got off his lap and went back to her cookie-munching. After a while she said, "Grandpa, the coyote falls off the cliff so far you can't even see him. When he hits, the whole earth shakes. But he always comes back, good as new. Why can he fall so far and not get hurt? Why couldn't King Kong fall and be just like new?"

Her grandparents and her mother had explained many times the distinction between a "live" and a "taped" show. It did not seem to make any difference how many times they explained. Somehow, in the years of watching TV, she had gotten the fixed idea that people in "live" shows actually suffered pain, sorrow, and death. The only shows she could endure seeing were those that her elders labeled as "taped." This worried Mr. Howller more than he admitted to his wife and daughter. Jill was a very bright child, but what if too many TV shows at too early an age had done her some irreparable harm? What if, a few years from now, she could easily see, and even define, the distinction between reality and unreality on the screen, but deep down in her there was a child that still could not distinguish?

"You know that the Roadrunner is a series of pictures that move. People draw pictures, and people can do anything with pictures. So the Roadrunner is drawn again and again, and he's back in the next show with his wounds all healed, and he's ready to make a jackass of himself again."

"A jackass? But he's a coyote."

"Now . . ."

Mr. Howller stopped. Jill was grinning.

"O.K., now you're pulling my leg."

"But is King Kong alive or is he taped?"

"Taped. Like the Disney I took you to see last week. *Bedknobs and Broomsticks.*"

"Then *King Kong* didn't happen?"

"Oh, yes, it really happened. But this is a movie they made about King Kong after what really happened was all over. So it's not exactly like it really was, and actors took the parts of Ann Redman and Carl Denham and all the others. Except King Kong himself. He was a toy model."

Jill was silent for a minute and then she said, "You mean, there really *was* a King Kong? How do you know, Grandpa?"

"Because I was there in New York when Kong went on his rampage. I was in the theater when he broke loose, and I was in the crowd that gathered around Kong's body after he fell off the Empire State Building. I was thirteen then, just seven years older than you are now. I was with my parents, and they were visiting my Aunt Thea. She was beautiful, and she had golden hair just like Fay Wray's—I mean, Ann Redman's. She'd married a very rich man, and they had a big apartment high up in the clouds. In the Empire State Building itself."

"High up in the clouds! That must've been fun, Grandpa!"

It would have been, he thought, if there had not been so much tension in that apartment. Uncle Nate and Aunt Thea should have been happy because they were so rich and lived in such a swell place. But they weren't. No one said anything to young Tim Howller, but he felt the suppressed anger, heard the bite of tone, and saw the tightening lips. His aunt and uncle were having trouble of some sort, and his parents were upset by it. But they all tried to pretend everything was as sweet as honey when he was around.

Young Howller had been eager to accept the pretense. He didn't like to think that anybody could be mad at his tall, blonde, and beautiful aunt. He was passionately in love with her; he ached for her in the daytime; at night he had fantasies about her of which he was ashamed when he awoke. But not for long. She was a thousand times more desirable than Fay Wray or Claudette Colbert or Elissa Landi.

But that night, when they were all going to see the première of *The Eighth Wonder of the World,* King Kong himself, he had managed to ignore whatever it was that was bugging his elders. And even they seemed to be having a good time. Uncle Nate, over young Howller's parents' weak protests, had purchased orchestra seats for them. These were twenty dollars apiece, big money in Depression days, enough to feed a family for a month. Everybody got all dressed up, and Aunt Thea looked too beautiful to be real. Young Howller was so excited that he thought his heart was going to climb up and out through his throat. For days the newspapers had been full of stories about King Kong—speculations, rather, since Carl Denham wasn't telling them much. And he, Tim Howller, would be one of the lucky few to see the monster first.

Boy, wait until he got back to the kids in seventh grade at Busiris, Illinois! Would their eyes ever pop when he told them all about it!

But his happiness was too good to last. Aunt Thea suddenly said she had a headache and couldn't possibly go. Then she and Uncle Nate went into their bedroom, and even in the front room, three rooms and a hallway distant, young Tim could hear their voices. After a while Uncle Nate, slamming doors behind him, came out. He was red-faced and scowling, but he wasn't going to call the party off. All four of them, very uncomfortable and silent, rode in a taxi to the theater on Times Square. But when they got inside, even Uncle Nate forgot the quarrel, or at least he seemed to. There was the big stage with its towering silvery curtains, and through the curtains came a vibration of excitement and of delicious danger. And even through the curtains the hot hairy ape-stink filled the theater.

"Did King Kong get loose just like in the movie?" Jill said.

Mr. Howller started. "What? Oh, yes, he sure did. Just like in the movie."

"Were you scared, Grandpa? Did you run away like everybody else?"

He hesitated. Jill's image of her grandfather had been cast in a heroic mold. To her he was a giant of Herculean strength and perfect courage, her defender and champion. So far he had managed to live up to the image, mainly because the demands she made were not too much for him. In time she would see the cracks and the sawdust oozing out. But she was too young to disillusion now.

"No, I didn't run," he said. "I waited until the theater was cleared of the crowd."

This was true. The big man who'd been sitting in the seat before him had leaped up yelling as Kong began tearing the bars out of his cage, had whirled and jumped over the back of his seat, and had hit young Howller on the jaw with his knee. And so young Howller had been stretched out senseless on the floor under the seats while the mob screamed and tore at each other and trampled the fallen.

Later he was glad that he had been knocked out. It gave him a good excuse for not keeping cool, for not acting heroically in the situation. He knew that if he had not been unconscious, he would have been as frenzied as the others, and he would have abandoned his parents, thinking only in his terror of his own salvation. Of course, his parents had deserted him, though they claimed that they had been swept away from him by the mob. This *could* be true; maybe his folks *had* actually tried to get to him. But he had not really thought they had, and for years he had looked down on them because of their flight. When he got older, he realized that he would have done the same thing, and he knew that his contempt for them was really a disguised contempt for himself.

He had awakened with a sore jaw and a headache. The police and the ambulance men were there and starting to take care of the hurt and to haul away the dead. He staggered past them out into the lobby and, not seeing his parents there, went outside. The sidewalks and the streets were plugged with thousands of men, women, and children, on foot and in cars, fleeing northward.

He had not known where Kong was. He should have been able to figure it out, since the frantic mob was leaving the midtown part of Manhattan. But he could think of only two things. Where were his parents? And was Aunt Thea safe? And then he had a third thing to consider. He discovered that he had wet his pants. When he had seen the great ape burst loose, he had wet his pants.

Under the circumstances, he should have paid no attention to this. Certainly no one else did. But he was a very sensitive and shy boy of thirteen, and for some reason the need for getting dry underwear and trousers seemed even more important than finding his parents. In retrospect he would tell himself that he would have gone south anyway. But he knew deep down that if his pants had not been wet he might not have dared return to the Empire State Building.

It was impossible to buck the flow of the thousands moving like lava up Broadway. He went east on 43rd Street until he came to Fifth Avenue, where he started southward. There was a crowd to fight against here, too, but it was much smaller than that on Broadway. He was able to thread his way through it, though he often had to go out into the street and dodge the cars. These, fortunately, were not able to move faster than about three miles an hour.

"Many people got impatient because the cars wouldn't go faster," he told Jill, "and they just abandoned them and struck out on foot."

"Wasn't it noisy, Grandpa?"

"Noisy? I've never heard such noise. I think that everyone in Manhattan, except those hiding under their beds, was yelling or talking. And every driver in Manhattan was blowing his car's horn. And then there were the sirens of the fire trucks and police cars and ambulances. Yes, it was noisy."

Several times he tried to stop a fugitive so he could find out what was going on. But even when he did succeed in halting someone for a few seconds, he couldn't make himself heard. By then, as he found out later, the radio had broadcast the news. Kong had chased John Driscoll and Ann Redman out of the theater and across the street to their hotel. They had gone up to Driscoll's room, where they thought they were safe. But Kong had climbed up, using windows as ladder steps, reached into the room, knocked Driscoll out, grabbed Ann, and had then leaped away with her. He had headed, as Carl Denham figured he would, toward the tallest structure on the island. On King Kong's own island, he lived on the highest point, Skull Mountain, where he was truly monarch of all he surveyed. Here he would climb to the top of the Empire State Building, Manhattan's Skull Mountain.

Tim Howller had not known this, but he was able to infer that Kong had traveled down Fifth Avenue from 38th Street on. He passed a dozen cars with their tops flattened down by the ape's fist or turned over on their sides or tops. He saw three sheet-covered bodies on the sidewalks, and he overheard a policeman telling a reporter that Kong had climbed up several buildings on his way south and reached into windows and pulled people out and thrown them down onto the pavement.

"But you said King Kong was carrying Ann Redman in the crook of his arm, Grandpa," Jill said. "He only had one arm to climb with, Grandpa, so . . . so wouldn't he fall off the building when he reached in to grab those poor people?"

"A very shrewd observation, my little chickadee," Mr. Howller said, using the W. C. Fields voice that usually sent her into giggles. "But his arms were long enough for him to drape Ann Redman over the arm he used to hang on with while he reached in with the other. And to forestall your next question, even if you had not thought of it, he could turn over an automobile with only one hand."

"But . . . but why'd he take time out to do that if he wanted to get to the top of the Empire State Building?"

"I don't know why *people* often do the things they do," Mr. Howller said. "So how would I know why an *ape* does the things he does?"

When he was a block away from the Empire State Building, a plane crashed onto the middle of the avenue two blocks behind him and burned furiously. Tim Howller watched it for a few minutes, then he looked upward and saw the red and green lights of the five planes and the silvery bodies slipping in and out of the searchlights.

"Five airplanes, Grandpa? But the movie . . ."

"Yes, I know. The movie showed about fourteen or fifteen. But the book says that there were six to begin with, and the book is much more accurate. The movie also shows King Kong's last stand taking place in the daylight. But it didn't; it was still nighttime."

The Army Air Force plane must have been going at least 250 mph as it dived down toward the giant ape standing on the top of the observation tower. Kong had put Ann Redman by his feet so he could hang onto the tower with one hand and grab out with the other at the planes. One had come too close, and he had seized the left biplane structure and ripped it off. Given the energy of the plane, his hand should have been torn off, too, or at least he should have been pulled loose from his hold on the tower and gone down with the plane. But he hadn't let loose, and that told something of the enormous strength of that towering body. It also told something of the relative fragility of the biplane.

Young Howller had watched the efforts of the firemen to extinguish the fire, and then he had turned back toward the Empire State Building. By then it was all over. All over for King Kong, anyway. It was, in after years, one of Mr. Howller's greatest regrets that he had not seen the monstrous dark body falling through the beams of the searchlights—blackness, then the flash of blackness through the whiteness of the highest beam, blackness, the flash through the next beam, blackness, the flash through the third beam, blackness, the flash through the lowest beam. Dot, dash, dot, dash, Mr. Howller was to think afterward. A code transmitted unconsciously by the great ape and received unconsciously by those who witnessed the fall. Or by those who would hear of it and think about it. Or was he going too far in conceiving this? Wasn't he always looking for codes? And, when he found them, unable to decipher them?

Since he had been thirteen, he had been trying to equate the great falls in man's myths and legends and to find some sort of intelligence in them. The fall of the tower of Babel, of Lucifer, of Vulcan, of Icarus, and, finally, of King Kong. But he wasn't equal to the task; he didn't have the genius to perceive what the falls meant, he couldn't screen out the—to use an electronic term—the "noise." All he could come up with were folk adages. What goes up must come down. The bigger they are, the harder they fall.

"What'd you say, Grandpa?"

"I was thinking out loud, if you can call that thinking," Mr. Howller said.

Young Howller had been one of the first on the scene, and so he got a place in the front of the crowd. He had not completely forgotten his parents or Aunt Thea, but the danger was over, and he could not make himself leave to search for them. And he had even forgotten about his soaked pants. The body was only about thirty feet from him. It lay on its back on the sidewalk, just as in the movie. But the dead Kong did not look as big or as dignified as in the movie. He was spread out more like an apeskin rug than a body, and blood and bowels and their contents had splashed out around him.

After a while Carl Denham, the man responsible for capturing Kong and bringing him to New York, appeared. As in the movie, Denham spoke his classical lines by the body: "It was Beauty. As always, Beauty killed the Beast."

This was the most appropriately dramatic place for the lines to be spoken, of course, and the proper place to end the movie.

But the book had Denham speaking these lines as he leaned over the parapet of the observation tower to look down at Kong on the sidewalk. His only audience was a police sergeant.

Both the book and the movie were true. Or half true. Denham did speak those lines way up on the 102nd floor of the tower. But, showman that he was, he also spoke them when he got down to the sidewalk, where the newsmen could hear them.

Young Howller didn't hear Denham's remarks. He was too far away. Besides, at that moment he felt a tap on his shoulder and heard a man say, "Hey, kid, there's somebody trying to get your attention!"

Young Howller went into his mother's arms and wept for at least a minute. His father reached past his mother and touched him briefly on the forehead, as if blessing him, and then gave his shoulder a squeeze. When he was able to talk, Tim Howller asked his mother what had happened to them. They, as near as they could remember, had been pushed out by the crowd, though they had fought to get to him, and had run up Broadway after they found themselves in the street because King Kong had appeared. They had managed to get back to the theater, had not been able to locate Tim, and had walked back to the Empire State Building.

"What happened to Uncle Nate?" Tim said.

Uncle Nate, his mother said, had caught up with them on Fifth Avenue and just now was trying to get past the police cordon into the building so he could check on Aunt Thea.

"She must be all right!" young Howller said. "The ape climbed up her side of the building, but she could easily get away from him, her apartment's so big!"

"Well, yes," his father had said. "But if she went to bed with her headache, she would've been right next to the window. But don't worry. If she'd been hurt, we'd know it. And maybe she wasn't even home."

Young Tim had asked him what he meant by that, but his father had only shrugged.

The three of them stood in the front line of the crowd, waiting for Uncle Nate to bring news of Aunt Thea, even though they weren't really worried about her, and waiting to see what happened to Kong. Mayor Jimmy Walker showed up and conferred with the officials. Then the governor himself, Franklin Delano Roosevelt, arrived with much noise of siren and motorcycle. A minute later a big black limousine with flashing red lights and a siren pulled up. Standing on the runningboard was a giant with bronze hair and strange-looking gold-flecked eyes. He jumped off the runningboard and strode up to the mayor, the governor, and the police commissioner and talked briefly with them. Tim Howller asked the man next to him what the giant's name was, but the man replied that he didn't know because he was from out of town also. The giant finished talking and strode up to the crowd, which opened for him as if it were the Red Sea and he were Moses, and he had no trouble at all getting through the police cordon. Tim then asked the man on the right of his parents if he knew the yellow-eyed giant's name. This man, tall and thin, was with a beautiful woman dressed up in an evening gown and a mink coat. He turned his head when Tim called to him and presented a hawklike face and eyes that burned so brightly that Tim wondered if he took dope. Those eyes also told him that here was a man who asked questions, not one who gave answers. Tim didn't repeat his question, and a moment later the man said, in a whispering voice that still carried a long distance, "Come on, Margo. I've work to do." And the two melted into the crowd.

Mr. Howller told Jill about the two men, and she said, "What about them, Grandpa?"

"I don't really know," he said. "Often I've wondered . . . Well, never mind. Whoever they were, they're irrelevant to what happened to King Kong. But I'll say one thing about New York—you sure see a lot of strange characters there."

Young Howller had expected that the mess would quickly be cleaned up. And it was true that the sanitation department had sent a big truck with a big crane and a number of men with hoses, scoop shovels, and brooms. But a dozen people at least stopped the cleanup almost before it began. Carl Denham wanted no one to touch the body except the taxidermists he had called in. If he couldn't exhibit a live Kong, he would exhibit a dead one. A colonel from Roosevelt Field claimed the body and, when asked why the Air Force wanted it, could not give an explanation. Rather, he refused to give one, and it was not until an hour later that a phone call from the White House forced him to reveal the real reason. A general wanted the skin for a trophy because Kong was the only ape ever shot down in aerial combat.

A lawyer for the owners of the Empire State Building appeared with a claim for possession of the body. His clients wanted reimbursement for the damage done to the building.

A representative of the transit system wanted Kong's body so it could be sold to help pay for the damage the ape had done to the Sixth Avenue Elevated.

The owner of the theater from which Kong had escaped arrived with his lawyer and announced he intended to sue Denham for an amount which would cover the sums he would have to pay to those who were inevitably going to sue him.

The police ordered the body seized as evidence in the trial for involuntary manslaughter and criminal negligence in which Denham and the theater owner would be defendants in due process.

The manslaughter charges were later dropped, but Denham did serve a year before being paroled. On being released, he was killed by a religious fanatic, a native brought back by the second expedition to Kong's island. He was, in fact, the witch doctor. He had murdered Denham because Denham had abducted and slain his god, Kong.

His Majesty's New York consul showed up with papers which proved that Kong's island was in British waters. Therefore, Denham had no right to anything removed from the island without permission of His Majesty's government.

Denham was in a lot of trouble. But the worst blow of all was to come next day. He would be handed notification that he was being sued by Ann Redman. She wanted compensation to the tune of ten million dollars for various physical indignities and injuries suffered during her two abductions by the ape, plus the mental anguish these had caused her. Unfortunately for her, Denham went to prison without a penny in his pocket, and she dropped the suit. Thus, the public never found out exactly what the "physical indignities and injuries" were, but this did not keep it from making many speculations. Ann Redman also sued John Driscoll, though for a different reason. She claimed breach of promise. Driscoll, interviewed by newsmen, made his famous remark that she should have been suing Kong, not him. This convinced most of the public that what it had suspected had indeed happened. Just how it could have been done was difficult to explain, but the public had never lacked wiseacres who would not only attempt the difficult but would not draw back even at the impossible.

Actually, Mr. Howller thought, the deed was not beyond possibility. Take an adult male gorilla who stood six feet high and weighed 350 pounds. According to Swiss zoo director Ernst Lang, he would have a full erection only two inches long. How did Professor Lang know this? Did he enter the cage during a mating and measure the phallus? Not very likely. Even the timid and amiable gorilla would scarcely submit to this type of handling in that kind of situation. Never mind. Professor Lang said it was so, and so it must be. Perhaps he used a telescope with gradations across the lens like those on a submarine's periscope. In any event, until someone entered the cage and slapped down a ruler during the action, Professor Lang's word would have to be taken as the last word.

By mathematical extrapolation, using the square-cube law, a gorilla twenty feet tall would have an erect penis about twenty-one inches long. What the diameter would be was another guess and perhaps a vital one, for Ann Redman anyway. Whatever anyone else thought about the possibility, Kong must have decided that he would never know unless he tried. Just how well he succeeded only he and his victim knew, since the attempt would have taken place before Driscoll and Denham got to the observation tower and before the searchlight beams centered on their target.

But Ann Redman must have told her lover, John Driscoll, the truth, and he turned out not to be such a strong man after all.

"What're you thinking about, Grandpa?"

Mr. Howller looked at the screen. The Roadrunner had been succeeded by the Pink Panther, who was enduring as much pain and violence as the poor old coyote.

"Nothing," he said. "I'm just watching the Pink Panther with you."

"But you didn't say what happened to King Kong," she said.

"Oh," he said, "we stood around until dawn, and then the big shots finally came to some sort of agreement. The body just couldn't be left there much longer, if for no other reason than that it was blocking traffic. Blocking traffic meant that business would be held up. And lots of people would lose lots of money. And so Kong's body was taken away by the police department, though it used the sanitation department's crane, and it was kept in an icehouse until its ownership could be thrashed out."

"Poor Kong."

"No," he said, "not poor Kong. He was dead and out of it."

"He went to heaven?"

"As much as anybody," Mr. Howller said.

"But he killed a lot of people, and he carried off that nice girl. Wasn't he bad?"

"No, he wasn't bad. He was an animal, and he didn't know the difference between good and evil. Anyway, even if he'd been human, he would've been doing what any human would have done."

"What do you mean, Grandpa?"

"Well, if you were captured by people only a foot tall and carried off to a far place and put in a cage, wouldn't you try to escape? And if these people tried to put you back in, or got so scared that they tried to kill you right now, wouldn't you step on them?"

"Sure I'd step on them, Grandpa."

"You'd be justified, too. And King Kong was justified. He was only acting according to the dictates of his instincts."

"What?"

"He was an animal, and so he can't be blamed, no matter what he did. He wasn't evil. It was what happened around Kong that was evil."

"What do you mean?" Jill said.

"He brought out the bad and the good in the people."

But mostly bad, he thought, and he encouraged Jill to forget about Kong and concentrate on the Pink Panther. And as he looked at the screen, he saw it through tears. Even after forty-two years, he thought, tears. This was what the fall of Kong had meant to him.

The crane had hooked the corpse and lifted it up. And there were two flattened-out bodies under Kong; he must have dropped them onto the sidewalk on his way up and then fallen on them from the tower. But how explain the nakedness of the corpses of the man and the woman?

The hair of the woman was long and, in a small area not covered by blood, yellow. And part of her face was recognizable.

Young Tim had not known until then that Uncle Nate had returned from looking for Aunt Thea. Uncle Nate gave a long wailing cry that sounded as if he, too, were falling from the top of the Empire State Building.

A second later young Tim Howller was wailing. But where Uncle Nate's was the cry of betrayal, and perhaps of revenge satisfied, Tim's was both of betrayal and of grief for the death of one he had passionately loved with a thirteen-year-old's love, for one whom the thirteen-year-old in him still loved.

"Grandpa, are there any more King Kongs?"

"No," Mr. Howller said. To say yes would force him to try to explain something that she could not understand. When she got older, she would know that every dawn saw the death of the old Kong and the birth of the new.

When Petals Fall

SYDNEY J. VAN SCYOC

With harsh logic and great feeling, Sydney J. Van Scyoc looks at the numbing horrors of senility, at a time when the world is waiting for the benefits of immortality.

IT was 2 A.M. when Kelta pushed the night buzzer at the personnel entrance. A minute later a narrow night face, male variety, appeared at the opening door. Kelta palmed her credentials at him. "Federal Inspector." Quickly she stepped past into the corridor, a tall, lean girl with straight brows and with purpose in her voice. "Take me to the central desk, please."

The orderly stared at her incredulously. "You can't come in here."

"I have. Now examine my credentials again and take me to the desk."

"You—" He frowned at the credential case in her hand and shook his head, reluctantly surrendering to her authority.

The corridor turned, then branched, and they approached a broad counter behind which appeared another night face, female variety, sandwiched unpalatably between stiff white collar and bun of rusty hair.

"Miss Hastings, this—"

"This Federal Inspector is bumping the aide on Ward Seven for the remainder of the shift," Kelta finished for him, presenting her credentials, sliding out of her coat. Beneath she wore white.

Hastings gaped at the emergent uniform, at the tall girl inside it. She turned the credentials, digested them biliously. Her face pulled itself together. "You can't enter this facility at this hour. Inspections are scheduled through Director Behrens herself. For daylight hours."

"Well, my approach is a little different. I'm Inspector West, transferred out of Federal District Four six months ago."

Intelligence invaded the stony eyes. "So."

"So," Kelta agreed, confident her reputation had preceded her, "I'm sure you know that if a Federal Inspector is denied entry, the facility may find its license suspended upon twenty-four hours' notice. That would involve relocating a number of patients very rapidly."

Hastings' face underwent a second unpleasant rearrangement. She moved to the end of the counter, punched at the commset there. She molded the privacy receiver against her ear. "Director, I'm sorry to disturb you at home, but there is a Federal Inspector here. West. She is trying to enter Seven." Her glance returned to Kelta. "Director wants the name of your superior."

"I'm sure she knows Pallan Holmes has been Supervising Inspector in this district for several years. But she may not know that if I'm not conducted to Seven within five minutes, my report to Holmes will reflect your lack of cooperation. Combined with what happened here three nights ago, that could have a deleterious effect upon the licensure of this institution."

Quickly Hastings relayed the ultimatum. A moment later she proffered the receiver. "Director Behrens will speak with you herself."

Kelta shook her head. "Tomorrow, after I've completed my inspection." She retrieved her credentials, dropped them into her bag. Deftly she flipped her dark hair off her collar, rolled it, and pinned it to her head.

Waited.

Five minutes later the door of Ward Seven slid open and Kelta stepped in. Her eyes swung up the steep walls. Tiers of care cradles, serviced by narrow, railed catwalks, reached to the ceiling. A deserted monitor desk commanded a view of both cradle walls of Ward Seven.

Hastings' voice rattled up the walls. "Ames?"

A face appeared upon an upper catwalk, eyes large.

"Inspection. You're dismissed for the night."

The aide's eyes slid to Kelta. She pattered down the stairs, stepped quickly behind the desk to retrieve her coat. Vanished through the sliding door.

Kelta stepped to the desk. Her eyes moved across the display of monitor panels. Over half those panels were dark tonight. The ones that were illuminated, indicating occupied cradles, were scattered randomly. "I see you haven't consolidated the survivors on the lower tiers."

Hastings glanced at the display without comment.

"Didn't it strike you at the time of the raid that there was an unusually high survival rate? Normally when a Messenger strikes, ninety-five percent of the patients are lost. In this case, better than forty percent were salvaged."

Hastings' eyes were impenetrable. "Evidently the girl failed to pull the tubes early enough in her shift."

Kelta nodded. "Possible." She dropped her coat over the back of the seat. "But I'm very interested in that survival rate." Her mouth moved in a quick, impersonal smile. "Please don't let anyone interrupt me tonight."

Hastings moved to fortify her position. "Director Behrens instructed me—"

"To see that I don't turn in an unfavorable report. And I'm telling you I don't want to be annoyed by anyone while I'm at work. I will sign out when day shift arrives at 6 A.M."

There was a recoiling in the stony eyes. "Night shift terminates at 4 A.M. on these wards."

Kelta's eyebrows rose. "Oh? Who takes the load between 4 and 6?"

"Monitor readout is switched to the central desk. I take it myself."

Kelta's eyes narrowed. "I see. Well, I'll relieve you of this one ward tonight."

The rocky eyes turned briefly to lava. Then Hastings withdrew.

Alone, Kelta dropped her bag beside the desk. She sat, touched the surface of the desk. Here, only three nights before, a Messenger of Mercy had sat watching these readout panels while her patients died in their cradles. Then, shortly before her shift ended, she had disappeared into the night. She hadn't been seen since.

Not by anyone who hunted her.

Kelta stood and mounted the catwalks, walked the tiers. The old lay in their cradles swaddled in senility, entubed at every orifice, gaping eyes deserted, lax mouths wordless. Forty-two of them doggedly fighting out the last moments of personal existence, blood circulated by machinery, minds erased by age, they waited for the miracle that could restore them to function, however minimal. Waited for someone, somewhere, to make the immortality-breakthrough before their bodies deteriorated to the point where even the machinery of Ward Seven would be useless to them.

But these particular patients seemed to have an edge on the elderly in other nursing homes across the country. Because when the Messenger had disentubed this ward three nights ago, forty-two of these patients had resisted death. Forty-two of a hundred had remained warm and breathing.

Now Kelta examined those forty-two. In most she found several unusual conditions. The skin that stretched across the wasted muscles and prominent bones was leathery, lacking the typical fragility of age. Turning the patients, she found no sign of bedsores. In these same patients, Kelta found the surfaces of the eyeballs subtly mottled. In most there were perceptible deformities of the limbs, bones of the forearms and forelegs oddly bent.

When Kelta had examined all the present occupants of the ward, she selected her three test cases. Grimly she disconnected them from the equipment that maintained them, leaving their tubes arcing loose like so many strands of half-cooked spaghetti. Then she returned to the monitor desk and sat.

Waiting.

Watching.

In all three cases, blood pressure fell—and stabilized. Heart action appeared—and stabilized. Temperature fell, four degrees—and stabilized. No distress lights flashed. Within their cradles the three patients drew breath without artificial aid.

Just as they had three nights before.

Kelta frowned, bobbed up to make visual check. She found respiration barely perceptible, pulse light but steady, skin surfaces slightly cool, but not with the chill of death. This was the chill of life.

Unnatural life. The lines of Kelta's face lengthened. Her lips set.

At 5:50 A.M. she reconnected her three subjects and settled behind the desk again. At six o'clock the door slid. A thirtyish woman in white stepped through, eyes anxious. Kelta stood. "Day duty?"

"I'm—yes, I'm Fisher." Fisher's eyes moved nervously up the tiers.

"How long have you been on Seven, Fisher?"

Fisher probed dry lips with pale tongue. "Three years."

"Notice anything unusual about the patients who survived the Messenger call?"

Again Fisher's eyes made the anxious trip up the tiers. "They're—well, they're different. They're—" Her voice died uncertainly.

Kelta nodded. "Any idea whether they're on special medication?"

Fisher shook her head. "A registered nurse administers medications. I'm not qualified."

Kelta nodded again, stood, flipped her coat off the back of the chair. "Well, I think you'll find everything in order. There were no emergencies."

Upstairs Hastings waited stiffly behind the desk while her relief moved busily behind her. "What time does Director Behrens normally sign in?" Kelta asked.

"Director arrives at 9:30."

"Good. Leave word that I'll be in to speak with her then."

Outside the world was dim, the walks almost empty. Kelta plunged through the dawn-fogged loneliness toward the transit stop, preoccupied. At the hotel she shelled out a dozen water tokens and showered. It refreshed her little.

Immortality. Someone was on the verge of the breakthrough, perhaps had already penetrated the barrier. There could be no other explanation. But she was not helpless in the face of this development. Not if the patients on Ward Seven, and probably on other wards as well, had been used in the way she suspected they had been used.

At 8:30 she hit the commset and reached the district headquarters. "Supervisor Holmes, please."

Pallan Holmes appeared upon the faceplate, a big man with a vague expression and curly locks that tumbled over his forehead. It became less vague when he met Kelta's eyes. "West," he acknowledged painfully.

"I've run across something a little unusual in my present assignment. I'm scheduling the day to deal with it. I may have to requisition someone to back me up later in the day."

Alarmed, Holmes pawed at his desklog. "You're at Leisure Gardens in Cincinnati?"

"No. Taylor-Welsh Home in Cleveland. I rearranged my schedule. I wanted to observe the aftermath of the Messenger strike three nights ago."

Holmes' voice rose in alarm. "West, Taylor-Welsh is one of the higher-caliber homes in our district. We've never had cause for complaint there. Management has always been fully cooperative with the department, and the department in turn—"

"The department has always been fully cooperative with management. You've even allowed Director Behrens to schedule 'impromptu' inspections at her own convenience."

Holmes swept at his curls, his eyes lost in agony. "West, it's our policy to cooperate with reputable facilities whenever we can. Particularly when they're as ably administered as Taylor-Welsh. I've known Director Behrens personally—"

"A convenient arrangement for everyone, though sometimes I

think that philosophy has something to do with the way I'm bounced from district to district. I'll call later if I need help. I'd appreciate it if you would hold Napp available."

Holmes' face twisted. "West, you're not—"

"You'll probably have a call from Director Behrens later this morning. I haven't interviewed her yet." Quickly Kelta broke connection, retreated from the commset.

It summoned a moment later. Kelta did not answer. Somehow she recognized the wounded tone of its cry.

At 9:35 she was admitted to Director Behrens' private office.

Director Behrens was a middle-aged woman with glossy green hair and matching green-lacquered fingernails. "The type of off-hours inspection you subjected this facility to last night would be far more appropriate to some undercapitalized vegetable farm," she snapped, green nails tapping the desktop once in sharp emphasis.

"Well, I guess you've already heard that I don't tailor my visits to suit management," Kelta said, sitting. "And I thought the Messenger raid unusual enough a circumstance to warrant an unusual type of visit."

Director Behrens' face creased bitterly. "Inspector, no home in the nation is invulnerable to those fanatics. I learned that three nights ago. Despite every precaution, they slipped through to work their devastation upon our business."

"And not upon your patients?"

Behrens' face colored slightly. "Our patients *are* our business. They've entrusted their future to us. In the past years, our district association has watched this scourge concentrate first upon one district, then upon another. Now apparently it is our turn. Seven homes ravaged in a bare four months. I completely fail to understand why the authorities have not prosecuted these people."

"The fact that none of them has ever been apprehended may have something to do with it."

"And *why* have none been apprehended? Over a period of five years? After thousands of deaths?"

Kelta shrugged. "The operation appears to be very well

managed. The Messenger appears with an apparently valid certificate from a local aide-training school. She works for a day, maybe for two or three days, even four. Then, before anyone on the staff has had time to become acquainted with her, she pulls the plug and disappears, never to be seen again. It later develops it was another Messenger who actually attended the training course, having borrowed the name and background of some local girl for enrollment purposes. This false identity was, of course, passed on to the strike Messenger at graduation. The local girl whose identity was usurped is always found to be in complete ignorance of the double-barreled impersonation. Presumably both Messengers change their appearance and resume their former lives.

"The leaders of the movement issue periodic statements of philosophy and intent—but never in such a way as to point to the identity of any member of the organization. You know, I've even heard it suggested that any member who has delivered her Message is immediately and permanently disaffiliated."

Behrens nodded impatiently. "Oh yes, I've heard all the theories. And I feel it should be made adequately clear to the public that when an incident of this nature occurs, the home is in no way at fault. Despite all my media releases, this home is losing patients at the rate of two dozen a day."

"Unfortunate." Kelta's tone became remote from the topic. "Now. My first question concerns the two-hour gap between night shift and day shift on the wards."

Behrens' green nails disappeared beneath whitening knuckles. "During those two hours all monitor systems are read at the central desk, Inspector. The nurse on duty can attend to any emergency within moments. Our patients are in no way endangered by this simple economy measure."

Kelta nodded. "I see. But I wonder why you economize in that particular way when no other reputable home leaves wards unattended during the early-morning hours."

"Inspector, there is nothing within regulations to prohibit this particular arrangement."

"No. As a matter of fact, there isn't. Now, I'm interested in the patients who survived the Messenger raid. Have you examined them yourself?"

"I never enter the wards."

"But I'm sure you know these patients show some interesting physical manifestations. A difference in skin texture and thickness, a mottling of the ocular surfaces, limb deformities. Are these attributable to some medication these patients receive?"

"You may speak with our staff physician tomorrow. He is out today."

Kelta shook her head. "I think I will learn just as much by examining your patient files."

Behrens stared at her. Her face whitened. "The condition of the patients on our wards is testimony enough to the care we render here."

"Well, I'm going to see the files anyway, Director. Immediately."

Director Behrens sat, stark and still. Then, abruptly, she stood, her eyes fierce. She stalked out.

Kelta sat back in the chair to wait. There would be a delay, she knew, while Director Behrens called Pallan Holmes. In a few cases, Kelta's supervising inspector had actually summoned her back to district headquarters before she had completed inspection. But she doubted that Pallan Holmes would respond that vigorously or directly.

Ten minutes later the door opened. A secretary tapped across the floor, pressed the control that brought the microviewer up from Director Behrens' desktop, inserted a plate of microrecords. "You'll be able to view better from this chair."

"Thank you." Kelta installed herself in the Director's chair. "Do these include files on the patients who died in the raid?"

"Why, no. These only include patients who are on Seven now."

"I want the others too."

The secretary wheeled, addressed a silent question to Director Behrens, who stood at the door. Tight-lipped, Behrens nodded.

Kelta flashed through the files in half an hour. Then she stacked the two plates. "Wrapping paper and tape, Director?"

Behrens stared at her, grappling for voice. "For what purpose?"

"I'm going to take these records with me. They're quite interesting."

"They're—you can't."

Kelta stood, tapping the plates. "I don't find any mention here of the medication being administered to the patients who survived the raid and not to the others on Seven. Something else I don't find is signed consent forms."

"Consent? For what?"

"For the drug that obviously *is* being dispensed to those patients sometime between 4 and 6 A.M. It's a criminal offense, you know, to use experimental drugs on patients who haven't been apprised of all details and who haven't signed consent forms while in clear mind."

"This home—Inspector, Taylor-Welsh would never risk the welfare of its patients in the fashion you intimate."

Kelta shook her head. "I'm not intimating. I'm stating. Studying these records, I see that the patients who survived the Messenger strike are actually on the average older than the patients who died. I disconnected several of the survivors myself this morning—for three hours. From their medical records, and from my personal observation, I can say they should have expired almost immediately. They didn't, any more than they expired when the Messenger disentubed them. They're receiving a drug that enables them to survive. But there's no such drug on the market. Therefore it's experimental. And there are no signed consent forms in these files."

Director Behrens' eyes flashed. "Young woman, it would be much more to the point for you to attempt to find the person who killed over fifty of our patients than to persecute the administration of a reputable home."

"I'm a facility inspector, Director. My job is to police the management of nursing homes. The local and state police forces will have to track the Messenger for you."

"And they'll never catch her! They never do! These children— they come into our facilities, devastate our business, and then they drop from sight! Idealists they call themselves!"

Kelta's brows rose. "Well, there *are* a lot of ways the time and money you expend here could be put to better use."

"These children might think differently if they were old themselves."

Kelta shrugged. "Wrapping paper and tape?"

There was another delay. Then the requested items appeared. Kelta secured the two plates into a small package. "I'm filing departmental action immediately to ensure that those patients aren't removed from the facility. If you need me, I'll be at the Southside Hotel for the rest of the day."

Before proceeding there, however, she locked the microplates into a security box in a bank vault. The key to the box she mailed to herself at district headquarters.

Reaching her room, she called Pallan Holmes again. He flashed on screen in a state of agitation, curls bobbing, distraught. "West, I've had two calls from Director Behrens at Taylor-Welsh in the past hour."

"I'll fill you in later," Kelta said quickly. "I have some very interesting evidence in safekeeping, but I need a backup man immediately. Is Napp available?"

"West, Taylor-Welsh is one of the most respected homes for the aged in our district. I've known Director Behrens—"

"Yes—personally for a number of years. Is Napp available? I want sound equipment with him, and I want him now."

Discussion ensued. Kelta prevailed. Napp was scheduled on the next flash west.

He arrived an hour later, appeared at Kelta's door, a burly young man with reddish-blond hair receding from a high, bulbous forehead. "You jarred me off writeup on a week's work. You're offering thrills?"

Kelta grinned. "I'm offering. You have the sound equipment?"

Napp nodded, stepping into the room, glancing around. "Here?"

Kelta chewed her lower lip. "No, elsewhere, I think. I want a remote button."

Napp nodded, setting down his case, rummaging in it. Kelta

studied the top of his head, hoping her evaluation of him had been accurate. "How much stock do you hold, Napp?"

Napp's brows furnished brief warmth to his balding upper forehead. "Pardon?"

"Stock. United Textile East. Singer Diversified. General Paper and Plastics."

Napp's grin cleared a dozen and a half solid white teeth. "You know, West, I've observed that ownership of stock tends to interfere with pursuit of duty. So I don't own any stock. But I hear others in the department own a little. I guess you've run into that, as much as you've bounced districts."

"Repeatedly. Now I think I'm about to be offered some myself." She accepted the small blue sound button along with his appraising glance. She clipped the button into the hair at the base of her neck. "Has this equipment been checked out recently?"

"I checked everything while I was waiting for flash time."

The call came minutes later. A smooth masculine voice, a matter of mutual interest to be discussed, a rendezvous arranged.

A rendezvous kept. Kelta arrived at the hotel bar, where a reserved booth awaited her, five minutes early. She wore a brief dress with buttercup skirt strips that flapped across her long thighs. She had touched her lips with color, but her brows remained straight and uncompromising.

That fact she obscured temporarily with an effusive smile when two sleek men in business blue were conducted to the booth, suits glossy, smiles glassy.

"Miss West?"

"Yes," she agreed brightly.

Manifestly prosperous, patently shrewd, they were Patrick and Nussman. "Our colleague, Dr. Vincinzi, will meet us in a few moments," Nussman reassured Kelta smoothly. "I think we may order without him."

They ordered. Drinks arrived.

Nussman leaned earnestly across the table. "Now, Miss West, it has been suggested that you are an excellent prospect for investment counseling. You hold a civil service position with good salary and security prospects. You're young, dedicated, very much involved with your profession. Too involved, I'm sure, to make careful analysis of the market yourself or to spend much time watching your stocks as they must be watched to derive maximum benefit from your investment program."

Kelta tilted her drink, examined the bottom of the glass through it, nodding. "My time is so completely filled I've never gotten around to investing at all. Which counseling service do you represent?"

"Ah." Nussman flourished an embossed card. "Actually we represent Robard Wheels East, a diversified industrial and service firm. Casters, utility wheels, rubber products—"

"Nursing homes."

Nussman's glib attempt to gloss over Kelta's interruption was interrupted in turn by the arrival of an elderly man, slight and visibly withdrawn. Patrick and Nussman bobbed up. "Dr. Vincinzi, Inspector Kelta West. We were just discussing Miss West's investment program."

"Which is currently nonexistent," Kelta added, her eyes on the older man. He joined them with obvious reluctance. "Do you represent Robard East too, Dr. Vincinzi?"

Vincinzi's forehead creased faintly. "Not in the way Patrick and Nussman do." His eyes met Kelta's briefly, then moved away, avoiding his associates.

Nussman reasserted himself. "Miss West, we're here because a mutual acquaintance suggested you might appreciate being introduced to a new investment plan. Our plan, you see—it's still in the pilot stage—is designed to help responsible younger citizens find their way into the market by granting them substantial blocks of Robard at nominal prices. In addition, you will be introduced to one of the investment firms we have found reliable in our own trading. They will handle your account without fee. In fact, it might be possible to arrange an extended program, a certain number of shares of Robard East being entered upon your account semiannually over a decade. Of course, you would be in no way obliged to retain the stock. You could trade or sell, although your counselors would advise you that Robard is a diversified concern with many excellent prospects."

Kelta nodded gravely. "Are you in the pharmaceutical line, Dr. Vincinzi?"

The older man's eyes came up, faded, wary.

Nussman hastened into the gap. "Now, Miss West, we can't discuss certain aspects of our enterprise at all. Pharmaceuticals are a very touchy field. If the nature of direction of certain researches are leaked too soon, the opportunity to sweep the market—at enormous profit—could be lost forever. That would considerably diminish what you might otherwise expect to realize from your own block of Robard."

"I see. How many nursing homes does Robard hold?"

Nussman's smooth forehead was briefly marred by irritation. "Robard holds half a dozen of the better homes in this state."

"And in how many of those are experiments in extended longevity being conducted?"

The three men were silent. Perspiration appeared upon Nussman's forehead.

"Only in the Taylor-Welsh home and Walden Gardens," Dr. Vincinzi said quietly, finally meeting and holding Kelta's eye.

"And how far has the research progressed, Doctor?"

Vincinzi's pale eyes were troubled. "I have developed a serum—with the help of my assistants and research staff, of course—that produces, as nearly as we can determine, virtual immortality. Unfortunately it does nothing to deter the progress of senility. It does not delay the onset or ameliorate the more distressing manifestations of senility even slightly. Virtually all it does is enable the body to survive as a body, not as a viable personality."

"Are your subjects vulnerable to accidental death?"

Vincinzi nodded slowly. "They are. Severe blood loss—loss amounting to eighty percent or more—will produce death. Incineration of body tissues likewise will produce death." He shrugged. "Little else will. I have in my possession mice who are up to twenty years old. They are helpless. Hopeless. But alive."

"Like the patients I examined this morning on Ward Seven."

Nussman moved uneasily. "Inspector, this is no place to discuss these matters. We made this appointment in order—"

Kelta's eyes were grave. "This is where we are going to discuss them. Doctor, have you considered the social aspects of your serum?"

"Present? Or future? I've considered both. I'm still considering them." Vincinzi shook his head. "When I went into this branch of research, I was a young man on the trail of conquest. Immortality —the unexplored frontier. If a breakthrough came in my time, it was my ticket to the future, to the centuries that lie ahead. My personality could survive, participate, contribute.

"Now I'm old. I see my development purely as a holding measure. There are hundreds of thousands of my generation in homes across this country, waiting. Most of them, if there were no startling development within the next few years, would die despite everything. But if my serum is marketed soon, they can continue to live. They can continue to wait—for the miracle that may someday restore them to consciousness and function." His eyes were suddenly intense. "Perhaps they will never contribute much to the future—perhaps *I* never will. But the sun shines. Water flows. Children play and roses bloom. The simple pleasures continue. Can we deny ourselves them? Could you deny yourself, after your productive years are past?"

Kelta was aware of Nussman and Patrick's alert silence. She frowned. The personal case, always the personal case. The two entrepreneurs hoped Dr. Vincinzi's personal case would persuade her.

She could only give the personal answer. She reached for her bag, flipped out a handful of tokens, spread them before her. "Water flows, Doctor Vincinzi? This represents my water allowance for the next week. It will get me through two showers, some personal laundry, and hopefully I'll be able to wash my face each morning. Of course I don't drink from the tap. I don't like to use sick leave unnecessarily.

"Personal exhibit number two, a photograph. My brother. He's twenty-two years old. He doesn't leave the apartment. That's because he's allergic to air—or to what passes for air. My parents have invested thousands of dollars in air filtration devices so he can survive inside the apartment.

"Exhibit number three, my radiation badge." She slipped it from around her neck. "It registers normal now. That's because I was reissued fourteen years ago, after the Dallas pile disaster. You'd be surprised how many young women are devoting themselves to careers or social causes because they'll never bear normal children."

She shook her head. "Your generation invested its time in a number of worthwhile purposes and in a number of frivolous ones. It created a number of problems we've all had to live with. Now, instead of passing on and leaving the one heritage any generation can leave—a clear field for the next generation to deal with those problems—it wants to linger. It wants present and future generations to maintain it indefinitely in thousands of storage homes all over the country. It wants precious resources expended upon it—water, power, pharmaceuticals, rubber, plastic and metal products."

Kelta smiled grimly. "You're not asking just for moral support. You're asking for our drinking water, our oxygen, our children playing. I say no. You've had your roses, Doctor. I hope you enjoyed them. You've had your time on earth too. Now it's our turn."

Nussman's features contracted ominously. "That sounds like the Messenger line."

"Is there anyone in the country who hasn't heard the Messenger line by now?"

Vincinzi touched Kelta's hand, his face grave. "You've answered my question, the one I've been asking myself—and sometimes these gentlemen—with increasing frequency these past few years. No man wants to go. But several mornings ago I stood on Ward Seven and saw fifty-eight dead. Fifty-eight, stiff and cold in their cradles. And a strange thought, an alien thought almost, entered my mind: death *is* a part of life."

"The rose petal drops." Kelta swung her head to meet two other pairs of eyes. They glittered, stark and cold. "As I see it, Robard has a choice. It can face charges of illegal experimentation upon human subjects and attempting to bribe a federal officer—I have a sound man upstairs recording this conversation—or it can close down its immortality project. Immediately."

Nussman and Patrick sat very still. Finally Nussman creaked back to life. "You can't prove anything. Even with sound tracks."

"I can prove a lot. I *will* prove a lot if I have to. You can make your stock offer to every member of the district staff—and it won't keep *me* quiet." Kelta stood. "The reason the department keeps me bouncing from district to district is that I don't silence."

"But we have a massive investment in this project!" Patrick exploded. "We've dropped billions into this!"

Kelta smiled tautly. "Now you're going to lose billions. Either way. If the government prosecutes, your chance to grab the market dissolves. Along with your corporate image. If you turn off the project, you might salvage at least the image."

Nussman shook his head stubbornly. "No. You misread public climate. Federal funds support our nursing homes. The old have public sympathy. Our serum will have public sympathy too, even if there has been some infraction of the law."

"Oh? Which public? For how long? Nursing homes originally drew public funds because their clients were human beings. Now the nursing homes have created a clientele of objects, and I see public sympathy changing. I see the public resenting the flow of money and resources into the maintenance of corpses. I see the public beginning to realize, with each Messenger strike, that the only parties who benefit from the present arrangement are the owners of these homes." She shook her head. "You have a choice. Dr. Vincinzi, I think maybe you've made yours."

The older man spoke through dry lips. "I believe I have now."

Upstairs Napp repacked his equipment. Kelta twitched the remote sound button out of her hair, dropped it into his palm, sagged into a chair. "I want the sound tracks dropped directly into a security box."

"Done." Napp's eyes were bright. "What do you think? Which light will they blink?"

Kelta shook her head. "I don't know. But I think we have them either way."

"You do?" Napp's brows went north, surprised. "Well, I can see Nussman and Patrick wading right through your charges and going ahead with their project, even from prison. There's still profit in corpses, even if it has to be shared."

Kelta shrugged. "In that case, I can see Messengers doing more than pulling tubes. I can see Messengers reversing blood flow back into the circulating equipment. Or creating a series of funeral pyres. And releasing more public statements, especially on the subject of the increased costs of maintaining the tubers.

"And I can see Vincinzi publicly denouncing the project if necessary. Maybe even delivering a Message to his experimental subjects himself. As a public demonstration of his feelings."

Napp's eyes widened. "Ah." His legs folded and he sat on the floor. "That *was* the Messenger line you were unwinding downstairs."

Kelta's eyes rested upon him. The normally decisive line of her mouth drooped with weariness.

"The Messenger line—you've been in this district what? Five months?" Napp asked.

"Six."

"And four months ago we began getting heavy Messages. As many in a few months as we'd gotten in two years before."

Kelta's expression remained opaque.

Napp frowned intently. "You know, a facility inspector would be an ideal coordinator for Messenger operations. A facility inspector has access to everything, schedules, floor plans, personnel records, the facilities themselves. A facility inspector—"

Kelta unfolded from her chair, rummaged in her bag. Came out with a handful of water tokens. "Napp, would you mind if I took a shower?"

Slowly Napp shook his head. "No. No, I'll go rent a security box." He grinned. "On the way back maybe I'll pick up a rose."

Kelta smiled. "All right. Buy a yard of sunshine too. We'll spread it on the floor."

"And a puddle of rainwater? Enjoy it while we can."

"And one child playing." She touched her radiation badge, trying to keep the smile on her lips.

Paleontology:
An Experimental Science

ROBERT R. OLSEN

Humor is so rare in science fiction that we can only stand and applaud when a fine example comes along. Robert Olsen is a geologist by profession and this is his first published work of fiction. It was inspired by a visit to Dinosaur National Monument and was produced in a white heat of creation in a motel room in Meeker, Colorado. "Possibly," the author writes, "the only science-fiction story written in Meeker, Colorado."

"Computer reconstruction of fossil organisms" by L.R. Smizer (speaker), C.D. Halloran, P. McBride, H.C. Smith, and P.C. Eberhart, Geological Society of America Abstracts with Programs (Cordilleran Section), 1979, p. 14.

ADVANCES in computer technology have recently made possible the reconstruction of fossil organisms from the organic material found in certain fossils, at least on a theoretical basis. Methods of tissue culture from single DNA molecules have recently been placed on a routine basis, but actual reproduction of fossil organisms depends on the preservation of fragments of the DNA chain as fossil material in rocks. The destructive nature

41

of most fossilization processes suggests that only fossils of late Tertiary age can be replicated using this technique.

In cases where abundant but fragmentary material is present in fossil form, the substance is separated from the host rock and then subjected to microanalysis to determine what parts of the DNA chain are present. Analyses of the structure of the fragments are fed into a computer, which attempts to match fragments of the chain in order to obtain a composite model of the DNA, which governs the form and development of the organism. New DNA can then be synthesized, either by the difficult process of building the molecule up from simpler amino acids, or, in the ideal case, by rejoining the fragments of DNA into one complete molecule. Though the latter process has recently been performed in the laboratory, it appears that those parts of the chain where the fragments were fused is always a weak spot in the structure, and susceptible to breakage in the presence of certain chemicals.

Preliminary experiments have been carried out on several species of Pleistocene land-snails and one Pliocene ginkgo. Though some of these experiments are still in the early stages of test-tube culture, two snails appear to have developed normally, as far as can be determined; and the ginkgo, recently transferred to a soil medium, shows normal growth.

*   *   *

"Fossils of *Tyrannosaurus nevadensis* and other saurians, Hell's Flat, Nevada" by C.C. Morrow, Geological Society of America Abstracts with Programs (Cordilleran Section), 1979, p. 19.

Excellent preservation of saurian fossils has long been known in western Utah and easternmost Nevada, and recently a most remarkable case of preservation has been discovered. In a nearly inaccessible part of the northern Shadow Peak Mountains, Upper Cretaceous rocks are exposed in a small canyon which overlooks the area known locally as Hell's Flat. The rocks, a series of continental sandstones and shales about thirty-five feet thick, are flat-lying and rest upon a surface carved in the Middle Cambrian Bonanza King Formation. Overlying the fossiliferous Cretaceous strata are resistant Late Tertiary volcanic and volcanistic rocks, which form the higher parts of the Shadow Peak Mountains.

The Cretaceous rocks are thought to represent a river channel cut into the older material, and consist of reddish to pale yellow, medium to fine grained sandstones and gray shales. The material is almost unconsolidated, which accounts in part for the remarkable state of preservation of the fossils.

The fossil material consists of assorted bones and skin fragments, mostly of *Tyrannosaurus nevadensis*, though three species of *Triceratops*, and an unidentified form similar to *Trachodon* but smaller and lighter in build. All fossils are the products of perfect preservation, and no chemical replacement or deletion of material has occurred. The extreme aridity of the area, among other factors, has apparently caused this remarkable phenomenon; for when a skin fragment was wetted and left overnight, a strong organic odor indicative of decay was noted the next morning. The skin material is exceptionally coarse and tough, and a gray-green color.

Several pounds of this remarkable material were collected. It should prove to be of wide interest in the study of the biochemistry of fossil organisms and the geochemistry of fossilization, subjects which have not until now received the attention they deserve, due to the lack of suitable material for experiment. This lack has now been remedied to an extent.

*   *   *

"Computer reconstruction of fossil DNA of *Tyrannosaurus nevadensis*" by L.R. Smizer (speaker), C.D. Halloran, P. McBride, H.C. Smith, and P.C. Eberhart, Geological Society of America Abstracts with Programs (Cordilleran Section), 1985, p. 21.

Computer reconstruction of the DNA structure of the Hell's Flat fossil material has now progressed to the point where some preliminary deductions can be made as to the biochemistry of the subject organism, *T. nevadensis*, and the chemistry of the fossil material.

Although *T. nevadensis*-derived material was the most abundant fraction of fossil matter, abundant organic constituents from the other saurian remains posed a difficult problem in the early stages of preparation. However, little DNA remained from the other fossil forms, and a pure sample of *T. nev.*-derived DNA was eventually isolated by molecular probe. No complete DNA molecules were found, the largest fragment containing roughly 45 percent of the total genetic information as subsequently deduced. Other major fragments, some in slightly damaged form, contained 30, 28, 17, 12, and 8 percent of the total information necessary to reconstruct the living organism. Thus, an excess of 40 percent exists in the information as received by the computer. Analysis revealed that though this surplus of information was not as great as might be desired, all the necessary information was indeed present on the fragments.

Following computer correlation and modeling of the major DNA molecule, experimentation commenced on the actual construction and culture of the molecule. Using techniques described in a previous paper (1983), the fragmentary DNA molecules were cleaned and joined together microsurgically, the molecule being implanted in the specially prepared nucleus of the egg cell of a cayman from which the host's DNA had been removed.

Chemically induced replication of the original DNA molecule has now been attained, and the embryo placed in a life-support system. Growth is quite rapid, and the birth-analog event is scheduled for August 1986, corresponding to a gestation period of 11 months.

* * *

"Ontogeny and development of an artificial specimen of *Tyrannosaurus nevadensis*," by C.D. Halloran (speaker), P. McBride, H.C. Smith, and P.C. Eberhart, Geological Society of America Abstracts with Programs (Cordilleran Section), 1987, p. 13.

The artificially created embryo of *Tyrannosaurus nevadensis*, which has been the subject of previous reports, was inserted in a life-support growth medium on June 12, 1985, in an attempt to cause the development of a mature individual of the species. The work was performed at the Craig University Paleontology Laboratory in Hastings, California.

Though the environment of growth of course differed markedly from that which the organism would experience in its natural state, growth was rapid and proceeded normally throughout the embryonic stage. Oxygen demanded increased markedly (47 percent) in the sixth month but was successfully met due to careful supervision of the environment. By the end of the seventh month, the embryo was roughly five inches long and weighed nine ounces. At this time, definite signs of electrical activity in the brain were noted, and the birth-analog event was considered to be imminent.

The young animal, a male, was removed from the life-support system on July 7, and placed in a terrarium stocked with insects and small reptiles of various kinds. At this time the animal was eight inches long and weighed thirteen ounces. Respiratory function was somewhat sluggish for the first seven hours but then attained a condition judged to be normal for this species. The animal was from the first a vigorous and aggressive predator, and devoured two small lizards during the first day of active life.

Seven weeks later the specimen, now the size of a large dog, succeeded in breaking through the wire-mesh wall of the terrarium and briefly roamed at large in the Paleontology Laboratory. Several other laboratory specimens, as well as two German Shepherd dogs, were lost at this time. Unfortunately also, the struggle to recapture the animal resulted in the tragic loss of Dr. Smizer, who was first to discover the creature's hiding place.

In conclusion, despite some difficulty, significant data are now being obtained from the specimen, which has been removed from the Paleontology Laboratory to more secure quarters at the Elephant Corral of the San Diego Zoo. Data already collected indicate the necessity of revising current views on the intelligence and aggressiveness of the theropods, as well as their level of activity.

*   *   *

"Behavioral anomalies of *Tyrannosaurus nevadensis*, as deduced from the Smizer specimen," by C.D. Halloran (speaker), H.C. Smith, and P.C. Eberhart, Geological Society of America Abstracts with Programs (Cordilleran Section), 1988, p. 8.

An ongoing program of study at the Paleontological Laboratory of Craig University has been concerned with the production of an artificial specimen of *Tyrannosaurus nevadensis*. Following successful production of a young specimen of the species by repair of fragmental fossil DNA, the animal was placed in the Elephant Corral of the San Diego Zoo after its strength proved to be too great for conventional laboratory care.

The San Diego facilities, modified to include two double-strength steel barriers ten feet apart, proved entirely adequate for the task of containing the *Tyrannosaurus* during its youth and early adulthood, providing that adequate repair and rebuilding of the inner cage was performed weekly. With maturity, the reddish-brown mottled scale pattern of the animal's youth is being gradually replaced by a greenish-brown cast that undoubtedly had some camouflage function during Cretaceous times. Molting was accomplished once monthly during the period of maximum growth, and was accompanied by unusual patterns of behavior. Instead of the usual reptilian pattern of lethargy and passivity during the molting period, the Smizer tyrannosaurus became unusually vicious and hyperactive. It was undoubtedly due to this phenomenon, plus an oversight in the maintenance of the inner cage, that the animal was able to attain the space between the inner and outer cages on December 8, resulting in the tragic death of Dr. McBride. It was reliably reported that Dr. McBride was standing at least four feet from the outer cage when the animal seized him with a foreleg and dragged him into the cage to be consumed. Since the reach of the animal's foreleg when fully extended at this stage of development was only five feet six inches, it would appear that the forelegs are more useful to the creature in food gathering than was previously thought.

The great muscular development of the hind legs of the tyrannosaurus also has a significant adaptive advantage in this particular creature. It has been frequently observed that upon securing living prey, the animal will stamp and crush the prey with its feet, thus presumably rendering the food more pliant. It is thought that this behavior is related to the habit of swallowing the food in one piece, as would a more modern reptile. Since the forelegs are of little use in this procedure, the rear legs have assumed the role of food-preparing devices.

* * *

"Results of computer reconstruction of DNA of the Smizer tyrannosaurus" by C.D. Halloran (speaker), H.C. Smith, and P.C. Eberhart, Geological Society of America Abstracts with Programs (Cordilleran Section), 1989, p. 27.

Since the Smizer specimen of *Tyrannosaurus nevadensis* has now reached physical maturity (although continued growth, in the manner of all reptiles, is expected), it is appropriate to examine how closely the artificially reconstituted DNA, pieced together from fragments of fossil DNA from Nevada, approximates the known genetic structure of the tyrannosaurs as previously deduced. Although certain anomalies have been observed which possibly are due to faulty reconstruction, the procedure seems to have been in large part successful, and promises to make possible further reconstitutions in the future.

Anomalies in the specimen may be divided into two classes: physical/developmental anomalies, and behavioral anomalies.

Although the Smizer specimen is now as large as the largest known fossil Tyrannosaurus of any species, the junior author feels that it has not attained full maturity; if this is so, it follows that through a defect in the DNA reconstruction, the size of this specimen is greater than it should be. This theory must wait for support with time and further growth of the specimen. The rapid growth of the animal both before and after the birth-analog event has caused some authorities to object to the speed of maturation. However, it should be remembered that since the specimen has been given sufficient or even excess food throughout its life, rapid development may be more a result of opportunity than genetic anomaly.

Though the animal exhibits behavioral aberrations as discussed in a previous paper, it is unknown whether this behavior was natural to the Cretaceous *Tyrannosaurus nevadensis* or not. Other aspects of behavior must be, as above, dependent on opportunity—as, for example, the Smizer tyrannosaurus' habit of sharpening its teeth on building concrete.

In conclusion, with the possible exception of anomalous size, the Smizer tyrannosaurus is a completely normal specimen of its type and suggests the great gains to be derived from further research into the reconstruction of fossil organisms from DNA fragments.

*   *   *

"Predatory habits of *Tyrannosaurus nevadensis smizer*" by H.C. Smith, Geological Society of America Abstracts with Programs (Cordilleran Section), 1989, p. 21.

Because *Tyrannosaurus nevadensis smizer* is a vigorous predator, and because of the creature's unusual size, great problems were encountered relating to the procurement of sufficient food to keep the animal both nourished and satisfied. Due to the lack of herbivorous dinosaurs of sufficient size to provide satisfactory prey for the tyrannosaurus (a lack which may soon be remedied—see Smith, in preparation, *Geol. Soc. Amer. Bull.*), smaller animals must be used. Normal behavior for the theropods is thought to have been for the creature to sleep for a matter of days after eating to repletion, after which the old kill would be revisited. However, with the artificial specimen, only small animals such as cattle and oxen were available for consumption. This resulted in a diminution of the resting periods of the creature, hence to increased activity, and therefore presumably to an increased demand for food.

Although the escape of the Smizer tyrannosaurus in March of this year, involving as it did the regrettable deaths of Dr. Halloran and Dr. Eberhart, was a serious setback to the project, it did involve unparalleled opportunity to observe the habits of the creature in a more natural setting. Fortunately, the creature proved to be very much afraid of automobiles, and while it is perhaps strange that it managed to escape from the San Diego area in view of this, the shyness on the part of the animal kept the loss of human life to a minimum.

Because of its unusual size, the dinosaur was observed by many people as it journeyed north toward Lake Elsinore. Having grown considerably by this time, the animal was forced to stop frequently for food, where it showed a definite preference for Hereford cattle. As many observers remarked, its behavior in rounding up the cattle preparatory to crushing several of them with its hind legs was quite remarkable in view of the often postulated low degree of intelligence of the saurians.

Although the creature is still at large, capture is expected at any time. Since the creature has recently shown a diminishing fear of automobiles, the Lake Elsinore region has recently been evacuated, and the situation is viewed as stable. Herds of cattle are driven into the area weekly to keep the specimen from roaming too far in its search for food.

* * *

"Death and postmortem examination of *Tyrannosaurus nevadensis smizer*" by H.C. Smith, Geological Society of America Abstracts with Programs (Cordilleran Section), 1990, p. 17.

Although the creature was naturally of inestimable scientific value, care of the reconstructed *Tyrannosaurus nevadensis* proved to be a formidable problem, particularly after its escape in March 1989. After the creature had moved north to the vicinity of Lake Elsinore, the onset of cool weather in October 1989 caused definite signs of restlessness in the animal. Finally, on November 4, in a cold rain, the creature began to move south rapidly. It was at this point that the civil authorities requested *(People of California vs. Smith)* that the creature be put to death. Although conscious of the immense amount of data yet unacquired, the author endeavored to comply.

Since traditional methods of attack had failed, causing many needless tragedies, it was felt that the only means of subduing the beast was to use weaknesses in its own reconstituted genetic structure against it. Since it was known that slight flaws existed in the structure of the DNA, the creature was injected with K-ryocyanin at close range by bazooka. Although this treatment would have no immediate effect, it would prevent the replication of new body cells by breaking down the structure of the DNA.

However, before the animal succumbed, it nearly succeeded in reaching the Mexican border, ultimately collapsing in downtown San Diego. At this time, the creature was reliably estimated to be five stories tall (as demonstrated by the absence of fatalities or damage above the sixth floor of the Union Building). This translates to an overall length of roughly 100 feet. This measurement was confirmed when shortly afterwards the creature fell dead in the street, where it could be measured. Death was caused by cellular deterioration brought on by the injection, and occurred one week and two days after injection.

In the future it is to be recommended that more caution be used in the selection of subjects for artificial regeneration, although the process itself must be considered totally successful. In particular, the procedure will be of great value in research into the behavior of extinct animals. Preferred specimens of predators should be more intelligent, and hence more tractable, than the great reptiles. For example, there is some controversy concerning the feeding habits of the early cave bears, with some writers maintaining that they were strictly carnivorous, as opposed to the omnivorous modern bears. The Paleontology Laboratory is currently caring for an embryo of *Arctotherium californicum*, commonly known as the giant cave bear, developed from fossil material found at Rancho La Brea; after the animal is born this fall, answers to this and many other questions will undoubtedly be found.

The Women Men Don't See

JAMES TIPTREE, JR.

*This story is true to its title. It is about the women men
don't see, who are around us yet invisible to the
masculine eye. James Tiptree, Jr., a writer of immense
talents, flexes his literary muscles, looks around at a
landscape he knows very well—then tells a story that has
the reader nodding his head and agreeing every foot of
the way.*

SEE her first while the Mexicana 727 is barreling down to
Cozumel Island. I come out of the can and lurch into her seat,
saying, "Sorry," at a double female blur. The near blur nods
quietly. The younger one in the window seat goes on looking out.
I continue down the aisle, registering nothing. Zero. I never would
have looked at them or thought of them again.

Cozumel airport is the usual mix of panicky Yanks dressed for
the sand pile and calm Mexicans dressed for lunch at the
Presidente. I am a used-up Yank dressed for serious fishing; I
extract my rods and duffel from the riot and hike across the field
to find my charter pilot. One Captain Estéban has contracted to
deliver me to the bonefish flats of Bélise three hundred kilometers
down the coast.

Captain Estéban turns out to be four feet nine of mahogany
Maya *puro*. He is also in a somber Maya suit. He tells me my

Cessna is grounded somewhere, and his Bonanza is booked to take a party to Chetumal.

Well, Chetumal is south; can he take me along and go on to Bélise after he drops them? Gloomily he concedes the possibility —*if* the other party permits, and *if* there are not too many *equipajes.*

The Chetumal party approaches. It's the woman and her young companion—daughter?—neatly picking their way across the gravel and yucca apron. Their Ventura two-suiters, like themselves, are small, plain, and neutral-colored. No problem. When the captain asks if I may ride along, the mother says mildly, "Of course," without looking at me.

I think that's when my inner tilt-detector sends up its first faint click. How come this woman has already looked me over carefully enough to accept on her plane? I disregard it. Paranoia hasn't been useful in my business for years, but the habit is hard to break.

As we clamber into the Bonanza, I see the girl has what could be an attractive body if there was any spark at all. There isn't. Captain Estéban folds a serape to sit on so he can see over the cowling and runs a meticulous check-down. And then we're up and trundling over the turquoise Jello of the Caribbean into a stiff south wind.

The coast on our right is the territory of Quintana Roo. If you haven't seen Yucatan, imagine the world's biggest absolutely flat green-gray rug. An empty-looking land. We pass the white ruin of Tulum and the gash of the road to Chichén Itza, a half-dozen coconut plantations, and then nothing but reef and low scrub jungle all the way to the horizon, just about the way the conquistadores saw it four centuries back.

Long strings of cumulus are racing at us, shadowing the coast. I have gathered that part of our pilot's gloom concerns the weather. A cold front is dying on the henequen fields of Mérida to west, and the south wind has piled up a string of coastal storms: what they call *llovisnas.* Estéban detours methodically around a couple of small thunderheads. The Bonanza jinks, and I look back with a vague notion of reassuring the women. They are calmly intent on what can be seen of Yucatan. Well, they were offered the copilot's view, but they turned it down. Too shy?

Another *llovisna* puffs up ahead. Estéban takes the Bonanza upstairs, rising in his seat to sight his course. I relax for the first time in too long, savoring the latitudes between me and my desk, the week of fishing ahead. Our captain's classic Maya profile attracts my gaze: forehead sloping back from his predatory nose, lips and jaw stepping back below it. If his slant eyes had been any more crossed, he couldn't have made his license. That's a handsome combination, believe it or not. On the little Maya chicks in their minishifts, with iridescent gloop on those cockeyes, it's also highly erotic. Nothing like the oriental doll thing; these people have stone bones. Captain Estéban's old grandmother could probably tow the Bonanza . . .

I'm snapped awake by the cabin hitting my ear. Estéban is barking into his headset over a drumming racket of hail; the windows are dark gray.

One important noise is missing—the motor. I realize Estéban is fighting a dead plane. Thirty-six hundred; we've lost two thousand feet!

He slaps tank switches as the storm throws us around; I catch something about *gasolina* in a snarl that shows his big teeth. The Bonanza reels down. As he reaches for an overhead toggle, I see the fuel gauges are high. Maybe a clogged gravity feed line; I've heard of dirty gas down here. He drops the set. It's a million to one nobody can read us through the storm at this range anyway. Twenty-five hundred—going down.

His electric feed pump seems to have cut in: the motor explodes—quits—explodes—and quits again for good. We are suddenly out of the bottom of the clouds. Below us is a long white line almost hidden by rain: the reef. But there isn't any beach behind it, only a big meandering bay with a few mangrove flats—and it's coming up at us fast.

This is going to be bad, I tell myself with great unoriginality. The women behind me haven't made a sound. I look back and see they're braced down with their coats by their heads. With a stalling speed around eighty, all this isn't much use, but I wedge myself in.

Estéban yells some more into his set, flying a falling plane. He is doing one jesus job, too—as the water rushes up at us he dives into a hair-raising turn and hangs us into the wind—with a long pale ridge of sandbar in front of our nose.

Where in hell he found it I'll never know. The Bonanza mushes down, and we belly-hit with a tremendous tearing crash—bounce —hit again—and everything slews wildly as we flat-spin into the mangroves at the end of the bar. Crash! Clang! The plane is wrapping itself into a mound of strangler fig with one wing up. The crashing quits with us all in one piece. And no fire. Fantastic.

Captain Estéban pries open his door, which is now in the roof. Behind me a woman is repeating quietly, "Mother. Mother." I climb up the floor and find the girl trying to free herself from her mother's embrace. The woman's eyes are closed. Then she opens them and suddenly lets go, sane as soap. Estéban starts hauling them out. I grab the Bonanza's aid kit and scramble out after them into brilliant sun and wind. The storm that hit us is already vanishing up the coast.

"Great landing, Captain."

"Oh, yes! It was beautiful." The women are shaky, but no hysteria. Estéban is surveying the scenery with the expression his ancestors used on the Spaniards.

If you've been in one of these things, you know the slow-motion inanity that goes on. Euphoria, first. We straggle down the fig tree and out onto the sandbar in the roaring hot wind, noting without alarm that there's nothing but miles of crystalline water on all sides. It's only a foot or so deep, and the bottom is the olive color of silt. The distant shore around us is all flat mangrove swamp, totally uninhabitable.

"Bahia Espiritu Santo." Estéban confirms my guess that we're down in that huge water wilderness. I always wanted to fish it.

"What's all that smoke?" The girl is pointing at the plumes blowing around the horizon.

"Alligator hunters," says Estéban. Maya poachers have left burn-offs in the swamps. It occurs to me that any signal fires we make aren't going to be too conspicuous. And I now note that our plane is well-buried in the mound of fig. Hard to see it from the air.

Just as the question of how the hell we get out of here surfaces in my mind, the older woman asks composedly, "If they didn't hear you, Captain, when will they start looking for us? Tomorrow?"

"Correct," Estéban agrees dourly. I recall that air-sea rescue is fairly informal here. Like, keep an eye open for Mario, his mother says he hasn't been home all week.

It dawns on me we may be here quite some while.

Furthermore, the diesel-truck noise on our left is the Caribbean piling back into the mouth of the bay. The wind is pushing it at us, and the bare bottoms on the mangroves show that our bar is covered at high tide. I recall seeing a full moon this morning in—believe it, St. Louis—which means maximal tides. Well, we can climb up in the plane. But what about drinking water?

There's a small splat! behind me. The older woman has sampled the bay. She shakes her head, smiling ruefully. It's the first real expression on either of them; I take it as the signal for introductions. When I say I'm Don Fenton from St. Louis, she tells me their name is Parsons, from Bethesda, Maryland. She says it so nicely I don't at first notice we aren't being given first names. We all compliment Captain Estéban again.

His left eye is swelled shut, an inconvenience beneath his attention as a Maya, but Mrs. Parsons spots the way he's bracing his elbow in his ribs.

"You're hurt, Captain."

"*Roto*—I think is broken." He's embarrassed at being in pain. We get him to peel off his Jaime shirt, revealing a nasty bruise in his superb dark-bay torso.

"Is there tape in that kit, Mr. Fenton? I've had a little first-aid training."

She begins to deal competently and very impersonally with the tape. Miss Parsons and I wander to the end of the bar and have a conversation which I am later to recall acutely.

"Roseate spoonbills," I tell her as three pink birds flap away.

"They're beautiful," she says in her tiny voice. They both have tiny voices. "He's a Mayan Indian, isn't he? The pilot, I mean."

"Right. The real thing, straight out of the Bonampak murals. Have you seen Chichén and Uxmal?"

"Yes. We were in Mérida. We're going to Tikal in Guatemala . . . I mean, we were."

"You'll get there." It occurs to me the girl needs cheering up. "Have they told you that Maya mothers used to tie a board on the infant's forehead to get that slant? They also hung a ball of tallow over its nose to make its eyes cross. It was considered aristocratic."

She smiles and takes another peak at Estéban. "People seem different in Yucatan," she says thoughtfully. "Not like the Indians around Mexico City. More, I don't know, independent."

"Comes from never having been conquered. Mayas got massacred and chased a lot, but nobody ever really flattened them. I bet you didn't know that the last Mexican-Maya war ended with a negotiated truce in nineteen thirty-five?"

"No!" Then she says seriously, "I like that."

"So do I."

"The water is really rising very fast," says Mrs. Parsons gently from behind us.

It is, and so is another *llovisna*. We climb back into the Bonanza. I try to rig my parka for a rain catcher, which blows loose as the storm hits fast and furious. We sort a couple of malt bars and my bottle of Jack Daniel's out of the jumble in the cabin and make ourselves reasonably comfortable. The Parsonses take a sip of whiskey each, Estéban and I considerably more. The Bonanza begins to bump soggily. Estéban makes an ancient one-eyed Maya face at the water seeping into his cabin and goes to sleep. We all nap.

When the water goes down, the euphoria has gone with it, and we're very, very thirsty. It's also damn near sunset. I get to work with a bait-casting rod and some treble hooks and manage to foul-hook four small mullets. Estéban and the women tie the Bonanza's midget life raft out in the mangroves to catch rain. The wind is parching hot. No planes go by.

Finally another shower comes over and yields us six ounces of water apiece. When the sunset envelops the world in golden smoke, we squat on the sandbar to eat wet raw mullet and Instant Breakfast crumbs. The women are now in shorts, neat but definitely not sexy.

"I never realized how refreshing raw fish is," Mrs. Parsons says pleasantly. Her daughter chuckles, also pleasantly. She's on Mamma's far side away from Estéban and me. I have Mrs. Parsons figured now; Mother Hen protecting only chick from male predators. That's all right with me. I came here to fish.

But something is irritating me. The damn women haven't complained once, you understand. Not a peep, not a quaver, no personal manifestations whatever. They're like something out of a manual.

"You really seem at home in the wilderness, Mrs. Parsons. You do much camping?"

"Oh goodness no." Diffident laugh. "Not since my girl scout days. Oh, look—are those man-of-war birds?"

Answer a question with a question. I wait while the frigate birds sail nobly into the sunset.

"Bethesda . . . Would I be wrong in guessing you work for Uncle Sam?"

"Why, yes. You must be very familiar with Washington, Mr. Fenton. Does your work bring you there often?"

Anywhere but on our sandbar the little ploy would have worked. My hunter's gene twitches.

"Which agency are you with?"

She gives up gracefully. "Oh, just GSA records. I'm a librarian."

Of course, I know her now, all the Mrs. Parsonses in records divisions, accounting sections, research branches, personnel and administration offices. Tell Mrs. Parsons we need a recap on the external service contracts for fiscal 'seventy-three. So Yucatan is on the tours now? Pity . . . I offer her the tired little joke. "You know where the bodies are buried."

She smiles deprecatingly and stands up. "It does get dark quickly, doesn't it?"

Time to get back into the plane.

A flock of ibis are circling us, evidently accustomed to roosting in our fig tree. Estéban produces a machete and a Maya hammock. He proceeds to sling it between tree and plane, refusing help. His machete stroke is noticeably tentative.

The Parsonses are taking a pee behind the tail vane. I hear one of them slip and squeal faintly. When they come back over the hull, Mrs. Parsons asks, "Might we sleep in the hammock, Captain?"

Estéban splits an unbelieving grin. I protest about rain and mosquitoes.

"Oh, we have insect repellent and we do enjoy fresh air."

The air is rushing by about force five and colder by the minute.

"We have our raincoats," the girl adds cheerfully.

Well, okay, ladies. We dangerous males retire inside the damp cabin. Through the wind I hear the women laugh softly now and then, apparently cozy in their chilly ibis roost. A private insanity, I decide. I know myself for the least threatening of men; my noncharisma has been in fact an asset jobwise, over the years. Are they having fantasies about Estéban? Or maybe they really are fresh-air nuts. . . . Sleep comes for me in invisible diesels roaring by on the reef outside.

We emerge dry-mouthed into a vast windy salmon sunrise. A diamond chip of sun breaks out of the sea and promptly submerges in cloud. I go to work with the rod and some mullet bait while two showers detour around us. Breakfast is a strip of wet barracuda apiece.

The Parsons continue stoic and helpful. Under Estéban's direction they set up a section of cowling for a gasoline flare in case we hear a plane, but nothing goes over except one unseen jet droning toward Panama. The wind howls, hot and dry and full of coral dust. So are we.

"They look first in the sea," Estéban remarks. His aristocratic frontal slope is beaded with sweat; Mrs. Parsons watches him concernedly. I watch the cloud blanket tearing by above, getting higher and dryer and thicker. While that lasts nobody is going to find us, and the water business is now unfunny.

Finally I borrow Estéban's machete and hack a long, light pole.

"There's a stream coming in there. I saw it from the plane. Can't be more than two, three miles."

"I'm afraid the raft's torn." Mrs. Parsons shows me the cracks in the orange plastic; irritatingly, it's a Delaware label.

"All right," I hear myself announce. "The tide's going down. If we cut the good end of that air tube, I can haul water back in it. I've waded flats before."

Even to me it sounds crazy.

"Stay by plane," Estéban says. He's right, of course. He's also clearly running a fever. I look at the overcast and taste grit and old barracuda. The hell with the manual.

When I start cutting up the raft, Estéban tells me to take the serape. "You stay one night." He's right about that, too; I'll have to wait out the tide.

"I'll come with you," says Mrs. Parsons calmly.

I simply stare at her. What new madness has got into Mother Hen? Does she imagine Estéban is too battered to be functional? While I'm being astounded, my eyes take in the fact that Mrs. Parsons is now quite rosy around the knees, with her hair loose and a sunburn starting on her nose. A trim, in fact a very neat shading-forty.

"Look, that stuff is horrible going. Mud up to your ears and water over your head."

"I'm really quite fit and I swim a great deal. I'll try to keep up. Two would be much safer, Mr. Fenton, and we can bring more water."

She's serious. Well, I'm about as fit as a marshmallow at this time of winter, and I can't pretend I'm depressed by the idea of company. So be it.

"Let me show Miss Parsons how to work this rod."

Miss Parsons is even rosier and more windblown, and she's not clumsy with my tackle. A good girl, Miss Parsons, in her nothing way. We cut another staff and get some gear together. At the last minute Estéban shows how sick he feels: he offers me the machete. I thank him, but, no; I'm used to my Wirkkala knife. We tie some air into the plastic tube for a float and set out along the sandiest looking line.

Estéban raises one dark palm. *"Buen viaje."* Miss Parsons has hugged her mother and gone to cast from the mangrove. She waves. We wave.

An hour later we're barely out of waving distance. The going is purely god-awful. The sand keeps dissolving into silt you can't walk on or swim through, and the bottom is spiked with dead mangrove spears. We flounder from one pothole to the next, scaring up rays and turtles and hoping to god we don't kick a moray eel. Where we're not soaked in slime, we're desiccated, and we smell like the Old Cretaceous.

Mrs. Parsons keeps up doggedly. I only have to pull her out once. When I do so, I notice the sandbar is now out of sight.

Finally we reach the gap in the mangrove line I thought was the creek. It turns out to open into another arm of the bay, with more mangroves ahead. And the tide is coming in.

"I've had the world's lousiest idea."

Mrs. Parsons only says mildly, "It's so different from the view from the plane."

I revise my opinion of the girl scouts, and we plow on past the mangroves toward the smoky haze that has to be shore. The sun is setting in our faces, making it hard to see. Ibises and herons fly up around us, and once a big hermit spooks ahead, his fin cutting a rooster tail. We fall into more potholes. The flashlights get soaked. I am having fantasies of the mangrove as universal obstacle; it's hard to recall I ever walked down a street, for instance, without stumbling over or under or through mangrove roots. And the sun is dropping, down, down.

Suddenly we hit a ledge and fall over it into a cold flow.

"The stream! It's fresh water!"

We guzzle and gargle and douse our heads; it's the best drink I remember. "Oh my, oh my—!" Mrs. Parsons is laughing right out loud.

"That dark place over to the right looks like real land."

We flounder across the flow and follow a hard shelf, which turns into solid bank and rises over our heads. Shortly there's a break beside a clump of spiny bromels, and we scramble up and flop down at the top, dripping and stinking. Out of sheer reflex my arm goes around my companion's shoulder—but Mrs. Parsons isn't there; she's up on her knees peering at the burnt-over plain around us.

"It's so good to see land one can walk on!" The tone is too innocent. *Noli me tangere.*

"Don't try it." I'm exasperated; the muddy little woman, what does she think? "That ground out there is a crust of ashes over muck, and it's full of stubs. You can go in over your knees."

"It seems firm here."

"We're in an alligator nursery. That was the slide we came up. Don't worry, by now the old lady's doubtless on her way to be made into handbags."

"What a shame."

"I better set a line down in the stream while I can still see."

I slide back down and rig a string of hooks that may get us breakfast. When I get back Mrs. Parsons is wringing muck out of the serape.

"I'm glad you warned me, Mr. Fenton. It *is* treacherous."

"Yeah." I'm over my irritation; god knows I don't want to *tangere* Mrs. Parsons, even if I weren't beat down to mush. "In its quiet way, Yucatan is a tough place to get around in. You can see why the Mayas built roads. Speaking of which—look!"

The last of the sunset is silhouetting a small square shape a couple of kilometers inland: a Maya *ruina* with a fig tree growing out of it.

"Lot of those around. People think they were guard towers."

"What a deserted-feeling land."

"Let's hope it's deserted by mosquitoes."

We slump down in the 'gator nursery and share the last malt bar, watching the stars slide in and out of the blowing clouds. The bugs aren't too bad; maybe the burn did them in. And it isn't hot any more, either—in fact, it's not even warm, wet as we are. Mrs. Parsons continues tranquilly interested in Yucatan and unmistakably uninterested in togetherness.

Just as I'm beginning to get aggressive notions about how we're going to spend the night if she expects me to give her the serape, she stands up, scuffs at a couple of hummocks, and says, "I expect this is as good a place as any, isn't it, Mr. Fenton?"

With which she spreads out the raft bag for a pillow and lies down on her side in the dirt with exactly half the serape over her and the other corner folded neatly open. Her small back is toward me.

The demonstration is so convincing that I'm halfway under my share of serape before the preposterousness of it stops me.

"By the way. My name is Don."

"Oh, of course." Her voice is graciousness itself. "I'm Ruth."

I get in, not quite touching her, and we lie there like two fish on a plate, exposed to the stars and smelling the smoke in the wind and feeling things underneath us. It is absolutely the most intimately awkward moment I've had in years.

The woman doesn't mean one thing to me, but the obtrusive recessiveness of her, the defiance of her little rump eight inches from my fly—for two pesos I'd have those shorts down and introduce myself. If I were twenty years younger. If I weren't so bushed . . . But the twenty years and the exhaustion are there, and it comes to me wryly that Mrs. Ruth Parsons has judged things to a nicety. If I *were* twenty years younger, she wouldn't be here. Like the butterfish that float around a sated barracuda, only to vanish away the instant his intent changes, Mrs. Parsons knows her little shorts are safe. Those firmly filled little shorts, so close . . .

A warm nerve stirs in my groin—and just as it does I become aware of a silent emptiness beside me. Mrs. Parsons is imperceptibly inching away. Did my breathing change? Whatever, I'm perfectly sure that if my hand reached, she'd be elsewhere—probably announcing her intention to take a dip. The twenty years bring a chuckle to my throat, and I relax.

"Good night, Ruth."

"Good night, Don."

And believe it or not, we sleep, while the armadas of the wind roar overhead.

Light wakes me—a cold white glare.

My first thought is 'gator hunters. Best to manifest ourselves as *turistas* as fast as possible. I scramble up, noting that Ruth has dived under the bromel clump.

"*Quién estás? A socorro!* Help, *señores!*"

No answer except the light goes out, leaving me blind.

I yell some more in a couple of languages. It stays dark. There's a vague scrabbling, whistling sound somewhere in the burn-off. Liking everything less by the minute, I try a speech about our plane having crashed and we need help.

A very narrow pencil of light flicks over us and snaps off.

"Eh-ep," says a blurry voice and something metallic twitters. They for sure aren't locals. I'm getting unpleasant ideas.

"Yes, help!"

Something goes crackle-crackle whish-whish, and all sounds fade away.

"What the holy hell!" I stumble toward where they were.

"Look," Ruth whispers behind me. "Over by the ruin."

I look and catch a multiple flicker which winks out fast.

"A camp?"

And I take two more blind strides; my leg goes down through the crust, and a spike spears me just where you stick the knife in to unjoint a drumstick. By the pain that goes through my bladder I recognize that my trick kneecap has caught it.

For instant basket case you can't beat kneecaps. First you discover your knee doesn't bend anymore, and so you try putting some weight on it, and a bayonet goes up your spine and unhinges your jaw. Little grains of gristle have got into the sensitive bearing surface. The knee tries to buckle and can't, and mercifully you fall down.

Ruth helps me back to the serape.

"What a fool, what a god-forgotten imbecile—"

"Not at all, Don. It was perfectly natural." We strike matches; her fingers push mine aside, exploring. "I think it's in place, but it's swelling fast. I'll lay a wet handkerchief on it. We'll have to wait for morning to check the cut. Were they poachers, do you think?"

"Probably," I lie. What I think they were is smugglers.

She comes back with a soaked bandanna and drapes it on. "We must have frightened them. That light . . . it seemed so bright."

"Some hunting party. People do crazy things around here."

"Perhaps they'll come back in the morning."

"Could be."

Ruth pulls up the wet serape, and we say goodnight again. Neither of us is mentioning how we're going to get back to the plane without help.

I lie staring south where Alpha Centauri is blinking in and out of the overcast and cursing myself for the sweet mess I've made. My first idea is giving way to an even less pleasing one.

Smuggling, around here, is a couple of guys in an outboard meeting a shrimp boat by the reef. They don't light up the sky or have some kind of swamp buggy that goes whoosh. Plus a big camp . . . paramilitary-type equipment?

I've seen a report of Guévarista infiltrators operating on the British Honduran border, which is about a hundred kilometers—sixty miles—south of here. Right under those clouds. If that's what looked us over, I'll be more than happy if they don't come back . . .

I wake up in pelting rain, alone. My first move confirms that my leg is as expected—a giant misplaced erection bulging out of my shorts. I raise up painfully to see Ruth standing by the bromels, looking over the bay. Solid wet nimbus is pouring out of the south.

"No planes today."

"Oh, good morning, Don. Should we look at that cut now?"

"It's minimal." In fact the skin is hardly broken, and no deep puncture. Totally out of proportion to the havoc inside.

"Well, they have water to drink," Ruth says tranquilly. "Maybe those hunters will come back. I'll go see if we have a fish—that is, can I help you in any way, Don?"

Very tactful. I emit an ungracious negative, and she goes off about her private concerns.

They certainly are private, too; when I recover from my own sanitary efforts, she's still away. Finally I hear splashing.

"It's a big fish!" More splashing. Then she climbs up the bank with a three-pound mangrove snapper—and something else.

It isn't until after the messy work of filleting the fish that I begin to notice.

She's making a smudge of chaff and twigs to singe the fillets, small hands very quick, tension in that female upper lip. The rain has eased off for the moment; we're sluicing wet but warm enough. Ruth brings me my fish on a mangrove skewer and sits back on her heels with an odd breathy sigh.

"Aren't you joining me?"

"Oh, of·course." She gets a strip and picks at it, saying quickly, "We either have too much salt or too little, don't we? I should fetch some brine." Her eyes are roving from nothing to noplace.

"Good thought." I hear another sigh and decide the girl scouts need an assist. "Your daughter mentioned you've come from Mérida. Seen much of Mexico?"

"Not really. Last year we went to Mazatlan and Cuernavaca. . . ." She puts the fish down, frowning.

"And you're going to see Tikál. Going to Bonampak too?"

"No." Suddenly she jumps up, brushing rain off her face. "I'll bring you some water, Don."

She ducks down the slide, and after a fair while comes back with a full bromel stalk.

"Thanks." She's standing above me, staring restlessly round the horizon.

"Ruth, I hate to say it, but those guys are not coming back and it's probably just as well. Whatever they were up to, we looked like trouble. The most they'll do is tell someone we're here. That'll take a day or two to get around; we'll be back at the plane by then."

"I'm sure you're right, Don." She wanders over to the smudge fire.

"And quit fretting about your daughter. She's a big girl."

"Oh, I'm sure Althea's all right. . . . They have plenty of water now." Her fingers drum on her thigh. It's raining again.

"Come on, Ruth. Sit down. Tell me about Althea. Is she still in college?"

She gives that sighing little laugh and sits. "Althea got her degree last year. She's in computer programming."

"I'm in Foreign Procurement Archives." She smiles mechanically, but her breathing is shallow. "It's very interesting."

"I know a Jack Wittig in Contracts, maybe you know him?" It sounds pretty absurd, there in the 'gator slide.

"Oh, I've met Mr. Wittig. I'm sure he wouldn't remember me."

"Why not?"

"I'm not very memorable."

Her voice is purely factual. She's perfectly right, of course. Who was that woman, Mrs. Jannings, Janny, who coped with my per diem for years? Competent, agreeable, impersonal. She had a sick father or something. But dammit, Ruth is a lot younger and better-looking. Comparatively speaking.

"Maybe Mrs. Parsons doesn't want to be memorable."

She makes a vague sound, and I suddenly realize Ruth isn't listening to me at all. Her hands are clenched around her knees, she's staring inland at the ruin.

"Ruth, I tell you our friends with the light are in the next county by now. Forget it, we don't need them."

Her eyes come back to me as if she'd forgotten I was there, and she nods slowly. It seems to be too much effort to speak. Suddenly she cocks her head and jumps up again.

"I'll go look at the line, Don. I thought I heard something—" She's gone like a rabbit.

While she's away I try getting up onto my good leg and the staff. The pain is sickening; knees seem to have some kind of hot line to the stomach. I take a couple of hops to test whether the Demerol I have in my belt would get me walking. As I do so, Ruth comes up the bank with a fish flapping in her hands.

"Oh, no, Don! *No!*" She actually clasps the snapper to her breast.

"The water will take some of my weight. I'd like to give it a try."

"You mustn't!" Ruth says quite violently and instantly modulates down. "Look at the bay, Don. One can't see a thing."

I teeter there, tasting bile and looking at the mingled curtains of sun and rain driving across the water. She's right, thank god. Even with two good legs we could get into trouble out there.

"I guess one more night won't kill us."

I let her collapse me back onto the gritty plastic, and she positively bustles around, finding me a chunk to lean on, stretching the serape on both staffs to keep rain off me, bringing another drink, grubbing for dry tinder.

"I'll make us a real bonfire as soon as it lets up, Don. They'll see our smoke, they'll know we're all right. We just have to wait." Cheery smile. "Is there any way we can make you more comfortable?"

Holy Saint Sterculius: playing house in a mud puddle. For a fatuous moment I wonder if Mrs. Parsons has designs on me. And then she lets out another sigh and sinks back onto her heels with that listening look. Unconsciously her rump wiggles a little. My ear picks up the operative word: *wait*.

Ruth Parsons is waiting. In fact, she acts as if she's waiting so hard it's killing her. For what? For someone to get us out of here, what else? . . . But why was she so horrified when I got up to try to leave? Why all this tension?"

My paranoia stirs. I grab it by the collar and start idly checking back. Up to when whoever it was showed up last night, Mrs. Parsons was, I guess, normal. Calm and sensible, anyway. Now she's humming like a high wire. And she seems to want to stay here and wait. Just as an intellectual pastime. Why?

Could she have intended to come here? No way. Where she planned to be was Chetumal, which is on the border. Come to think, Chetumal is an odd way round to Tikál. Let's say the scenario was that she's meeting somebody in Chetumal. Somebody who's part of an organization. So now her contact in Chetumal knows she's overdue. And when those types appeared last night, something suggested to her that they're part of the same organization. And she hopes they'll put one and one together and come back for her?

"May I have the knife, Don? I'll clean the fish."

Rather slowly I pass the knife, kicking my subconscious. Such a decent ordinary little woman, a good girl scout. My trouble is that

I've bumped into too many professional agilities under the careful stereotypes. *I'm not very memorable. . . .*

What's in Foreign Procurement Archives? Wittig handles classified contracts. Lots of money stuff; foreign currency negotiations, commodity price schedules, some industrial technology. Or—just as a hypothesis—it could be as simple as a wad of bills back in that modest beige Ventura, to be exchanged for a packet from say, Costa Rica. If she were a courier, they'd want to get at the plane. And then what about me and maybe Estéban? Even hypothetically, not good.

I watch her hacking at the fish, forehead knotted with effort, teeth in her lip. Mrs. Ruth Parsons of Bethesda, this thrumming, private woman. How crazy can I get? *They'll see our smoke. . . .*

"Here's your knife, Don. I washed it. Does the leg hurt very badly?"

I blink away the fantasies and see a scared little woman in a mangrove swamp.

"Sit down, rest. You've been going all out."

She sits obediently, like a kid in a dentist chair.

"You're stewing about Althea. And she's probably worried about you. We'll get back tomorrow under our own steam, Ruth."

"Honestly I'm not worried at all, Don." The smile fades; she nibbles her lip, frowning out at the bay.

"Ruth, you know you surprised me when you offered to come along. Not that I don't appreciate it. But I rather thought you'd be concerned about leaving Althea. Alone with our good pilot, I mean. Or was it only me?"

This gets her attention at last.

"I believe Captain Estéban is a very fine type of man."

The words surprise me a little. Isn't the correct line more like "I trust Althea," or even, indignantly, "Althea is a good girl"?

"He's a man. Althea seemed to think he was interesting."

She goes on staring at the bay. And then I notice her tongue flick out and lick that prehensile upper lip. There's a flush that isn't sunburn around her ears and throat too, and one hand is gently rubbing her thigh. What's she seeing, out there in the flats?

Captain Estéban's mahogany arms clasping Miss Althea Parsons' pearly body. Captain Estéban's archaic nostrils snuffling in Miss Parsons' tender neck. Captain Estéban's copper buttocks pumping into Althea's creamy upturned bottom . . . The hammock, very bouncy. Mayas know all about it.

Well, well. So Mother Hen has her little quirks.

I feel fairly silly and more than a little irritated. *Now* I find out. . . . But even vicarious lust has much to recommend it, here in the mud and rain. I settle back, recalling that Miss Althea the computer programmer had waved good-bye very composedly. Was she sending her mother to flounder across the bay with me so she can get programmed in Maya? The memory of Honduran mahogany logs drifting in and out of the opalescent sand comes to me. Just as I am about to suggest that Mrs. Parsons might care to share my rain shelter, she remarks serenely, "The Mayas seem to be a very fine type of people. I believe you said so to Althea."

The implications fall on me with the rain. *Type.* As in breeding, bloodline, sire. Am I supposed to have certified Estéban not only as a stud but as a genetic donor?

"Ruth, are you telling me you're prepared to accept a half-Indian grandchild?"

"Why, Don, that's up to Althea, you know."

Looking at the mother, I guess it is. Oh, for mahogany gonads.

Ruth has gone back to listening to the wind, but I'm not about to let her off that easy. Not after all that *noli me tangere* jazz.

"What will Althea's father think?"

Her face snaps around at me, genuinely startled.

"Althea's father?" Complicated semismile. "He won't mind."

"He'll accept it too, eh?" I see her shake her head as if a fly were bothering her, and add with a cripple's malice, "Your husband must be a very fine type of a man."

Ruth looks at me, pushing her wet hair back abruptly. I have the impression that mousy Mrs. Parsons is roaring out of control, but her voice is quiet.

"There isn't any Mr. Parsons, Don. There never was. Althea's father was a Danish medical student. . . . I believe he has gained considerable prominence."

"Oh." Something warns me not to say I'm sorry. "You mean he doesn't know about Althea?"

"No." She smiles, her eyes bright and cuckoo.

"Seems like rather a rough deal for her."

"I grew up quite happily under the same circumstances."

Bang, I'm dead. Well, well, well. A mad image blooms in my mind: generations of solitary Parsons women selecting sires, making impregnation trips. Well, I hear the world is moving their way.

"I better look at the fish line."

She leaves. The glow fades. *No.* Just no, no contact. Good-bye, Captain Estéban. My leg is very uncomfortable. The hell with Mrs. Parsons' long-distance orgasm.

We don't talk much after that, which seems to suit Ruth. The odd day drags by. Squall after squall blows over us. Ruth singes up some more fillets, but the rain drowns her smudge; it seems to pour hardest just as the sun's about to show.

Finally she comes to sit under my sagging serape, but there's no warmth there. I doze, aware of her getting up now and then to look around. My subconscious notes that she's still twitchy. I tell my subconscious to knock it off.

Presently I wake up to find her penciling on the water-soaked pages of a little notepad.

"What's that, a shopping list for alligators?"

Automatic polite laugh. "Oh, just an address. In case we—I'm being silly, Don."

"Hey." I sit up, wincing. "Ruth, quit fretting. I mean it. We'll all be out of this soon. You'll have a great story to tell."

She doesn't look up. "Yes . . . I guess we will."

"Come on, we're doing fine. There isn't any real danger here, you know. Unless you're allergic to fish?"

Another good-little-girl laugh, but there's a shiver in it.

"Sometimes I think I'd like to go . . . really far away."

To keep her talking I say the first thing in my head.

"Tell me, Ruth. I'm curious why you would settle for that kind of lonely life, there in Washington? I mean, a woman like you—"

"Should get married?" She gives a shaky sigh, pushing the notebook back in her wet pocket.

"Why not? It's the normal source of companionship. Don't tell me you're trying to be some kind of professional man-hater."

"Lesbian, you mean?" Her laugh sounds bitter. "With my security rating? No, I'm not."

"Well, then. Whatever trauma you went through, these things don't last forever. You can't hate all men."

The smile is back. "Oh, there wasn't any trauma, Don, and I *don't* hate men. That would be as silly as—as hating the weather." She glances wryly at the blowing rain.

"I think you have a grudge. You're even spooky of me."

Smooth as a mouse bite she says, "I'd love to hear about your family, Don."

Touché. I give her the edited version of how I don't have one anymore, and she says she's sorry, how sad. And we chat about what a good life a single person really has, and how she and her friends enjoy plays and concerts and travel, and one of them is head cashier for Ringling Brothers, how about that?

But it's coming out jerkier and jerkier like a bad tape, with her eyes going round the horizon in the pauses and her face listening for something that isn't my voice. What's wrong with her? Well, what's wrong with any furtively unconventional middle-aged woman with an empty bed? And a security clearance. An old habit of mind remarks unkindly that Mrs. Parsons represents what is known as the classic penetration target.

"—so much more opportunity now." Her voice trails off.

"Hurrah for women's lib, eh?"

"The lib?" Impatiently she leans forward and tugs the serape straight. "Oh, that's doomed."

The word apocalyptic jars my attention.

"What do you mean, doomed?"

She glances at me as if I weren't hanging straight either and says vaguely, "Oh . . ."

"Come on, why doomed? Didn't they get that equal-rights bill?"

Long hesitation. When she speaks again her voice is different. "Women have no rights, Don, except what men allow us. Men are more aggressive and powerful, and they run the world. When the next real crisis upsets them, our so-called rights will vanish like—like that smoke. We'll be back where we always were: property. And whatever has gone wrong will be blamed on our freedom, like the fall of Rome was. You'll see."

Now all this is delivered in a gray tone of total conviction. The last time I heard that tone, the speaker was explaining why he had to keep his file drawers full of dead pigeons.

"Oh, come on. You and your friends are the backbone of the system; if you quit, the country would come to a screeching halt before lunch."

No answering smile.

"That's fantasy." Her voice is still quiet. "Women don't work that way. We're a—a toothless world." She looks around as if she wanted to stop talking. "What women do is survive. We live by ones and twos in the chinks of your world-machine."

"Sounds like a guerrilla operation." I'm not really joking, here in the 'gator den. In fact, I'm wondering if I spent too much thought on mahogany logs.

"Guerrillas have something to hope for." Suddenly she switches on the jolly smile. "Think of opossums, Don. Did you know there are opossums living all over? Even in New York City."

I smile back with my neck prickling. I thought I was the paranoid one.

"Men and women aren't different species, Ruth. Women do everything men do."

"Do they?" Our eyes meet, but she seems to be seeing ghosts between us in the rain. She mutters something that could be "My Lai" and looks away. "All the endless wars . . ." Her voice is a whisper. "All the huge authoritarian organizations for doing unreal things. Men live to struggle against each other; we're just part of the battlefields. It'll never change unless you change the whole world. I dream sometimes of—of going away—" She checks and abruptly changes voice. "Forgive me, Don, it's so stupid saying all this."

"Men hate wars too, Ruth," I say as gently as I can.

"I know." She shrugs and climbs to her feet. "But that's your problem, isn't it?"

End of communication. Mrs. Ruth Parsons isn't even living in the same world with me.

I watch her move around restlessly, head turning toward the ruins. Alienation like that can add up to dead pigeons, which would be GSA's problem. It could also lead to believing some joker who's promising to change the world. Which could just probably be my problem if one of them was over in that camp last night, where she keeps looking. *Guerrillas have something to hope for . . . ?*

Nonsense. I try another position and see that the sky seems to be clearing as the sun sets. The wind is quieting down at last too. Insane to think this little woman is acting out some fantasy in this swamp. But that equipment last night was no fantasy; if those lads have some connection with her, I'll be in the way. You couldn't find a handier spot to dispose of a body. . . . Maybe some Guévarista is a fine type of man?

Absurd. Sure . . . The only thing more absurd would be to come through the wars and get myself terminated by a mad librarian's boyfriend on a fishing trip.

A fish flops in the stream below us. Ruth spins around so fast she hits the serape. "I better start the fire," she says, her eyes still on the plain and her head cocked, listening.

All right, let's test.

"Expecting company?"

It rocks her. She freezes, and her eyes come swiveling around at me like a film take captioned Fright. I can see her decide to smile.

"Oh, one never can tell!" She laughs weirdly, the eyes not changed. "I'll get the—the kindling." She fairly scuttles into the brush.

Nobody, paranoid or not, could call *that* a normal reaction.

Ruth Parsons is either psycho or she's expecting something to happen—and it has nothing to do with me; I scared her pissless.

Well, she could be nuts. And I could be wrong, but there are some mistakes you make only once. Reluctantly I unzip my body belt, telling myself that if I think what I think, my only course is to take something for my leg and get as far as possible from Mrs. Ruth Parsons before whoever she's waiting for arrives.

In my belt also is a .32 caliber asset Ruth doesn't know about—and it's going to stay there. My longevity program leaves the shoot-outs to TV and stresses being somewhere else when the roof falls in. I can spend a perfectly safe and also perfectly horrible night out in one of those mangrove flats . . . am I insane?

At this moment Ruth stands up and stares blatantly inland with her hand shading her eyes. Then she tucks something into her pocket, buttons up and tightens her belt.

That does it.

I dry-swallow two 100-mg. tabs, which should get me ambulatory and still leave me wits to hide. Give it a few minutes. I make sure my compass and some hooks are in my own pocket and sit waiting while Ruth fusses with her smudge fire, sneaking looks away when she thinks I'm not watching.

The flat world around us is turning into an unearthly amber and violet light show as the first numbness seeps into my leg. Ruth has crawled under the bromels for more dry stuff; I can see her foot. Okay. I reach for my staff.

Suddenly the foot jerks, and Ruth yells—or rather, her throat makes that *Uh-uh-uhhh* that means pure horror. The foot disappears in a rattle of bromel stalks.

I lunge upright on the crutch and look over the bank at a frozen scene.

Ruth is crouching sideways on the ledge, clutching her stomach. They are about a yard below, floating on the river in a skiff. While I was making up my stupid mind, her friends have glided right under my ass. There are three of them.

They are tall and white. I try to see them as men in some kind of white jumpsuits. The one nearest the bank is stretching out a long white arm toward Ruth. She jerks and scuttles farther away.

The arm stretches after her. It stretches and stretches. It stretches two yards and stays hanging in air. Small black things are wiggling from its tip.

I look where their faces should be and see black hollow dishes with vertical stripes. The stripes move slowly. . . . .

There is no more possibility of their being human—or anything else I've ever seen. What has Ruth conjured up?

The scene is totally silent. I blink, blink—this cannot be real. The two in the far end of the skiff are writhing those arms around an apparatus on a tripod. A weapon? Suddenly I hear the same blurry voice I heard in the night.

"Guh-give," it groans. "G-give . . ."

Dear god, it's real, whatever it is. I'm terrified. My mind is trying not to form a word.

And Ruth—Jesus, of course—Ruth is terrified too; she's edging along the bank away from them, gaping at the monsters in the skiff, who are obviously nobody's friends. She's hugging something to her body. Why doesn't she get over the bank and circle back behind me?

"G-g-give." That wheeze is coming from the tripod. "Pee-eeze give." The skiff is moving upstream below Ruth, following her. The arm undulates out at her again, its black digits looping. Ruth scrambles to the top of the bank.

"Ruth!" My voice cracks. "Ruth, get over here behind me!"

She doesn't look at me, only keeps sidling farther away. My terror detonates into anger.

"Come back here!" With my free hand I'm working the .32 out of my belt. The sun has gone down.

She doesn't turn but straightens up warily, still hugging the thing. I see her mouth working. Is she actually trying to *talk* to them?

"Please . . ." She swallows. "Please speak to me. I need your help."

"RUTH!!"

At this moment the nearest white monster whips into a great S-curve and sails right onto the bank at her, eight feet of snowy rippling horror.

And I shoot Ruth.

I don't know that for a minute—I've yanked the gun up so fast

that my staff slips and dumps me as I fire. I stagger up, hearing
Ruth scream "No! No! No!"

The creature is back down by his boat, and Ruth is still farther
away, clutching herself. Blood is running down her elbow.

"Stop it, Don! They aren't attacking you!"

"For god's sake! Don't be a fool, I can't help you if you won't
get away from them!"

No reply. Nobody moves. No sound except the drone of a jet
passing far above. In the darkening stream below me the three
white figures shift uneasily; I get the impression of radar dishes
focusing. The word spells itself in my head: *Aliens.*

Extraterrestrials.

What do I do, call the President? Capture them singlehanded
with my peashooter? . . . I'm alone in the arse end of nowhere
with one leg and my brain cuddled in meperidine hydrochloride.

"Prrr-eese," their machine blurs again. "Wa-wat hep . . ."

"Our plane fell down," Ruth says in a very distinct, eerie voice.
She points up at the jet, out toward the bay. "My—my child is
there. Please take us *there* in your boat."

Dear god. While she's gesturing, I get a look at the thing she's
hugging in her wounded arm. It's metallic, like a big glimmering
distributor head. What—?

Wait a minute. This morning: when she was gone so long, she
could have found that thing. Something they left behind. Or
dropped. And she hid it, not telling me. That's why she kept going
under that bromel clump—she was peeking at it. Waiting. And
the owners came back and caught her. They want it. She's trying
to bargain, by god.

"—Water," Ruth is pointing again. "Take us. Me. And him."

The black faces turn toward me, blind and horrible. Later on I
may be grateful for that "us." Not now.

"Throw your gun away, Don. They'll take us back." Her voice is
weak.

"Like hell I will. You—who are you? What are you doing
here?"

"Oh god, does it matter? He's frightened," she cries to them.
"Can you understand?"

She's as alien as they, there in the twilight. The beings in the skiff are twittering among themselves. Their box starts to moan. "Ss-stu-dens," I make out. "S-stu-ding . . . not—huhparm-ing . . . w-we . . . buh . . ." It fades into garble and then says "G-give . . . we . . . g-go . . ."

Peace-loving cultural-exchange students—on the interstellar level now. Oh, no.

"Bring that thing here, Ruth—right now!"

But she's starting down the bank toward them, saying, "Take me."

"Wait! You need a tourniquet on that arm."

"I know. Please put the gun down, Don."

She's actually at the skiff, right by them. They aren't moving. "Jesus Christ." Slowly, reluctantly I drop the .32. When I start down the slide, I find I'm floating; adrenaline and Demerol are a bad mix.

The skiff comes gliding toward me, Ruth in the bow clutching the thing and her arm. The aliens stay in the stern behind their tripod, away from me. I note the skiff is camouflaged tan and green. The world around us is deep shadowy blue.

"Don, bring the water bag!"

As I'm dragging down the plastic bag, it occurs to me that Ruth really is cracking up; the water isn't needed now. But my own brain seems to have gone into overload. All I can focus on is a long white rubbery arm with black worms clutching the far end of the orange tube, helping me fill it. This isn't happening.

"Can you get in, Don?" As I hoist my numb legs up, two long white pipes reach for me. *No you don't.* I kick and tumble in beside Ruth. She moves away.

A creaky hum starts up, it's coming from a wedge in the center of the skiff. And we're in motion, sliding toward dark mangrove files.

I stare mindlessly at the wedge. Alien technological secrets? I can't see any, the power source is under that triangular cover, about two feet long. The gadgets on the tripod are equally cryptic, except that one has a big lens. Their light?

As we hit the open bay, the hum rises and we start planing faster and faster still. Thirty knots? Hard to judge in the dark. Their hull seems to be a modified trihedral much like ours, with a remarkable absence of slap. Say twenty-two feet. Schemes of capturing it swirl in my mind: I'll need Estéban.

Suddenly a huge flood of white light fans out over us from the tripod, blotting out the aliens in the stern. I see Ruth pulling at a belt around her arm, which is still hugging the gizmo.

"I'll tie that for you."

"It's all right."

The alien device is twinkling or phosphorescing slightly. I lean over to look, whispering, "Give that to me, I'll pass it to Estéban."

"No!" She scoots away, almost over the side. "It's theirs, they need it!"

"What? Are you crazy?" I'm so taken aback by this idiocy I literally stammer. "We have to, we—"

"They haven't hurt us. I'm sure they could." Her eyes are watching me with feral intensity; in the light her face has a lunatic look. Numb as I am, I realize that the wretched woman is poised to throw herself over the side if I move. With the gizmo.

"I think they're gentle," she mutters.

"For Christ's sake, Ruth, they're *aliens!*"

"I'm used to it," she says absently. "There's the island! Stop! Stop here!"

The skiff slows, turning. A mound of foliage is tiny in the light. Metal glints—the plane.

"Althea! Althea! Are you all right?"

Yells, movement on the plane. The water is high, we're floating over the bar. The aliens are keeping us in the lead with the light hiding them. I see one pale figure splashing toward us and a dark one behind, coming more slowly. Estéban must be puzzled by that light.

"Mr. Fenton is hurt, Althea. These people brought us back with the water. Are you all right?"

"A-okay." Althea flounders up, peering excitedly. "You all right? Whew, that light!" Automatically I start handing her the idiotic water bag.

"Leave that for the captain," Ruth says sharply. "Althea, can you climb in the boat? Quickly, it's important."

"Coming!"

"No, no!" I protest, but the skiff tilts as Althea swarms in. The aliens twitter, and their voice box starts groaning. "Gu-give . . . now . . . give . . ."

"*Que llega?*" Estéban's face appears beside me, squinting fiercely into the light.

"Grab it, get it from her—that thing she has—" but Ruth's voice rides over mine. "Captain, lift Mr. Fenton out of the boat. He's hurt his leg. Hurry, please."

"Goddamn it, wait!" I shout, but an arm has grabbed my middle. When a Maya boosts you, you go. I hear Althea saying, "Mother, your arm!" and fall onto Estéban. We stagger around in water up to my waist; I can't feel my feet at all.

When I get steady, the boat is yards away, the two women, head-to-head, murmuring.

"Get them!" I tug loose from Estéban and flounder forward. Ruth stands up in the boat facing the invisible aliens.

"Take us with you. Please. We want to go with you, away from here."

"Ruth! Estéban, get that boat!" I lunge and lose my feet again. The aliens are chirruping madly behind their light.

"Please take us. We don't mind what your planet is like; we'll learn—we'll do anything! We won't cause any trouble. Please. Oh *please*." The skiff is drifting farther away.

"Ruth! Althea! You're crazy, wait—" But I can only shuffle nightmarelike in the ooze, hearing that damn voice box wheeze, "N-not come . . . more . . . not come. . . ." Althea's face turns to it, open-mouthed grin.

"Yes, we understand," Ruth cries. "We don't want to come back. Please let us go with you!"

I shout and Estéban splashes past me shouting too, something about radio.

"Yes-s-s" groans the voice.

Ruth sits down suddenly, clutching Althea. At that moment Estéban grabs the edge of the skiff beside her.

"Hold them, Estéban! Don't let her go."

He gives me one slit-eyed glance over his shoulder, and I recognize his total uninvolvement. He's had a good look at that camouflage paint and the absence of fishing gear. I make a desperate rush and slip again. When I come up Ruth is saying, "We're going with these people, Captain. Please take your money out of my purse, it's in the plane. And give this to Mr. Fenton."

She passes him something small; the notebook. He takes it slowly.

"Estéban! Don't!"

He has released the skiff.

"Thank you so much," Ruth says as they float apart. Her voice is shaky; she raises it. "There won't be any trouble, Don. Please send this cable. It's to a friend of mine, she'll take care of everything." Then she adds the craziest touch of the entire night. "She's a grand person; she's director of nursing training at N.I.H."

As the skiff drifts, I hear Althea add something that sounds like "Right on."

Sweet Jesus . . . Next minute the humming has started; the light is receding fast. The last I see of Mrs. Ruth Parsons and Miss Althea Parsons is two small shadows against that light, like two opossums. The light snaps off, the hum deepens—and they're going, going, gone away.

In the dark water beside me Estéban is instructing everybody in general to *chingarse* themselves.

"Friends, or something," I tell him lamely. "She seemed to want to go with them."

He is pointedly silent, hauling me back to the plane. He knows what could be around here better than I do, and Mayas have their own longevity program. His condition seems improved. As we get in I notice the hammock has been repositioned.

In the night—of which I remember little—the wind changes. And at seven thirty next morning a Cessna buzzes the sandbar under cloudless skies.

By noon we're back in Cozumel. Captain Estéban accepts his fees and departs laconically for his insurance wars. I leave the Parsons' bags with the Caribe agent, who couldn't care less. The cable goes to a Mrs. Priscilla Hayes Smith also of Bethesda. I take myself to a medico and by three PM I'm sitting on the Cabañas terrace with a fat leg and a double margarita, trying to believe the whole thing.

The cable said, *Althea and I taking extraordinary opportunity for travel. Gone several years. Please take charge our affairs. Love, Ruth.*

She'd written it that afternoon, you understand.

I order another double, wishing to hell I'd gotten a good look at that gizmo. Did it have a label, Made by Betelgeusians? No matter how weird it was, *how* could a person be crazy enough to imagine—?

Not only that, but to hope, to plan? *If I could only go away.* . . . That's what she was doing, all day. Waiting, hoping, figuring how to get Althea. To go sight unseen to an alien world. . . .

With the third margarita I try a joke about alienated women, but my heart's not in it. And I'm certain there won't be any bother, any trouble at all. Two human women, one of them possibly pregnant, have departed for, I guess, the stars; and the fabric of society will never show a ripple. I brood; do all Mrs. Parsons' friends hold themselves in readiness for any eventuality, including leaving Earth? And will Mrs. Parsons somehow one day contrive to send for Mrs. Priscilla Hayes Smith, that grand person?

I can only send for another cold one, musing on Althea. What suns will Captain Estéban's sloe-eyed offspring, if any, look upon? "Get in, Althea, we're taking off for Orion." "A-okay, Mother." Is that some system of upbringing? *We survive by ones and twos in the chinks of your world-machine.* . . . *I'm used to aliens.* . . . She'd meant every word. Insane. How could a woman choose to live among unknown monsters, to say good-bye to her home, her world?

As the margaritas take hold, the whole mad scenario melts down to the image of those two small shapes sitting side by side in the receding alien glare.

Two of our opossums are missing.

1984 Revisited

It has been twenty-five years since George Orwell wrote
a novel of the future entitled 1984. This ominous year is
part of the world's languages now, so much so that
government agencies avoid any predictions that might
fall in this fatal year. Less seriously, Punch devoted most
of an issue to a satirical look at 1984 and made some
strong attempts to see if Orwell's predictions might be
coming true. For this special number of the magazine
Brian Aldiss produced an all too wintry look at the
future of Britain controlled by new world rulers Orwell
never considered. Clive James is brief and entertaining
with some heretofore unfaced speculation about the
future of Concorde, while Alan Coren, deputy editor of
Punch, most logically outlines some reasons why Orwell's 1984 will never arrive in our lifetimes.

Listen with Big Brother

BRIAN W. ALDISS

FOG hung in layers over Southmoor. Christopher Woodham paid
off the pedicab.

"It's six minutes past four," he said aloud. "I've arrived home."

He could see a light moving in the house, where Ruth was
preparing for the evening's ordeal. Before daylight drained away,
he made an inspection of the grounds, checking that the
remaining goat had hay, that the hens and goose were secure. The

half-acre of garden had been turned into a small-holding ten years ago; Ruth no longer grew prize chrysanthemums, but her marrows were renowned.

A shaggy figure loomed in the mist. Woodham was immediately on the alert. Despite enforced personal bugging, lawlessness was current, particularly in areas of high unemployment.

"It's me, Chris. I was checking the pump."

Fred Laws had been in the aircraft industry until the Fall. Now he was a general trader, operating just within the law, and helping with odd jobs for wealthy friends like Woodham. He was a big man; he wore an old helmet painted in stripes.

"Hello, Fred. I'm getting the batteries."

They went to the windmill which Laws had built. Laws made deaf-and-dumb signs as they walked through the chicken enclosure. At the windmill, which worked a generator charging the batteries that supplied much of the Woodhams' power, Laws said, "What's wrong here?" and leaned against the metal superstructure.

Covered by the vibrations which played through his body, canceling his personal bugging system, he said softly, "It's your big night tonight, isn't it? Are you going to have any trouble with him?"

Woodham shook his head, conscious of the wires about his neck and chest and the recorder in the small of his back.

Laws motioned him to press against the superstructure too, saying, "I was in Oxford today. I've got a haunch of venison, guaranteed from Magdalen Deer Park, if that would help you with him."

"They like sausages. Ruth has got sausages." Woodham hated these stealthy conversations which everyone indulged in, knowing they were wired for sound. He bent down and read the voltmeter. The batteries were ready. The windmill could generate 75 kilowatts in a forty kph wind.

As Woodham took two of the batteries off charge, preparing to drag them to the house on a sled, Laws said in a hearty, artificial voice, "Everything's fine, then, Chris. I'm glad we live in heroic times! I'm fitter than I was ten years ago, sitting in an office from nine till five, lining up for a coronary. Outdoor life suits me. And thank heavens cigarettes have disappeared. Remember those disgusting fags we used to smoke? If this is a relapse into barbarism, I'm for it!"

"Yes, heroic times . . . I never think of that wasteful old consumer society we escaped from," said Woodham, despising himself for pandering to whatever member of the Conservationist Party might examine his tape tomorrow. He genuinely hated what everyone called the Fall of Europe, whereas Laws, nefarious by nature, genuinely enjoyed it. Laws would be in trouble one day; on that day, it might help not to have accepted his hijacked venison.

The men parted, Laws vanishing into mist as Woodham lugged his batteries towards the house.

*   *   *

With the batteries linked to the emergency lighting, the room filled with yellow light.

Woodham grunted. "We'll have a log fire, so that it's warm here when he arrives."

Ruth blew out her candle. "What a relief when we have power through the grid again. A lot of use the Severn Barrage is!"

Assuming an official voice, he said, "The tidal power harnessed in the Bristol Channel goes to operate essential industry—Britain must export or die. We'll be getting a domestic supply next year, when the Solent barrage comes on the national grid." He pulled a face, to show her that what he was saying was strictly for the bugmen.

She held a strip of paper before his eyes, on which she had written, "FOOD STORE CLOSED AGAIN TODAY SOL-DIERS GUARDING."

She smiled wearily. Ruth had stood the challenge of the last years remarkably well. The girl he had married, so dependent on mother's helps, shopping sprees, TV, and hairdressers, had disappeared; in her place was this quiet, dependable woman, thin of cheek but adept at gutting an occasional illegal rabbit. He patted her bottom as she went into the kitchen.

The room looked well enough, Woodham thought. They had brought out all their Arab knick-knacks. Vessels of bronze and copper, one inscribed "A Souvenir of Esfahan," stood on the mantelpiece, a fine hanging was draped down the wall, and an aroma which passed for Arab incense hung in the air. They had put themselves out for an honored guest. It was now dark; nobody would see how shabby and paintless the place had become.

"Heroic times indeed!" he said aloud. There was always a hope that you might *bore* a bugman to death. . . .

*   *   *

The magical sound of a *car* on the drive.

"Seven-fifteen precisely and guest arrived," Woodham said.

He hurried to the door. A uniformed Pakistani was opening the car door—Rolls? Cadillac? Some other old-fashioned name?—and in no time, smelling sweet and herbal, impeccably tailored Munich-style, Shaikh Mahmoud Gheleb was striding into the Woodham house.

He seemed to throw off light and elegance, from the strands of burnished gold in his neat dark beard to the rings on his fingers. Although Ruth kept out of the way for etiquette's sake, the distinguished visitor had not forgotten *alva* for her, with Sumatran cigars for Woodham. Moreover, he was delighted with the room—surprised to discover how civilized it was, charmed by its warmth and the feel of genial Olde England.

Ruth's meal went equally well. Before they ate, a fragrance drifted in from the kitchen, and the Shaikh confided how much he enjoyed British sausages. Lo and behold, in came Ruth, bearing a great plate of goat sausages and poached goose eggs, bedded on rice! The two men belched delicately afterwards, as they finished their vintage apple wine, and Shaikh Gheleb confided that Britain was easily his favorite tourist country. No, no, he even liked the cold damp winters; they made a pleasant change after the heat of Jiddah.

"I fear you are playing the polite guest, Shaikh. This is a miserable little country, which people leave when they can get work permits for yours." The rules were strict but clear: it was only seditious to run down one's country to a fellow-countryman; to a prosperous foreigner, advantage might be gained.

Yet his was a tactless remark. For the Shaikh could have rejoined that at least there was still a thin stream of Israeli refugees coming into Britain. The man was too courteous for such crudity; he said, "We never forget how hospitable Britain was, in the days of her prosperity, to workers from all over the world, no matter what color their skin."

It was time for business. Ruth was working the manual-power record-player, but music could not drown out voices for little microphones clamped round the neck. Woodham seized the Turkish coffee mill and ground it with difficulty against the top of his spine.

"Forgive this absurdity of posture, Shaikh, but you know how law-abiding this country is. I have a confidence to share with you which I do not wish to get into the central computers. You forgive me, I hope, since the confidence could be mutually profitable?"

"The pleasure of your home is sufficient, but your confidence would be an added benefit. So let's talk turkey. You have some reclamation systems you can sell my firm? Oil by-products?"

"No. Not quite." Grating away till his head hummed, speaking low so that Ruth's bugging would not catch his words he said, "As you know, I own a recycling plant in Abingdon—part-own, since the government has compulsory shares. We recycle two things: paper and glass. We mainly turn the glass into cullet, which then goes to a glass factory to make more glass. The paper we turn into cardboard and protein."

The Shaikh nodded. "I understand you are making steaks from the recycled paper."

"Yes, and they are palatable when flavored with dog or cat meat essence—you probably know that the British are no longer allowed pets since 1982, but laboratory animals exist, which we acquire cheaply. Now, my technicians have discovered a way of making crude but cheap containers out of a modified cullet. They're like tin cans, such as we used to drink beer from, before the Fall. I plan to can our steaks and sell them as a cheap storable food-source."

"Where do I come in?"

Woodham glanced at the clock. It was later than he thought. In an hour, curfew, and the day's tape poured in one loud high-speed scream into the computer terminal on the phone . . . its contents to be picked over at leisure by the buggers of Whitehall. He ground the mill more furiously at the thought.

"We need one vital thing which you can supply, Shaikh. A refrigeration unit. They can't be obtained in Europe, even on the black market. Get me one of those, and I will guarantee you 25% of my profits. Here are some figures." He handed over a prepared sheet.

Shaikh Gheleb appraised the figures with a keen eye, then said, "It's difficult. You understand the Arab Bloc is at war with Japan. For me to get a permit for exports to Europe will be extremely complex in the circumstances."

"For 30% perhaps?"

"Can you not obtain the permit through legal channels, since your objective is to increase productivity?"

The very words caused Woodham to tremble. He blurted out a Party slogan: "Expansionist Thinking set Britain sinking!"

The Shaikh nodded. "But they would accept a *fait accompli*, the authorities, right? Particularly if it were guaranteed by an Arab industrialist? That would entail a capital risk for me. . . ."

"35%?"

Leaning forward confidentially, the Shaikh said, "One further doubt . . . This—this food product . . ."

"Yes? We shall market it initially as 'The Cullet Cutlet'—if we obtain your support, that is."

"This Cullet Cutlet . . . it cannot be very tasty. Where will you find a market sufficiently undiscriminating to buy your product?"

"Ah! We have just such a market! As you probably know, Shaikh, our massive unemployment has forced many Englishmen to form mercenary armies or join the British Legion. There are, I'm proud to say, three British mercenary battalions fighting for the Arab Superstate in the Pacific right now."

"And four fighting for the Japanese . . ."

"That's seven battalions in the Pacific theater alone. Cullet Cutlet will find a ready market, rest assured."

"Okay. 60%."

*   *   *

As they were saying farewell, Woodham glanced at the clock. Just gone ten. Half-an-hour to Curfew and Off-load. He would have twenty minutes of suspicious blanket-noise on his tape, but that could be explained away. Meanwhile, the deal had been completed. Mentally, he saw himself booking passages on a Korean sailboat and heading with Ruth for sunny retirement by the Red Sea. The Shaikh and he embraced with warmth, although Woodham was conscious of his own strong body odor.

The night was thick outside. Shaikh Gheleb produced a torch and shone it towards his vehicle.

Both men exclaimed. The chauffeur lay gagged and bound in the car. His eyes rolled helplessly. His body was lashed round with a green fencing wire which Woodham recognized.

Crime against property, foreign property! The car was propped up on bricks. Its tires, synthesized from precious Arabian oil, had been removed. And on the doors of the vehicle were scrawled the words "Heroic Times!"

There was still a place for unspoken crime, even in the best-organized society.

The Rise of Airstrip One

CLIVE JAMES

MINTRUTH INFOBUMF UPDATE 2121221122

REFERENCE: CONCORDE

Concorde's cost estimates having reached their planned 1973 year's end level of £100,000,000, the government expelled France from the project and instituted the modification phase of the aircraft's development schedule. Contrary to rumors spread by the Environmental Lobby (Mintruth Infobumf Update 1122211221 Reference Liquidated Organizations) these modifications had been fully allowed for in the cost-estimate projections.

The aircraft's payload shortfall (the pre-production prototype of the post-preproduction production version could carry a hundred people from Heathrow to Gatwick, a hundredweight from Gatwick to Prestwick, and a hundred grammes from Prestwick to Rejkavik) was comfortably inside forecasts. Nevertheless, for margin considerations, and taking advantage of the breathing space conferred by the cancellation of all remaining options by foreign airlines, engine power was uprated by one hundred percent in a development programme beginning 1975.

As anticipated, fuel consumption rose by a related figure.

As planned, tankage was increased by a proportional volume. As expected, payload shortfall, a function of the increased fuel weight, recurred. Concorde's cost estimates having reached their planned 1983 year's end level of £1,000,000,000, the first production version of the pre-post-preproduction prototype was rolled out. Weighing a quarter of a million tons, it proved able to carry an airletter from one end of Heathrow to the other at a speed of 27 mph, provided the airletter contained no enclosures. The planned post-modification phase was begun, and continues.

Owing to Circumstances Beyond Our Control 1984 Has Been Unavoidably Detained . . .

ALAN COREN

Winston Smith lay on his mean little bed in his mean little room and stared at his mean little telescreen. The screen stared back, blank. Smith eased himself from the side of his mean little blonde, walked across his dun and threadbare carpet, and kicked the silent cathode. A blip lurched unsteadily across it, and disappeared. Smith sighed, and picked up the telephone.

"Would you get me Rentabrother Telehire?" he said.

"They're in the book," said the operator.

"I haven't got a book," said Smith. "They didn't deliver it."

"It's no good blaming me," said the operator. "It's a different department."

"I'm not blaming you," said Smith. "I just thought you might get me the number."

"I was just going off," said the operator, "on account of the snow."

"It's not snowing," said Smith.

"Not *now*, it isn't," said the operator. "I never said it was snowing *now*."

"Perhaps I might have a word with the Supervisor," said Smith.

"She's not here," said the operator. "She gets her hair done Fridays."

"I only need the Rentabrother number," said Smith. "Perhaps you could find it for me. You must have a book."

"I'd have to bend," said the operator.

"I'd be awfully grateful," said Smith.

"I've just done me nails."

"Please," said Smith.

There was a long pause, during which a woman came on and began ordering chops, and someone gave Smith a snatch of weather forecast for Heligoland. After that, there was a bit of recipe for sausage toad. Eventually, after two further disconnections, the operator came back.

"It's 706544," she snapped.

Smith put the receiver down, and dialed 706544.

"809113," shouted a voice, "Eastasian Cats Home."

He got a Samoan ironmonger after that, and then a French woman who broke down and screamed. At last "Rentabrother Telehire," said a man.

"Winston Smith here," said Smith, "72a, Osbaldeston Road. I'm afraid my telescreen seems to be out of order."

"What am I supposed to do?" said the man. "We're up to our necks."

"But I'm not being watched," said Smith. "Big Brother is supposed to be monitoring me at all times."

"Ring Big Bleeding Brother, then," said the man. "Maybe he's not suffering from staff shortages, seasonal holidays, people off sick. Maybe he's not awaiting deliveries. Not to mention we had a gull get in the stockroom, there's stuff all over, all the labels come off, broken glass. People ringing up all hours of the day and night. You realize this is my tea-time?"

"I'm terribly sorry," said Smith. "It's just that . . ."

"Might be able to fit you in Thursday fortnight," said the man. "Can't promise nothing, though. Got a screwdriver, have you?"

"I'm not sure," said Smith.

"Expect bleeding miracles, people," said the man, and rang off.

Smith put the phone down, and was about to return to the bed when there was a heavy knocking on the door, and before he or the little blonde could move, it burst from its hinges and two enormous constables of the thought police hurtled into the room. They recovered, and looked around, and took out notebooks.

"Eric Jervis," cried the larger of the two, "we have been monitoring your every action for the past six days, and we have reason to believe that the bicycle standing outside with the worn brake blocks is registered in your name. What have you to say?"

"I'm not Eric Jervis," said Smith.

They stared at him.

"Here's a turn-up," said the shorter officer.

"Ask him if he's got any means of identity," murmured the larger.

"Have you any means of identity?" said the constable.

"I'm waiting for a new identity card," said Smith. "It's in the post."

"I knew he'd say that," said the larger officer.

"We're right in it now," said his colleague. "Think of the paperwork."

They put their notebooks away.

"You wouldn't know where this Eric Jervis is, by any chance?" said the taller.

"I'm afraid not," said Smith.

"Who's that on the bed, then?"

"It's certainly not Eric Jervis," said Smith.

They all looked at the little blonde.

"He's got us there," said the shorter constable.

"I've just had a thought," said the taller, "I don't think people are supposed to, er, do it, are they?"

"Do what?"

"You know, men," the thought policeman looked at his boots, "and women."

"I don't see what that's got to do with worn brake blocks," said his colleague.

They tipped their helmets.

"Mind how you go," they said.

Smith let them out, and came back into the room.

"I'll just nip down the corner," he said to the little blonde, "and pick up an evening paper. Shan't be a tick."

It was crowded on the street. It was actually the time of the two-minutes hate, but half the public telescreens were conked out, and anyway the population was largely drunk, or arguing with one another, or smacking kids round the head, or running to get a bet on, or dragging dogs from lamp-posts, or otherwise preoccupied, so nobody paid much attention to the suspended telescreens, except for the youths throwing stones at them. Smith edged through, and bought a paper, and opened it.

"COME OFF IT BIG BROTHER," screamed the headline, above a story blaming the Government for rising food prices, the shortage of underwear, and the poor showing of the Oceanic football team. It wasn't, Smith knew, the story the Government hacks had given to the printers, but you could never get the printers to listen to anyone, and when challenged, they always blamed the shortage of type, claiming that they could only put the words together from the letters available, and who cared, anyhow? The Government, with so much else on its plate, had given up bothering.

It was as Winston Smith turned to go back to his flat that he felt a frantic plucking at his knee and heard a soprano scream ring through the street. He looked down and saw a tiny youth spy jumping up and down below him.

"Winston Smith does dirty things up in Fourteen B," howled the child. "Come and get him; he's got a nude lady up there."

The youth spy might have elaborated on these themes, had its mother not reached out and given it a round arm swipe that sent it flying into the gutter; but, even so, the damage had been done, and before Smith had time to protest, he found himself picked up bodily by a brace of uniformed men and slung into the back of a truck which, siren wailing, bore him rapidly through the evening streets towards the fearful pile of the Ministry of Love.

"Smith, W," barked the uniformed man to whom Smith was manacled, at the desk clerk.

"What's he done?" said the clerk. "I was just off home."

"They caught him at a bit of how's your father," said Smith's captor.

"It's Friday night," said the desk clerk. "I go to bingo Fridays." He turned to Smith. "Don't let it happen again, lad. You can go blind."

"I've written him in me book," said the guard. "It's no good saying go home. I'd have to tear the page out." He put his free hand on Smith's arm. "Sorry about this, son. It'd be different if I had a rubber. We're awaiting deliveries."

"You'd better take him up to Room 101, then," said the clerk.

"NOT ROOM 101," screamed Smith, "NOT THE TORTURE CHAMBER, PLEASE, I NEVER DID ANYTHING, I HARDLY KNOW THE WOMAN, CAN'T ANYONE HELP ME, DON'T SEND ME UP. . . ."

"Stop that," said the clerk sharply. "You'll start the dog off."

Smith was dragged, shrieking, to the elevator.

"Ah, Smith, Winston," cried the white-coated man at the door of Room 101. "Won't you come in? Rats, I believe, are what you, ha-ha-ha, fear most of all. Big brown rats. Big brown pink-eyed rats . . ."

"NO," screamed Smith, "NOT RATS, ANYTHING BUT RATS, NO, NO, NO."

". . . Rats with long slithery tails, Smith, fat, hungry rats, rats with sharp little . . ."

"Oh, do shut up, Esmond," interrupted his assistant wearily. "You know we haven't got any rats. We haven't seen a rat since last December's delivery."

"No rats?" gasped Smith.

Esmond sighed and shook his head. Then he suddenly brightened.

"We've got mice, though," he cried. "Big, fat, hungry, pink-eyed . . ."

"I don't mind mice," said Smith.

They looked at him.

"You're not making our job any easier, you know," muttered Esmond.

"Try him on toads," said Esmond's assistant. "Can't move in the stockroom for toads."

"That's it!" exclaimed Esmond. "Toads. Big, fat, slimy . . ."

"I quite like toads," said Smith.

There was a long pause.

"Spiders?"

"Lovely little things," said Smith. "If it's any help, I can't stand moths."

"Moths," cried Esmond. "Where do you think you are, bloody Harrod's? We can't get moths for love nor money."

"Comes in here, big as you please, asking for moths," said Esmond's assistant.

Smith thought for a while.

"I'm not all that keen on stoats," he said at last.

"At last," said Esmond. "I thought we'd be here all night. Give him a stoat, Dennis."

So they put Winston Smith in Room 101 with a stoat. It was an old stoat, and it just sat on the floor, wheezing, and as far as Smith was concerned, things could have been, all things considered, a lot worse.

Lost and Found

THOMAS BAUM

What if things had been different . . . ? What if I could change the past? These questions have troubled writers for a very long time. So many pact-with-the-devil and three-wish stories have been written, so many time travelers have gone back to straighten out their earlier lives, that it takes a writer of immense talent and strong resolution to venture into an area where so many others have gone before. Happily, Thomas Baum, a novelist and a screenwriter, has these talents in excess.

ON a recent evening in February, *If Winter Comes*, the Pulitzer Prize drama by Sidney Wise, was revived at the Morosco Theater, New York. That morning the playwright rose early, as always, and took his wife, Marcia, her breakfast in bed. While he was taking his shower, his son, Howard, arrived with a batch of congratulatory telegrams sent over by Nate Folger, Sidney Wise's producer, and when Sidney Wise came in from the bathroom, his wife was reading them aloud, in a pinched, postnasal voice, to the ceiling.

"‘AGE CANNOT WITHER YOUR INFINITE VARIETY. IF WINTER COMES STILL MY FAVORITE. GEORGE.’ George who?" demanded Marcia Wise, reaching for a tissue.

"George Hartshorne," said Sidney Wise, with his customary

patience. "He does interviews for the *Times*. I'm having lunch with him today."

"I see. So that's why you're rushing off when I need you—to be interviewed." She blew her nose violently. " 'CROW KEEPS WELL IN THE FREEZER. I PLAN TO EAT SOME TONIGHT. STANLEY DULLES.' "

"He panned *If Winter Comes* in 1948," Sidney Wise explained. "We became friends later."

"How would I know?" said Marcia Wise. "Since I don't know any of your friends. 'IF WINTER COMES, CAN SPRING BE FAR BEHIND?' "

"Depends which way you're facing," said the playwright.

" 'SPRING WESTERMAN,' " read Marcia Wise. "Isn't that that awful actress from *Five'll Get You Ten* who's always trying to get you to write her another play? The one they all said you were sleeping with?"

"And you believed it," said Sidney Wise, parting a few uncombed locks of gray from his wife's forehead. The morning sun fell across her pale, handsome features, deepening the fine wrinkles, lighting the dry pools of fatigue beneath her eyes. "Did you take your temperature?" he said.

"No. And don't tell me I shouldn't go to Washington." She looked him briefly up and down. "Is that what you're wearing tonight? Your green blazer? I thought it was red you wore to the"—her lip curled fastidiously—"to the tragedies."

"No." The phone by the bed gave half a ring; he heard his son Howard answer in the study. "I guess you've forgotten. I wore this the night *If Winter Comes* first opened. Then to *Let's Talk About the Money* I wore a blue suit. Then *Border Disputes* opened and by chance I wore green again, and Leonard Lyons started saying I wore green to my serious plays and blue to my comedies, so when *Come Up for Air* opened—"

"You wore blue. So people would know to laugh. Spare me, Sidney, the biannual recitation of your *oeuvre*. I take it, then, you plan to go directly to the theater? I can't count on you to drive us to the airport?"

"I wish you'd reconsider this trip," said Sidney Wise. "Washington seems somehow like such a long way to go."

"Precisely," said Marcia Wise. "While your face is all over the New York papers, we'll be seeing the sights. Surely I don't have to remind you, Sidney, how hard these openings are on Howard."

"I think you exaggerate that."

"Exaggerate? God, when I think what a relief, all those people *not* coming up to us backstage asking if we're related to the playwright—did I ever tell you, Sidney," she said cheerfully, "that at the last opening someone wanted to know how it felt to be your mother?"

"You didn't go to the last opening," said Sidney Wise, transferring his wallet from the pocket of his corduroy jacket. He buttoned his ceremonial green blazer, bending to kiss his wife, who interposed a wad of tissue. Turning sadly, the playwright went out of the bedroom and down the hall to his study, where his son, Howard, was just hanging up the phone. At Howard's feet sat an airline bag, a rolled playscript projecting from one end.

"That was Nate Folger," said Howard Wise. "He'll meet you and George Hartshorne at Frankie & Johnnie's in half an hour. Turns out the *Times* is giving you a whole page Sunday. Save me that section, will you, Dad, since I'll be in Washington? Hey, that jacket still fits."

"Do you want to come to lunch, Howard?"

"With you? And the *Times*? You must be joking." Howard Wise rolled his eyes at his father's manuscript shelf, the *Playbills* framed on the study wall. "I'd feel like an idiot. Besides, I've got plane tickets to pick up. I'll ride as far as Fiftieth, though, and you can tell me what's wrong with *Reflected Glory*." He held up the airline bag with the playscript, following his father into the vestibule. Outside the brownstone, a cab was waiting.

"Morosco Theater," said Sidney Wise to the driver, moving over to make room for Howard.

"You didn't have to tell me," said the driver. "*If Winter Comes*. It's a privilege, Mr. Wise."

"You're very kind," said the playwright. The cab swung down Fifth Avenue.

"My wife sees all your plays," the driver said. "I can tell you this, too, yours are the only plays she ever sees. These other plays today, she says, are too damned confusing, and if she wants to be confused, my wife says, she can always talk to me."

Howard Wise leaned forward. "That, my good man, is why Sidney Wise is the only playwright in America whose name still sells tickets."

"I can believe it," said the driver.

"Drama you can sink your teeth into," said Howard Wise. "Comedy that makes you laugh, not scratch your head. The theater's greatest two-way threat since 1616."

"Are you his press agent?" asked the driver. "Not that my wife wouldn't agree."

"I'm his son." Howard leaned back, beaming at his father. "Son Howard. L'il Howie. The One Who Walks in Shadow. So what did you think, Dad?"

"Of that eulogy?"

"Of *Reflected Glory*." He jerked the playscript out of the airline bag. "Wait. Don't say it. It happened again. Six POWs come back from Vietnam. Timely? Sure-fire? Believe me, Dad, I don't set *out* to rip you off. This time I got halfway through before it hit me, before I remembered those six GIs returning from Japan. OK. Say what you always say. I should have taken a different tack. All right, but I was so goddamn depressed. Who, I said to myself, is really going to remember *If Winter Comes*? So the day I finish the longhand drafts, Nate Folger announces the revival. I almost killed myself."

"Bad poets imitate," Sidney Wise said helpfully, "good poets steal."

"*Reflected Glory*, I'm afraid, isn't what T. S. Eliot had in mind." Howard Wise leafed through the script. "The lieutenant's speech in act one? The comic relief? I don't have to tell you: practically word for word from *Come Up for Air*. Even when I think I'm inventing stuff, it turns out I'm copying you."

"You can rewrite," Sidney Wise suggested. "It's still a valid subject, it's only a first draft—"

"No! Thanks, Dad, but no. Don't you get it? It's always been this way, and it's getting worse. Can't you grasp what I'm up against? How you should never expect anything from me, because

I'll never be any good on my own? How I'm doomed to be the poor man's Sidney Wise? On my deathbed I'll probably recite your deathbed words! Let me off here," said Howard to the driver, "and then drive extra carefully. This is precious cargo you're carrying: Broadway's pride, every playwright's yardstick, the man who's said it all, who makes you laugh one night and cry the next, a great man and a really conscientious father and the greatest model any son could want!"

The cab door slammed. Sliding over, Sidney Wise watched his son sprint tearfully across the avenue, against the light. The playwright held his breath as for a moment Howard was lost to view, then blinked as he saw him again, safe on the sidewalk in front of the airline office, blowing his nose. I should do endorsements, thought Sidney Wise; I should pick up a bundle from Kleenex, give up writing plays and make everybody happy. He saw himself in his study, addressing the cameras. *You think I make audiences cry? Look what I do to my loved ones.* He passed a hand across his eyes. With each opening, things got a little worse. And was it his fault? It was not. Could a man be blamed if his success hurt others? It did not hurt others. Others hurt others. That was the truth. When had he ever believed it? I should have taken her temperature, he thought, drumming his fist suddenly on his knee. Flying off to Washington: even hysterical sniffles could lead to the flu.

"Family first," said the driver.

"Pardon me?" Sidney Wise glanced up; they were in the theater district.

"My wife says she can tell you're devoted to your family, and not just because she read it in some magazine. She says it shows in your plays."

"It's true," said the playwright, with sudden vehemence.

"She could tell it was."

"Nothing," insisted Sidney Wise, reaching for his wallet as the cab slowed, "not even a man's work, is worth the sacrifice of his family."

"I couldn't agree more. Is it true, Mr. Wise, that you've made more people laugh than any person in history?"

"What? No. You're thinking of Lucille Ball," said Sidney Wise. Where was his wallet? He slapped his pockets.

"Lucille Ball! Hey, that's terrific. My wife'll crack up when she hears that."

"Listen, I'm awfully sorry. I seem to have come away without my wallet. Although I distinctly remember transferring it from my corduroy jacket. If you'll give me your name and address, I'll mail you the fare."

"Forget it, Mr. Wise—this has been payment enough. Well, look, you can see for yourself what you did: you transferred the wallet, but then you put on the corduroy jacket anyway. I do that all the time. Here we are, Mr. Wise, Booth Theater!"

"But I said the Morosco—"

"The Morosco? No way. Check your tickets. What, is there a special matinee today? Must be fun for you, seeing somebody else's play for a change. Like I say, my wife sees every play that comes along, good, bad or indifferent. Watch the door, now. It's been a pleasure, Mr. Wise!"

The cab sped away; he stepped onto the curb. He was on the north side of 45th Street; revolving, he stared across at the Morosco. The lobby was dark, no cashier in the box office, no lettering on the billboard, no posters or show cards anywhere: not a sign that *If Winter Comes* was opening that night. He walked up to the theater, yanked on the doors; they were locked. He rattled them again and heard giggles; turning, he saw his producer, Nate Folger, with Spring Westerman, the actress. "What's happened to my play?" he said.

Spring Westerman checked another giggle; she looked at Nate Folger. "Actually, I don't get it. Do you get it, Nate?"

"I think I get it," said Nate Folger. "Arthur Miller's play closed here. But you're right, Spring, it isn't funny." The producer rested a hand on Sidney Wise's shoulder. "*Hob rachmones*, Sidney. The man had no business writing a comedy. Any more," he added, pointing him toward Frankie & Johnnie's, "than you'd have writing *Death of a Salesman*."

Sidney Wise examined his jacket sleeves. "Nate—"

"What is it, Sidney? Problems with the new play?"

"Nate, I'm talking about *If Winter Comes.*"

"*If Winter Comes?* That's a title for a comedy?"

"My Pulitzer Prize!"

"Sidney." A door opened; Folger guided them up the stairs to the restaurant. "It's a discredited award. I'll show you the article: Ninety-nine percent of all so-called tragedy is based on trivial misunderstandings between the sexes and between the generations. In another twenty-five years those'll all be gone, resolved forever, and you know what'll be left? Comedy, Sidney. Your comedies. *Let's Talk About the Money, Come Up for Air, Who Needs It?, Leaps and Bounds, Five'll Get You Ten*—the all-time comedy grosser, lest we forget—plus whatever you come up with next."

"Don't you *want* to write me another show?" said Spring Westerman, as they all sat down—in vain Sidney Wise looked around the restaurant for Hartshorne, the man from the *Times.* "Don't you *want* to work with me again?"

"Of course he does. That's what we're here to discuss. *Ten'll Get You Twenty—there's* a comedic title. We're four," said Nate Folger to the waiter. "Oh, Marcia! Here we are, baby!"

At the sound of his wife's name, Sidney Wise, who had been peering at his calendar watch, jerked upright.

"Hello, dears." Marcia Wise, in a gray body shirt and black palazzo pants, kissed Nate Folger, kissed Spring Westerman and sat down. "You both look fantastic. Sidney, why are you staring at me like that?"

"I wasn't. I'm not," said Sidney Wise, gazing at his wife's hair, a perfect, bushy, salt-and-pepper arch.

"He still can't get used to it," said Marcia Wise to Spring Westerman. "To Sidney, a natural is an ad for pubic hair. If Sidney had his way, I'd never go out of the house except in a *babushka.*"

"Takes more than jealousy to hold this broad," said Nate Folger. "When are you coming to read for me, gorgeous?"

"When my husband keels over. Why? Do you think in a million years Sidney would let me *work* for my living?"

"Yes!" said Sidney Wise, watching his wife's hand dive beneath the tablecloth.

"If Sidney had his *way*, I'd be one of those jealous, carping semi-invalids you see married to writers, up to my nostrils in Lady Scott, poor Howard would be some kind of thankless freak and Mr. Jokes here would be locked in his study writing heart-renders." She goosed him.

"Wrong!" said Sidney Wise.

"Wrong. I know, Sidney. You wouldn't know how to begin." She moved her fingers in a circle.

"I love your hair," protested Sidney Wise, groping under the table for her hand.

"And I love you," said Marcia Wise, moving it away.

"And I'm about to throw up," said Nate Folger. "Between Sidney's tragic muse—"

"Do you want to know Sidney's idea of tragedy?" said Marcia Wise brightly. "When the Knicks lose a close one." Reaching under the table again, she covered her husband's hand with her own, pressing it lovingly between her legs. She stood up. "Will you all excuse me?"

"Marcia?" said Sidney Wise, getting up.

"Where's she going?" said Nate Folger.

"Excuse me," said Sidney Wise, crouching to hide his erection. Marcia was halfway across the restaurant.

"What's going on?" said Nate Folger.

"I thought we were going to talk about my part," said Spring Westerman, as Sidney Wise lunged away from the table. The stairway door swung to. The playwright glanced back at Folger and Spring Westerman and pushed it open. From the shadow of the landing a pair of arms flung themselves about his neck.

"You horny toad. I saw you gawking at me."

They kissed fiercely, squirming together. People went by them on the stairs.

"Get rid of those two leeches. I'll meet you home in twenty minutes. You sex machine," she said, breaking loose and running down the steps. The downstairs door opened and closed. With another glance inside the restaurant—Folger and Spring Westerman were hunched around in their seats—he straightened his tie and descended after her. Emerging, he saw a cab pulling away from the curb, toward Broadway; he quickly hailed another. In the rear window the Morosco Theater receded, dark, posterless. The cab went up Sixth Avenue and across 50th and up Madison, arriving at his street before he recalled he was without his wallet. Asking the driver to wait, and handing him his watch as collateral, the playwright raced up the stairs to his front door and inside, calling his wife's name. There was no answer. He hurried to the bedroom, picturing her naked on the bed, waiting on hands and knees. He opened the door; there was no one. The covers were on the bed, the telegrams were gone, his green blazer, with his wallet—he searched rapidly through his closet—was gone. He went to the window. The cab was gone. He heard a voice.

"Right, I can see it works better without it. Hartshorne noticed, too? I don't know why I even put it in now. The producer is always right, I'll remember that—"

Turning from the window, Sidney Wise went down the hall to his study. His son's back was to him; a bound script of *Reflected Glory* was open on the desk. From the wall, a single photograph, snapped after the opening of *Five'll Get You Ten*, looked down, Nate Folger and Spring Westerman flanking himself and Marcia, who was balancing a glass of champagne and planting a kiss on his ear.

"Right, Nate. I'll get the changes to the typist. Right. You, too." Hanging up, Howard spun around. "Hi, Sid. You startled me. Sleep well?"

"Quite well," said Sidney Wise, glancing down at his pajamas.

"Wish I could learn to sleep past noon. If I don't write in the morning, I feel guilty the rest of the day." He picked up the script from the desk. "Guess what, Sid."

"Good news."

"Nate has definitely decided to do my play."

"I heard. I overheard. Congratulations, Howard."

Howard smiled. "You don't seem terribly pleased."

"Pleased? Of course I am. I couldn't be more pleased. He's suggested some changes, I gathered."

"Well, he showed it to Hartshorne and Dulles. That old ploy of consulting the critics in advance. Nate wants me to take out a speech in the first act. He thinks it might get laughs."

"The lieutenant's speech."

"Yes, the lieutenant's speech." Howard frowned. "I wasn't aware you'd read the script, Sid."

"I took the liberty."

"I see. Well, actually, I'm glad you did. I was going to ask you to. I wanted another . . . playwright's opinion." Howard glided toward the door. "Let's sit down one day and talk about it, shall we?"

Sidney Wise took a step forward. "I'll miss the lieutenant's speech," he said.

Howard pointed, pistol fashion. "It's yours."

"That's what I mean," said Sidney Wise hastily. "Any author hates to lose a tribute. An *hommage*, wasn't that the spirit? Especially from one's flesh and blood."

Howard eyed him peculiarly. "You've lost me, Sid."

"Well, you said it yourself just now: the fact that it resembled— what the hell, Howard—the fact that it was lifted, almost word for word, from my play."

"From *Five'll Get You Ten*? Are you serious? Where? How? I defy you to show me."

"I don't mean *Five'll Get You Ten*."

"Then what in God's name do you mean? Come on, Sid. Just because you wrote one money-making comedy in your life, anything funny I attempt is an imitation? Is there a Parkinson's Law for playwrights: The less you've done, the more it counts? I guess, then, the best thing *is* to be a one-play playwright—is that the idea? Are the rest of us a bunch of suckers, trying for the whole shelf? Because it's all one play anyway, right? OK, Sid. OK. Have it your way. I'm forever in your debt."

The closing door muted his sniff of laughter. Pinching his eyes with finger and thumb, so that a black globule of light swam, butterfly style, across his retinas, Sidney Wise heard his son's voice, below the study window, shouting for a cab. The cab door slammed and he stood there in his slippers and pajamas, by the shelf from which his works had vanished, all but one, and that of such accidental consequence that *The Reader's Encyclopedia* listed it by its title only, omitting any separate entry for the author of *Five'll Get You Ten.* He closed the reference book and replaced it on the shelf, flooded by sudden nostalgia. The asylums—he saw it now—were filled with people who had misplaced their lives, raging paranoids, grieving catatonics; he must not lose control. Returning to the bedroom, he showered and dressed, avoiding, as he wriggled into his corduroy jacket, the mirror on his closet door, as though afraid he might be unable to locate his reflection. He must hold on. He was the same man, with the same abilities. His drafts, his carbons, his finished scripts, his *Five Tragedies,* his *Five Comedies,* had dwindled to a single pile of words, words that had brought him money but no lasting fame (without success, he tried to recall the author of *Abie's Irish Rose*), words that, as he gingerly opened the cover of his one, published, profitable play, seemed, hideously, about to slide off the pages into his lap; but he was still Sidney Wise. In a plaintive voice he began to read aloud, savoring the familiar repartee, swaying with eyes closed as he reeled off the speeches to the empty room.

He opened his eyes.

Carrying himself gently, like a brimming bowl, to his desk, he sat down, took a stack of blank paper from his drawer and rolled a sheet into his typewriter.

IF WINTER COMES
a play in three acts
by Sidney Wise

He typed feverishly, getting up from his desk only once, during a love scene in act two, when he mistook a clatter in the pipes for the sound of his wife walking about in the bedroom. At 60 words a minute, with occasional brief pauses to relax his writer's cramp, he was able to transfer the play from his memory to 87 pages of typescript in less than four hours. By five o'clock, a manila package under his arm, he was in midtown again, ten minutes later stepping off the 12th-floor elevator of the old MGM Building, Broadway and 45th Street. A delivery boy was emerging from Nate Folger's small suite of offices; Sidney Wise squeezed past him into the anteroom. Folger's secretary, taking him for a messenger, thrust out her hand for the package; hearing footsteps, Sidney Wise looked up to see his wife, in jeans and baggy sweater and a pair of wire-frame glasses hanging from a chain, her gray hair pulled back in a disorderly bun, standing in the doorway to one of the offices. "Sidney, what is it? We're very, very busy."

"I brought you and Nate a new play," he said.

"Howard?" called Nate Folger from the other office.

"You thought I'd never write another," said Sidney Wise to his wife.

"Sidney, of all days—"

"Howard, I thought we were meeting you at the airport." Nate Folger swung around the corner, stopping in his tracks. *"Oy.* Sidney."

"Yes, *oy* Sidney." He handed Folger the script. "I'd like you to read this."

"Sidney, we're in a terrific hurry."

"Please. Nate? Please? Humor me."

Folger looked at Marcia Wise; she nodded. "It's all right, Nate. I'll tell him." Folger turned with the manuscript, closing his door; Sidney Wise stepped past his wife into her office. It was large, one of two windows looking out onto 45th Street, the other onto Broadway and the Allied Chemical Tower, with its electric sash of news. The headline read, "27 POWS TO ARRIVE CLARK AIR BASE TOMORROW."

"I've decided to go to Washington with Howard," said Marcia Wise.

"To Washington," Sidney Wise repeated, looking down at 45th Street. A workman was strapped to the Morosco billboard, installing a giant E at the end of REFLECTED GLORY BY HOWARD WIS. "Yes, of course. For the tryouts of Howard's play."

"Nate is joining us tomorrow," said Marcia Wise. "We won't be back until the New York previews. Don't say you didn't expect this."

"I expected it," said Sidney Wise, as the phone rang. He picked it up. "*Miz Wise? It ain't no Miz Wise here. Miz Wise done fled the plantation.*" He hung up. "Hartshorne and Dulles, I hear, are set to give it raves."

"Sidney, I don't care that you've made my life miserable. It's your absolute callousness toward *him.*"

"I know. Marcia, I had a lovely premonition today—"

"Barging in here, on the day his first play opens out of town—bringing a manuscript—haven't you ever heard of Oedipal Victor?"

"I thought his name was Howard."

"Your jokes are pathetic. Can't you see the guilt you're inflicting? Don't you realize how hard it was for him to finish this play, because you tried so many times and never succeeded once? Don't you know, finally, after all these years, what you're doing to your son?"

"He knows," said a voice from the doorway.

"Oh, Lord. Howard, please wait outside."

"He knows precisely what he's doing. The bloody sadist."

"Go downstairs and get us a cab."

"I'm not going with you," said Howard Wise, throwing himself onto the office couch.

"Howard, don't overreact—"

"I'm supposed to take a plane? A thing that flies in the sky? After seeing *him?*"

Sidney Wise took a step toward the couch. "Howard, you needn't worry about that anymore."

"Don't talk to me, you flop! Don't say anything!"

"I appreciate your distress, Howard. I'm sorry my failure, up till now, has been so complete. I think I've made a move to redress the unpleasantness I've caused you, and I'm confident that in the not too distant future the Broadway stage will make room for two Wises, father and son, to the greater glory of both—"

"For God's sake, will somebody make him stop!"

"Nate?" said Sidney Wise, looking up at the doorway. "Perhaps you can tell him."

Nate Folger, entering, blinked once. "Let's go," he said to Marcia and Howard Wise.

"Nate?" said Sidney Wise.

"You two have a plane to catch. Howard? Let's go." He motioned toward the door.

"My play, Nate?"

Nate Folger turned. "What about it, Sidney?"

"Tell me what you thought. Tell them."

Folger looked uneasily at Marcia and Howard. "We're living in the Seventies, Sidney. The world has come a long way since World War Two."

"You mean you just glanced at it, Nate? You didn't read it all the way through."

"Sidney, don't push it. I'm giving you my opinion. Do you want another opinion? I think you ought to see a doctor. And Howard: I don't want you ever showing a script of yours again without my permission. To anyone."

"I never did!" Howard Wise jumped up from the couch. "You mean to him? My father? Never! Deliberately! Why in God's name would I? Oh, for God's sake—you mean he copied it?"

"I'm not really sure. Maybe not on purpose, though what does that ever mean? The style. The structure. The subject. One or two scenes, though not so anyone could sue."

"Oh, my Lord," said Marcia Wise.

"Don't worry, baby, it'll never get on. He didn't write it for that."

Marcia Wise nodded. "You're a very sick man, Sidney."

"Sick? He's malignant!"

"A very troubled man. Do you know how troubled?"

"I believe I do," said Sidney Wise.

"Do you? Do you really, Sidney? Do you really understand?"

The three of them were at the door. Sidney Wise sank down on the couch. "You'll miss your plane," he said.

The door closed. Elevators rose and sank. Sidney Wise stared at the ceiling. An elevator went past the floor, dropped again. The walls hummed and fell silent. In the darkening room he sat jackknifed on the couch, staring at the posters on the wall, at his shoes, his head sinking slowly toward his knees. It snapped up. With difficulty he rose, looking at the clock on his wife's shelf. The windows were black, striped with neon glare. He stood over his wife's desk, holding a pencil in one hand, slowly tearing a piece of memo paper from a pad by the phone. His fingers felt numb, thickly gloved, as he pressed the pencil to the paper. He wrote a word; the pencil dropped. SORRY. He closed his fingers around the pencil again. Crossing out his wife's printed name, he wrote his own above it, small: SIDNEY. He weighted the paper with the phone, pulled the clock cord out of its socket and walked over to the window. "ALL" He pushed the window up as far as it would go. "ALL DEAD." The wind blew in from Times Square, the news ribbon blurred and sharpened, the sound of horns rose from Broadway. "D.C. SHUTTLE CRASHES ON TAKE-OFF LA GUARDIA. . . ."

"Mr. Wise."

He let down the window, turned around.

"Mr. Wise?"

It was Nate Folger's secretary.

"Mr. Wise, won't you miss your curtain?"

"Is it that late?" said the playwright.

"You were so quiet in here."

"Thank you for reminding me," he said, buttoning his green blazer. He moved past her through the anteroom into the corridor. An elevator was waiting. He stepped out through the lobby onto Broadway and 45th Street. At the Morosco, the last straggler was going past the ticket taker. Inside the theater, as he entered, he saw a group of people by the coat check, Nate Folger, Spring Westerman, Hartshorne, Dulles, others—Spring Westerman was crying. They saw him.

"Sidney."

"Oh, God. Oh, Sidney, it's so horrible—"

He started past them, looking toward the stage.

"Nate, he's in shock."

"Sidney, don't go in."

"Where were they going, Sidney?"

"To Washington," he said.

"But why? Why weren't they here?"

"Nate, leave him alone."

"They had their reasons," said the playwright.

"We've scrapped all the interviews: we'll take care of every-thing. Just go home, Sidney, we'll come with you—"

"That won't be necessary." He gazed down the aisle.

"You loved them, Sidney. You loved them so."

"Yes," said Sidney Wise, taking a *Playbill* from the usher. He pointed toward the stage, the empty first-act set. "*If Winter Comes*," he said, drying his eyes.

"Sidney."

"Stop him."

He went down the aisle.

"Sidney, you don't have to go through with this—"

"It's all right." Folger's hand was on his arm; he patted it. The commotion had prompted the audience to glance around; a wave of applause broke over the orchestra. He acknowledged it, sitting down as the lights dimmed, Folger, Hartshorne and Spring Westerman sinking stiffly beside him in unison, half-turning their heads, in uneasy disbelief, to stare at the playwright's grateful, trembling smile. The applause faded to a hush. "In fact," said Sidney Wise, very nearly depriving the first two rows of the first line of his play, "I wouldn't have missed this for the world."

The Four-Hour Fugue

ALFRED BESTER

From the man who brought us Tiger! Tiger! *and* The
Demolished Man *comes this fascinating look at a
science neglected until now in science fiction. The
science of odor, the sense of smell.*

BY now, of course, the Northeast Corridor was the Northeast
slum, stretching from Canada to the Carolinas and as far west as
Pittsburgh. It was a fantastic jungle of rancid violence inhabited
by a steaming, restless population with no visible means of
support and no fixed residence, so vast that census-takers, birth-
control supervisors and the social services had given up all hope. It
was a gigantic raree-show that everyone denounced and enjoyed.
Even the privileged few who could afford to live highly protected
lives in highly expensive Oases and could live anywhere else they
pleased never thought of leaving. The jungle grabbed you.

There were thousands of everyday survival problems, but one of
the most exasperating was the shortage of fresh water. Most of the
available potable water had long since been impounded by
progressive industries for the sake of a better tomorrow, and there
was very little left to go around. Rainwater tanks on the roofs, of
course. A black market, naturally. That was about all. So the
jungle stank. It stank worse than the court of Queen Elizabeth,
which could have bathed but didn't believe in it. The Corridor

just couldn't bathe, wash clothes, or clean house, and you could smell its noxious effluvium from ten miles out at sea. Welcome to the Fun Corridor.

Sufferers near the shore would have been happy to clean up in salt water, but the Corridor beaches had been polluted by so much crude oil seepage for so many generations that they were all owned by deserving oil reclamation companies. *Keep Out! No Trespassing!* And armed guards. The rivers and lakes were electrically fenced; no need for guards, just skull and crossbones signs and if you didn't know what they were telling you, tough.

Not to believe that everybody minded stinking as they skipped merrily over the rotting corpses in the streets, but a lot did and their only remedy was perfumery. There were dozens of competing companies producing perfumes, but the leader, far and away, was the Continental Can Company, which hadn't manufactured cans in two centuries. They'd switched to plastics and had the good fortune about a hundred stockholders' meetings back to make the mistake of signing a sales contract with and delivering to some cockamamie perfume brewer an enormous quantity of glowing neon containers. The corporation went bust and CCC took it over in hopes of getting some of their money back. That take-over proved to be their salvation when the perfume explosion took place; it gave them entrée to the most profitable industry of the times.

But it was neck-and-neck with the rivals until Blaise Skiaki joined CCC; then it turned into a runaway. Blaise Skiaki. Origins: French, Japanese, Black African and Irish. Education: BA, Princeton; ME, MIT; PhD, Dow Chemical. (It was Dow that had secretly tipped CCC that Skiaki was a winner, and lawsuits brought by the competition were still pending before the ethics board.) Blaise Skiaki: Age, thirty-one; unmarried, straight, genius.

His sense of scent was his genius, and he was privately referred to at CCC as "The Nose." He knew everything about perfumery: the animal products, ambergris, castor, civet, musk; the essential oils distilled from plants and flowers; the balsams extruded by tree and shrub wounds, benzoin, opopanax, Peru, Talu, storax, myrrh;

the synthetics created from the combination of natural and chemical scents, the latter mostly the esters of fatty acids.

He had created for CCC their most successful sellers: "Vulva," "Assuage," "Oxter" (a much more attractive brand name than "Armpitto"), "Preparation F," "Tongue War," et cetera. He was treasured by CCC, paid a salary generous enough to enable him to live in an Oasis and, best of all, granted unlimited supplies of fresh water. No girl in the Corridor could resist the offer of taking a shower with him.

But he paid a high price for these advantages. He could never use scented soaps, shaving creams, pomades, or depilatories. He could never eat seasoned foods. He could drink nothing but pure water. All this, you understand, to keep The Nose pure and uncontaminated so that he could smell around in his sterile laboratory and devise new creations. He was presently composing a rather promising unguent provisionally named "Correctum," but he'd been on it for six months without any positive results and CCC was alarmed by the delay. His genius had never before taken so long.

There was a meeting of the top-level executives, names withheld on the grounds of corporate privilege.

"What's the matter with him anyway?"

"Has he lost his touch?"

"It hardly seems likely."

"Maybe he needs a rest."

"Why, he had a week's holiday last month."

"What did he do?"

"Ate up a storm, he told me."

"Could that be it?"

"No. He said he purged himself before he came back to work."

"Is he having trouble here at CCC? Difficulties with middle-management?"

"Absolutely not, Mr. Chairman. They wouldn't dare touch him."

"Maybe he wants a raise."

"No. He can't spend the money he makes now."

"Has our competition got to him?"

"They get to him all the time, General, and he laughs them off."

"Then it must be something personal."

"Agreed."

"Woman-trouble?"

"My God! We should have such trouble."

"Family-trouble?"

"He's an orphan, Mr. Chairman."

"Ambition? Incentive? Should we make him an officer of CCC?"

"I offered that to him the first of the year, sir, and he turned me down. He just wants to play in his laboratory."

"Then why isn't he playing?"

"Apparently he's got some kind of creative block."

"What the hell is the matter with him anyway?"

"Which is how you started this meeting."

"I did not."

"You did."

"Not."

"Governor, will you play back the bug."

"Gentlemen, gentlemen, please! Obviously Dr. Skiaki has personal problems which are blocking his genius. We must solve that for him. Suggestions?"

"Psychiatry?"

"That won't work without voluntary cooperation. I doubt whether he'd cooperate. He's an obstinate gook."

"Senator, I beg you! Such expressions must not be used with reference to one of our most valuable assets."

"Mr. Chairman, the problem is to discover the source of Dr. Skiaki's block."

"Agreed. Suggestions?"

"Why, the first step should be to maintain twenty-four-hour surveillance. All of the gook's—excuse me—the good doctor's activities, associates, contacts."

"By CCC?"

"I would suggest not. There are bound to be leaks which would only antagonize the good gook—doctor!"

"Outside surveillance?"

"Yes, sir."

"Very good. Agreed. Meeting adjourned."

Skip-Tracer Associates were perfectly furious. After one month they threw the case back into CCC's lap, asking for nothing more than their expenses.

"Why in hell didn't you tell us that we were assigned to a pro, Mr. Chairman, sir? Our tracers aren't trained for that."

"Wait a minute, please. What d'you mean, 'pro'?"

"A professional Rip."

"A what?"

"Rip. Gorill. Gimpster. Crook."

"Dr. Skiaki a crook? Preposterous."

"Look, Mr. Chairman, I'll frame it for you and you draw your own conclusions. Yes?"

"Go ahead."

"It's all detailed in this report anyway. We put double tails on Skiaki every day to and from your shop. When he left they followed him home. He always went home. They staked in double shifts. He had dinner sent in from the Organic Nursery every night. They checked the messengers bringing the dinners. Legit. They checked the dinners; sometimes for one, sometimes for two. They traced some of the girls who left his penthouse. All clean. So far, all clean, yes?"

"And?"

"The crunch. Couple of nights a week he leaves the house and goes into the city. He leaves around midnight and doesn't come back until four, more or less."

"Where does he go?"

"We don't know because he shakes his tails like the pro that he is. He weaves through the Corridor like a whore or a fag cruising for trade—excuse me—and he always loses our men. I'm not taking anything away from him. He's smart, shifty, quick and a real pro. He has to be; and he's too much for Skip-Tracers to handle."

"Then you have no idea of what he does or who he meets between midnight and four?"

"No, sir. We've got nothing and you've got a problem. Not ours any more."

"Thank you. Contrary to the popular impression, corporations are not altogether idiotic. CCC understands that negatives are also results. You'll receive your expenses and the agreed-upon fee."

"Mr. Chairman, I—"

"No, no, please. You've narrowed it down to those missing four hours. Now, as you say, they're our problem."

*   *   *

CCC summoned Salem Burne. Mr. Burne always insisted that he was neither a physician nor a psychiatrist; he did not care to be associated with what he considered to be the dreck of the professions. Salem Burne was a witch doctor; more precisely, a warlock. He made the most remarkable and penetrating analyses of disturbed people, not so much through his coven rituals of pentagons, incantations, incense, and the like as through his remarkable sensitivity to Body English and his acute interpretation of it. And this might be witchcraft after all.

Mr. Burne entered Blaise Skiaki's immaculate laboratory with a winning smile and Dr. Skiaki let out a rending howl of anguish.

"I told you to sterilize before you came."

"But I did, Doctor. Faithfully."

"You did not. You reek of anise, ilang-ilang and methyl anthranilate. You've polluted my day. Why?"

"Dr. Skiaki, I assure you that I—" Suddenly Salem Burne stopped. "Oh my God!" he groaned. "I used my wife's towel this morning."

Skiaki laughed and turned up the ventilators to full force. "I understand. No hard feelings. Now let's get your wife out of here. I have an office about half a mile down the hall. We can talk there."

They sat down in the vacant office and looked at each other. Mr. Burne saw a pleasant, youngish man with cropped black hair, small expressive ears, high telltale cheekbones, slitty eyes that would need careful watching and graceful hands that would be a dead giveaway.

"Now, Mr. Burne, how can I help you?" Skiaki said while his hands asked, "Why the hell have you come pestering me?"

"Dr. Skiaki, I'm a colleague in a sense; I'm a professional witch doctor. One crucial part of my ceremonies is the burning of various forms of incense, but they're all rather conventional. I was hoping that your expertise might suggest something different with which I could experiment."

"I see. Interesting. You've been burning stacte, onycha, galbanum, frankincense . . . that sort of thing?"

"Yes. All quite conventional."

"Most interesting. I could, of course, make many suggestions for new experiments, and yet—" Here Skiaki stopped and stared into space.

After a long pause the warlock asked, "Is anything wrong, Doctor?"

"Look here," Skiaki burst out. "You're on the wrong track. It's the burning of incense that's conventional and old-fashioned, and trying different scents won't solve your problem. Why not experiment with an altogether different approach?"

"And what would that be?"

"The Odophone principle."

"Odophone?"

"Yes. There's a scale that exists among scents as among sounds. Sharp smells correspond to high notes and heavy smells with low notes. For example, ambergris is in the treble clef while violet is in the bass. I could draw up a scent scale for you, running perhaps two octaves. Then it would be up to you to compose the music."

"This is positively brilliant, Dr. Skiaki."

"Isn't it?" Skiaki beamed. "But in all honesty I should point out that we're collaborators in brilliance. I could never have come up with the idea if you hadn't presented me with a most original challenge."

They made contact on this friendly note and talked shop enthusiastically, lunched together, told each other about them-

selves and made plans for the witchcraft experiments in which
Skiaki volunteered to participate despite the fact that he was no
believer in diabolism.

"And yet the irony lies in the fact that he is indeed devil-
ridden," Salem Burne reported.

The Chairman could make nothing of this.

"Psychiatry and diabolism use different terms for the same
phenomenon," Burne explained. "So perhaps I'd better translate.
Those missing four hours are fugues."

The Chairman was not enlightened. "Do you mean the musical
expression, Mr. Burne?"

"No, sir. A fugue is also the psychiatric description of a more
advanced form of somnambulism . . . sleepwalking."

"Blaise Skiaki walks in his sleep?"

"Yes, sir, but it's more complicated than that. The sleepwalker
is a comparatively simple case. He is never in touch with his
surroundings. You can speak to him, shout at him, address him by
name, and he remains totally oblivious."

"And the fugue?"

"In the fugue the subject is in touch with his surroundings. He
can converse with you. He has awareness and memory for the
events that take place within the fugue, but while he is within his
fugue he is a totally different person from the man he is in real
life. And—and this is most important, sir—after the fugue he
remembers nothing of it."

"Then in your opinion Dr. Skiaki has these fugues two or three
times a week."

"That is my diagnosis, sir."

"And he can tell us nothing of what transpires during the
fugue?"

"Nothing."

"Can you?"

"I'm afraid not, sir. There's a limit to my powers."

"Have you any idea what is causing these fugues?"

"Only that he is driven by something. I would say that he is
possessed by the devil, but that is the cant of my profession.
Others may use different terms—compulsion or obsession. The

terminology is unimportant. The basic fact is that something possessing him is compelling him to go out nights to do—what? I don't know. All I do know is that this diabolical drive most probably is what is blocking his creative work for you."

*   *   *

One does not summon Gretchen Nunn, not even if you're CCC whose common stock has split twenty-five times. You work your way up through the echelons of her staff until you are finally admitted to the Presence. This involves a good deal of backing and forthing between your staff and hers, and ignites a good deal of exasperation, so the Chairman was understandably put out when at last he was ushered into Miss Nunn's workshop, which was cluttered with the books and apparatus she used for her various investigations.

Gretchen Nunn's business was working miracles; not in the sense of the extraordinary, anomalous or abnormal brought about by a superhuman agency, but rather in the sense of her extraordinary and/or abnormal perception and manipulation of reality. In any situation, she could and did achieve the impossible begged by her desperate clients, and her fees were so enormous that she was thinking of going public.

Naturally the Chairman had anticipated Miss Nunn as looking like Merlin in drag. He was flabbergasted to discover that she was a Watusi princess with velvety black skin, aquiline features, great black eyes, tall, slender, twentyish, ravishing in red.

She dazzled him with a smile, indicated a chair, sat in one opposite and said, "My fee is one hundred thousand. Can you afford it?"

"I can. Agreed."

"And your difficulty—is it worth it?"

"It is."

"Then we understand each other so far. Yes, Alex?"

The young secretary who had bounced into the workshop said, "Excuse me. LeClerque insists on knowing how you made the positive identification of the mold as extraterrestrial."

Miss Nunn clicked her tongue impatiently. "He knows that I never give reasons. I only give results."

"Yes'N."

"Has he paid?"

"Yes'N."

"All right, I'll make an exception in his case. Tell him that it was based on the levo and dextro probability in amino acids and tell him to have a qualified exobiologist carry on from there. He won't regret the cost."

"Yes'N. Thank you."

She turned to the Chairman as the secretary left. "You heard that. I only give results."

"Agreed, Miss Nunn."

"Now your difficulty. I'm not committed yet. Understood?"

"Yes, Miss Nunn."

"Go ahead. Everything. Stream of consciousness, if necessary."

An hour later she dazzled him with another smile and said, "Thank you. This one is really unique. A welcome change. It's a contract, if you're still willing."

"Agreed, Miss Nunn. Would you like a deposit or an advance?"

"Not from CCC."

"What about expenses? Should that be arranged?"

"No. My responsibility."

"But what if you have to—if you're required to—if—"

She laughed. "My responsibility. I never give reasons and I never reveal methods. How can I charge for them? Now don't forget; I want that Skip-Trace report."

A week later Gretchen Nunn took the unusual step of visiting the Chairman in his office at CCC. "I'm calling on you, sir, to give you the opportunity of withdrawing from our contract."

"Withdraw? But why?"

"Because I believe you're involved in something far more serious than you anticipated."

"But what?"

"You won't take my word for it?"

"I must know."

Miss Nunn compressed her lips. After a moment she sighed.

"Since this is an unusual case I'll have to break my rules. Look at this, sir." She unrolled a large map of a segment of the Corridor and flattened it on the Chairman's desk. There was a star in the center of the map. "Skiaki's residence," Miss Nunn said. There was a large circle scribed around the star. "The limits to which a man can walk in two hours," Miss Nunn said. The circle was crisscrossed by twisting trails all emanating from the star. "I got this from the Skip-Trace report. This is how the tails traced Skiaki."

"Very ingenious, but I see nothing serious in this, Miss Nunn."

"Look closely at the trails. What do you see?"

"Why . . . each ends in a red cross."

"And what happens to each trail before it reaches the red cross?"

"Nothing. Nothing at all, except—except that the dots change to dashes."

"And that's what makes it serious."

"I don't understand, Miss Nunn."

"I'll explain. Each cross represents the scene of a murder. The dashes represent the backtracking of the actions and whereabouts of each murder victim just prior to death."

"Murder!"

"They could trace their actions just so far back and no further. Skip-Trace could tail Skiaki just so far forward and no further. Those are the dots. The dates join up. What's your conclusion?"

"It must be coincidence," the Chairman shouted. "This brilliant, charming young man. Murder? Impossible!"

"Do you want the factual data I've drawn up?"

"No, I don't. I want the truth. Proof-positive without any inferences from dots, dashes and dates."

"Very well, Mr. Chairman. You'll get it."

She rented the professional beggar's pitch alongside the entrance to Skiaki's Oasis for a week. No success. She hired a Revival Band and sang hymns with it before the Oasis. No success. She finally made the contact after she promoted a job with the Organic Nursery. The first three dinners she delivered to the penthouse she came and went unnoticed; Skiaki was entertaining a series of girls, all scrubbed and sparkling with gratitude. When she made the fourth delivery he was alone and noticed her for the first time.

"Hey," he grinned. "How long has this been going on?"

"Sir?"

"Since when has Organic been using girls for delivery boys?"

"I am a delivery person, sir," Miss Nunn answered with dignity. "I have been working for the Organic Nursery since the first of the month."

"Knock off the sir bit."

"Thank you, s—Dr. Skiaki."

"How the devil do you know that I've got a doctorate?"

She'd slipped. He was listed at the Oasis and the Nursery merely as B. Skiaki, and she should have remembered. As usual, she turned her mistake into an advantage. "I know all about you, sir. Dr. Blaise Skiaki, Princeton, MIT, Dow Chemical. Chief Scent Chemist at CCC."

"You sound like *Who's Who*."

"That's where I read it, Dr. Skiaki."

"You read me up in *Who's Who*? Why on earth?"

"You're the first famous man I've ever met."

"Whatever gave you the idea that I'm famous, which I'm not."

She gestured around. "I knew you had to be famous to live like this."

"Very flattering. What's your name, love?"

"Gretchen, sir."

"What's your last name?"

"People from my class don't have last names, sir."

"Will you be the delivery b—person tomorrow, Gretchen?"

"Tomorrow is my day off, Doctor."

"Perfect. Bring dinner for two."

*   *   *

So the affair began and Gretchen discovered, much to her astonishment, that she was enjoying it very much. Blaise was indeed a brilliant, charming young man, always entertaining, always considerate, always generous. In gratitude he gave her (remember he believed she came from the lowest Corridor class) one of his most prized possessions, a five-carat diamond he had synthesized at Dow. She responded with equal style; she wore it in her navel and promised that it was for his eyes only.

Of course he always insisted on her scrubbing up each time she visited, which was a bit of a bore; in her income bracket she probably had more fresh water than he did. However, one convenience was that she could quit her job at the Organic Nursery and attend to other contracts while she was attending to Skiaki.

She always left his penthouse around eleven-thirty but stayed outside until one. She finally picked him up one night just as he was leaving the Oasis. She'd memorized the Salem Burne report and knew what to expect. She overtook him quickly and spoke in an agitated voice, "Mistuh. Mistuh."

He stopped and looked at her kindly without recognition. "Yes, my dear?"

"If yuh gone this way kin I come too? I scared."

"Certainly, my dear."

"Thanks, mistuh. I gone home. You gone home?"

"Well, not exactly."

"Where you gone? Y'ain't up to nothin' bad, is you? I don't want no part."

"Nothing bad, my dear. Don't worry."

"Then what you up to?"

He smiled secretly. "I'm following something."

"Somebody?"

"No, something."

"What kine something?"

"My, you're curious, aren't you? What's your name?"

"Gretchen. How 'bout you?"

"Me?"

"What's your name?"

"Wish. Call me Mr. Wish." He hesitated for a moment and then said, "I have to turn left here."

"Thas OK, Mistuh Wish. I go left, too."

She could see that all his senses were prickling, and reduced her prattle to a background of unobtrusive sound. She stayed with him as he twisted, turned, sometimes doubling back, through streets, alleys, lanes and lots, always assuring him that this was her way home too. At a rather dangerous-looking refuse dump he gave her a fatherly pat and cautioned her to wait while he explored its safety. He explored, disappeared and never reappeared.

"I replicated this experience with Skiaki six times," Miss Nunn reported to CCC. "They were all significant. Each time he revealed a little more without realizing it and without recognizing me. Burne was right. It is fugue."

"And the cause, Miss Nunn?"

"Pheromone trails."

"What?"

"I thought you gentlemen would know the term, being in the chemistry business. I see I'll have to explain. It will take some time so I insist that you do not require me to describe the induction and deduction that led me to my conclusion. Understood?"

"Agreed, Miss Nunn."

"Thank you, Mr. Chairman. Surely you all know hormones, from the Greek *hormaein*, meaning 'to excite.' They're internal secretions which excite other parts of the body into action. Pheromones are external secretions which excite other creatures into action. It's a mute chemical language.

"The best example of the pheromone language is the ant. Put a lump of sugar somewhere outside an ant hill. A forager will come across it, feed and return to the nest. Within an hour the entire commune will be single-filing to and from the sugar, following the pheromone trail first laid down quite undeliberately by the first discoverer. It's an unconscious but compelling stimulant."

"Fascinating. And Dr. Skiaki?"

"He follows human pheromone trails. They compel him; he goes into fugue and follows them."

"Ah! An outré aspect of The Nose. It makes sense, Miss Nunn. It really does. But what trails is he compelled to follow?"

"The death-wish."

"Miss Nunn!"

"Surely you're aware of this aspect of the human psyche. Many people suffer from an unconscious but powerful death-wish, especially in these despairing times. Apparently this leaves a pheromone trail which Dr. Skiaki senses, and he is compelled to follow it."

"And then?"

"Apparently he grants the wish."

"Apparently! Apparently!" the Chairman shouted. "I ask you for proof-positive of this monstrous accusation."

"You'll get it, sir. I'm not finished with Blaise Skiaki yet. There are one or two things I have to wrap up with him, and in the course of that I'm afraid he's in for a shock. You'll have your proof-pos—"

That was a half-lie from a woman half in love. She knew she had to see Blaise again, but her motives were confused. To find out whether she really loved him, despite what she knew? To find out whether he loved her? To tell him the truth about herself? To warn him or save him or run away with him? To fulfill her contract in a cool, professional style? She didn't know. Certainly she didn't know that she was in for a shock from Skiaki.

"Were you born blind?" he murmured that night.

She sat bolt upright in the bed. "What? Blind? What?"

"You heard me."

"I've had perfect sight all my life."

"Ah. Then you don't know, darling. I rather suspected that might be it."

"I certainly don't know what you're talking about, Blaise."

"Oh, you're blind all right," he said calmly. "But you've never known because you're blessed with a fantastic freak facility. You have extrasensory perception of other people's senses. You see through other people's eyes. For all I know you may be deaf and hear through their ears. You may feel with their skin. We must explore it sometime."

"I never heard of anything more absurd in all my life," she said angrily.

"I can prove it to you, if you like, Gretchen."

"Go ahead, Blaise. Prove the impossible."

"Come into the lounge."

In the living room he pointed to a vase. "What color is that?"

"Brown, of course."

"What color is that?" A tapestry.

"Gray."

"And that lamp?"

"Black."

"QED," Skiaki said. "It has been demonstrated."

"What's been demonstrated?"

"That you're seeing through my eyes."

"How can you say that?"

"Because I'm color-blind. That's what gave me the clue in the first place."

"What?"

He took her in his arms to quiet her trembling. "Darling Gretchen, the vase is green. The tapestry is amber and gold. The lamp is crimson. I can't see the colors but the decorator told me and I remember. Now why the terror? You're blind, yes, but you're blessed with something far more miraculous than mere sight; you see through the eyes of the world. I'd change places with you anytime."

"It can't be true," she cried.

"It's true, love."

"What about when I'm alone?"

"When are you alone? When is anybody in the Corridor ever alone?"

She snatched up a shift and ran out of the penthouse, sobbing hysterically. She ran back to her own Oasis nearly crazed with terror. And yet she kept looking around and there were all the colors: red, orange, yellow, green, indigo, blue, violet. But there were also people swarming through the labyrinths of the Corridor as they always were, twenty-four hours a day.

Back in her apartment she was determined to put the disaster to the test. She dismissed her entire staff with stern orders to get the hell out and spend the night somewhere else. She stood at the door and counted them out, all amazed and unhappy. She slammed the door and looked around. She could still see.

"The lying son-of-a-bitch," she muttered and began to pace

furiously. She raged through the apartment, swearing venomously. It proved one thing: never get into personal relationships. They'll betray you, they'll try to destroy you, and she'd made a fool of herself. But why, in God's name, did Blaise use this sort of dirty trick to destroy her? Then she smashed into something and was thrown back. She recovered her balance and looked to see what she had blundered into. It was a harpsichord.

"But . . . but I don't own a harpsichord," she whispered in bewilderment. She started forward to touch it and assure herself of its reality. She smashed into the something again, grabbed it and felt it. It was the back of a couch. She looked around frantically. This was not one of her rooms. The harpsichord. Vivid Brueghels hanging on the walls. Jacobean furniture. Linenfold paneled doors. Crewel drapes.

"But . . . this is the . . . the Raxon apartment downstairs. I must be seeing through their eyes. I must . . . he was right. I . . ." She closed her eyes and looked. She saw a mélange of apartments, streets, crowds, people, events. She had always seen this sort of montage on occasion but had always thought it was merely the total visual recall which was a major factor in her extraordinary abilities and success. Now she knew the truth.

She began to sob again. She felt her way around the couch and sat down, despairing. When at last the convulsion spent itself she wiped her eyes courageously, determined to face reality. She was no coward. But when she opened her eyes she was shocked by another bombshell. She saw her familiar room in tones of gray. She saw Blaise Skiaki standing in the open door smiling at her.

"Blaise?" she whispered.

"The name is Wish, my dear. Mr. Wish. What's yours?"

"Blaise, for God's sake, not me! Not me. I left no death-wish trail."

"What's your name, my dear? We've met before?"

"Gretchen," she screamed. "I'm Gretchen Nunn and I have no death-wish."

"Nice meeting you again, Gretchen," he said in glassy tones, smiling the glassy smile of Mr. Wish. He took two steps toward her. She jumped up and ran behind the couch.

"Blaise, listen to me. You are not Mr. Wish. There is no Mr. Wish. You are Dr. Blaise Skiaki, a famous scientist. You are chief chemist at CCC and have created many wonderful perfumes."

He took another step toward her, unwinding the scarf he wore around his neck.

"Blaise, I'm Gretchen. We've been lovers for two months. You must remember. Try to remember. You told me about my eyes tonight . . . being blind. You must remember that."

He smiled and whirled the scarf into a cord.

"Blaise, you're suffering from fugue. A blackout. A change of psyche. This isn't the real you. It's another creature driven by a pheromone. But I left no pheromone trail. I couldn't. I've never wanted to die."

"Yes, you do, my dear. Only happy to grant your wish. That's why I'm called Mr. Wish."

She squealed like a trapped rat and began darting and dodging while he closed in on her. She feinted him to one side, twisted to the other with a clear chance of getting out the door ahead of him, only to crash into three grinning goons standing shoulder to shoulder. They grabbed and held her.

Mr. Wish did not know that he also left a pheromone trail. It was a pheromone trail of murder.

"Oh, it's you again," Mr. Wish sniffed.

"Hey, old buddy-boy, got a looker this time, huh?"

"And loaded. Dig this layout."

"Great. Makes up for the last three which was nothin'. Thanks, buddy-boy. You can go home now."

"Why don't I ever get to kill one?" Mr. Wish exclaimed petulantly.

"Now, now. No sulks. We got to protect our bird dog. You lead. We follow and do the rest."

"And if anything goes wrong, you're the setup," one of the goons giggled.

"Go home, buddy-boy. The rest is ours. No arguments. We already explained the standoff to you. We know who you are, but you don't know who we are."

"I know who I am," Mr. Wish said with dignity. "I am Mr. Wish and I still think I have the right to kill at least one."

"All right, all right. Next time. That's a promise. Now blow."

As Mr. Wish exited resentfully, they ripped Gretchen naked and let out a huge wow when they saw the five-carat diamond in her navel. Mr. Wish turned and saw its scintillation too.

"But that's mine," he said in a confused voice. "That's only for my eyes. I—Gretchen said she would never—" Abruptly Dr. Blaise Skiaki spoke in a tone accustomed to command: "Gretchen, what the hell are you doing here? What's this place? Who are these creatures? What's going on?"

When the police arrived they found three dead bodies and a composed Gretchen Nunn sitting with a laser pistol in her lap. She told a perfectly coherent story of forcible entry, an attempt at armed rape and robbery, and how she was constrained to meet force with force. There were a few loopholes in her account. The bodies were not armed, but if the men had said they were armed Miss Nunn, of course, would have believed them. The three were somewhat battered, but goons were always fighting. Miss Nunn was commended for her courage and cooperation.

After her final report to the Chairman (which was not the truth, the whole truth and nothing but the truth) Miss Nunn received her check and went directly to the perfume laboratory, which she entered without warning. Dr. Skiaki was doing strange and mysterious things with pipettes, flasks and reagent bottles. Without turning he ordered, "Out. Out. Out."

"Good morning, Dr. Skiaki."

He turned, displaying a mauled face and black eyes, and smiled. "Well, well, well. The famous Gretchen Nunn, I presume. Voted Person of the Year three times in succession."

"No, sir. People from my class don't have last names."

"Knock off the sir bit."

"Yes-s—Mr. Wish."

"Oi!" He winced. "Don't remind me of that incredible insanity. How did everything go with the Chairman?"

"I snowed him. You're off the hook."

"Maybe I'm off his hook, but not my own. I was seriously thinking of having myself committed this morning."

"What stopped you?"

"Well, I got involved in this patchouli synthesis and sort of forgot."

She laughed. "You don't have to worry. You're saved."

"You mean cured?"

"No, Blaise. Not any more than I'm cured of my blindness. But we're both saved because we're aware. We can cope now."

He nodded slowly but not happily.

"So what are you going to do today?" she asked cheerfully. "Struggle with patchouli?"

"No," he said gloomily. "I'm still in one hell of a shock. I think I'll take the day off."

"Perfect. Bring two dinners."

The Scream

KATE WILHELM

This more than slightly chilling glimpse of the future has the solid taste and feel of reality. The solidity of the world that Kate Wilhelm's magic has created here is so strong that the image and the story will echo in memory long after the reader has closed the book.

THE sea had turned to copper; it rose and fell gently, the motion starting so deep that no ripple broke the surface of the slow swells. The sky was darkening to a deep blue-violet, with rose streaks in the west and a high cirrocumulus formation in the east that was a dazzling white mountain crowned with brilliant reds and touches of green. No wind stirred. The irregular dark strip that was Miami Beach separated the metallic sea from the fiery sky. We were at anchor eight miles offshore aboard the catamaran *Loretta*. She was a forty-foot, single-masted, inboard motorboat.

Evinson wanted to go on in, but Trainor, whose boat it was, said no. Too dangerous: sand, silt, wrecks, God knew what we might hit. We waited until morning.

We had to go in at Biscayne Bay; the Bal Harbour inlet was clogged with the remains of the bridge on old A1A. Trainor put in at the Port of Miami. All the while J.P. kept taking his water samples, not once glancing at the ruined city; Delia kept a running check for radiation, and Bernard took pictures. Corrie and I tried

131

to keep out of the way, and Evinson didn't. The ancient catamaran was clumsy, and Trainor was kept busy until we were tied up, then he bowed sarcastically to Evinson and went below.

Rusting ships were in the harbor, some of them on their sides half in water, half out. Some of them seemed afloat, but then we saw that without the constant dredging that had kept the port open, silt and sand had entered, and the bottom was no more than ten to fifteen feet down. The water was very clear. Some catfish lay unmoving on the bottom, and a school of big-eyed mullet circled at the surface, the first marine life we had seen. The terns were diving here, and sandpipers ran with the waves. J.P.'s eyes were shining as he watched the birds. We all had been afraid that there would be no life of any kind.

Our plan was to reconnoiter the first day, try to find transportation: bicycles, which none of us had ridden before, skates, canoes, anything. Miami and the beaches covered a lot of miles, and we had a lot of work; without transportation the work would be less valuable—if it had any value to begin with.

Bernard and Delia went ahead to find a place to set up our base, and the rest of us started to unload the boat. In half an hour we were drenched with sweat. At first glance the city had seemed perfectly habitable, just empty of people, but as we carried the boxes to the hotel that Bernard had found, the ruins dominated the scene. Walls were down, streets vanished under sand and palmettos and sea grapes. The hotel was five stories, the first floor covered with sand and junk: shells, driftwood, an aluminum oar eaten through with corrosion. Furniture was piled against walls haphazardly, like heaps of rotting compost. The water had risen and fallen more than once, rearranging floatables. It was hellishly hot, and the hotel stank of ocean and decay and dry rot and heat. No one talked much as we all worked, all but Trainor, who had worked to get us here and who now guzzled beer with his feet up. Evinson cursed him monotonously. We carried our stuff to the hotel, then to the second floor, where we put mosquito netting at the windows of three connecting rooms that would be used jointly. We separated to select our private rooms and clear them and secure them against the mosquitoes that would appear by the millions as soon as the sun went down.

After a quick lunch of soy wafers and beer we went out singly to get the feel of the city and try to locate any transportation we could.

I started with a map in my hand, and the first thing I did was put it back inside my pack. Except for the general areas, the map was worthless. This had been a seawalled city, and the seawalls had gone: a little break here, a crack somewhere else, a trickle of water during high tide, a flood during a storm, the pressure building behind the walls, on the land side, and inevitably the surrender to the sea. The water had undermined the road system and eaten away at foundations of buildings, and hurricane winds had done the rest. Some streets were completely filled in with rubble; others were pitted and undercut until shelves of concrete had shifted and slid and now rested crazily tilted. The white sand had claimed some streets so thoroughly that growth had had a chance to naturalize, and there were strip-forests of palm trees, straggly bushes with pink and yellow flowers, and sea grapes. I saw a mangrove copse claiming the water's edge and stopped to stare at it for a long time, with curious thoughts flitting through my brain about the land and the sea in a survival struggle in which man was no more than an incidental observer, here, then gone. The afternoon storm broke abruptly, and I took shelter in a building that seemed to have been a warehouse.

The stench of mold and decay drove me out again as soon as the storm abated. Outside, the sun had baked everything, the sun and rain sterilizing, neutralizing, keeping the mold at bay, but inside the cavernous buildings the soggy air was a culture for mold spores, and thirty years, forty, had not been long enough to deplete the rich source of nutrients. There was food available on the shelves, the shelves were food, the wood construction materials, the glues and grouts, the tiles and vinyls, the papers neatly filed, the folders that held them, pencils, everything finally was food for the mold.

I entered two more buildings, same thing, except that one of

them had become a bat cave. They were the large fruit bats, not
dangerous, and I knew they were not, but I left them the building
without contest.

At the end of the first day we had three bicycles and a
flat-bottomed rowboat with two oars. I hadn't found anything of
value. The boat was aluminum, and although badly corroded, it
seemed intact enough. Trainor slouched in while J.P. was cooking
dinner and the rest of us were planning our excursions for the next
day.

"You folks want boats? Found a storehouse full of them."

He joined us for dinner and drew a map showing the warehouse
he had found. His freehand map was more reliable than the
printed ones we had brought with us. I suspected that he was
salvaging what he could for his own boat. Unless he was a fool,
that was what he was doing. When Evinson asked him what else
he had seen that day, he simply shrugged.

"How's chances of a swim?" I asked Delia after we ate.

"No radiation. But you'd better wait for Corrie to run some
analyses. Too much that we don't know about it to chance it yet."

"No swimming, damn it!" Evinson said sharply. "For God's
sake, Sax." He issued orders rapidly for the next day, in effect
telling everyone to do what he had come to do.

Strut and puff, you little bastard, I thought at him. No one
protested.

*   *   *

The same ruins lay everywhere in the city. After the first hour it
was simply boring. My bicycle was more awkward than going on
foot, since I had to carry it over rubble as much as I got to ride it.
I abandoned it finally. I found the Miami River and dutifully got
a sample. It was the color of tea, very clear. I followed the river a
long time, stopped for my lunch, and followed it some more.
Ruins, sand, junk, palm trees. Heat. Silence. Especially silence. I
was not aware of when I began to listen to the silence, but I
caught myself walking cautiously, trying to be as quiet as the city,
not to intrude in any way. The wind in the dry fronds was the only

thing I heard. It stopped, then started again, and I jerked around. I went inside a building now and then, but they were worse than the ruined streets. Rusty toys, appliances, moldering furniture, or piles of dust where the termites had been, chairs that crumbled when I touched them, and the heat and silence.

I got bored with the river and turned in to what had been a garden park. Here the vegetation was different. A banyan tree had spread unchecked and filled more than a city block. A flock of blackbirds arose from it as I approached. The suddenness of their flight startled me and I whirled around, certain that someone was behind me. Nothing. Vines and bushes had grown wild in the park and were competing with trees for space—a minijungle. There were thousands of parakeets, emerald green, darting, making a cacophony that was worse than the silence. I retraced my steps after a few minutes. There might have been water in there, but I didn't care. I circled the park and kept walking.

The feeling that I was being followed grew stronger, and I stopped as if to look more closely at a weed, listening for steps. Nothing. The wind in some pampas grass, the louder rustle of palm fronds, the return of the blackbirds. And in the distance the raucous cries of gulls. The feeling didn't go away, and I walked faster and sweated harder.

I got out my kit and finished the last of the beer in the shade of a live oak with branches eighty feet long spreading out sideways in all directions. Whatever had poisoned Miami and reduced its population to zero hadn't affected the flora. The wind started, the daily storm. I sat in the doorway of a stinking apartment building and watched sheets of water race down the street. After the storm passed I decided to go back and try to get Corrie to bed with me. It never occurred to me to snuggle up to Delia, who seemed totally asexual. Delia and J.P., I thought.

Corrie was alone, and she said no curtly. She was as hot as I was and as tired. But she had a working lab set up, complete with microscopes and test tubes and flasks of things over Bunsen burners. She glanced contemptuously at the collecting bottle that I handed her. They knew about me, all of them.

"What did I do wrong?"

"Label it, please. Location, depth, source, time of day. Anything else you can think of that might be helpful."

Her tone said, and leave me alone because I have real work to do. She turned back to her microscope.

"So I'm not a hydrologist. I'm a pamphlet writer for Health, Education and Welfare."

"I know." She glanced at me again. "But why didn't they send a real hydrologist?"

"Because we don't have one."

She stood up and walked to the window netting and looked out. Her shirt was wet under her sleeves and down her back, her hair clung to her cheeks and the nape of her neck. "Why?" she whispered. "Why? Why? Why?"

"If they knew that we wouldn't be here."

She walked back to her chair and sat down again, drawing the microscope toward her once more.

"Is the bay all right?"

"Yes." She adjusted the focus and forgot about me. I left.

The warehouse where Trainor had found the boats was half a dozen blocks up the waterfront. I walked and sweated. Trainor had dragged some small boats outside, and I chose the smallest of them and took it down to the water. I rowed out into the bay, undressed, and swam for half an hour; then I started to row, going no place in particular.

The water was marvelously calm, and I felt cooler and less tense after the swim. I stopped to dive a couple of times around a sunken yacht; it had been stripped. I stopped again, this time ashore at what looked like a copy of the Parthenon. It had been a museum. The water lapped about the foundation; marble stairs and massive fountains indicated that it had been a grandiose thing. A statue had toppled and I considered it. A female form—vaguely female, anyway. Rounded, curving, voluptuous-looking, roughly hewn out of granite, it was touching somehow. The eye-hollows were facing out to sea, waiting, watching the water, waiting. The essence of woman as childbearer, woman as nourisher, woman as man's sexual necessity. Her flesh would be warm and yielding. She would be passive, accept his seed, and let it come to life within her. Those great round arms would hold a child, let it suckle at the massive breasts. I wished I could stand the statue upright again. When it fell one of thé arms had broken; it lay apart from the bulk of the work. I tried to lift it: too heavy. I ran my hand over the rough rock and I wanted to sit on the floor by the woman and talk to her, cry a little, rest my cheek against that breast. I began to feel suffocated suddenly and I turned and ran from the museum without looking for anything else. The sun was setting, the sky crimson and blue and green, incredible colors that looked like cheap art.

It was dark when I got back to headquarters. All the others were there already, even Trainor. Delia was cooking. I watched her as she added water to the dehydrated stew and stirred it over canned heat. She was angular, with firm muscles and hardly any breasts at all. Her hips were slim, boyish, her legs all muscle and bone. I wondered again about her sexuality. I had seen her studying Trainor speculatively once, but nothing had come of it, and I had seen almost the same expression on her face a time or two when she had been looking at Corrie.

I turned my attention to Corrie—a little better, but still not really woman, not as the statue had signified woman. Corrie was softer than Delia, her hips a bit rounder, her breasts bouncier, not much, but Delia's never moved at all. Corrie had more of a waistline. My thoughts were confusing to me, and I tried to think of something else, but that damn statue kept intruding. I should have talked to her, I found myself thinking. And, she would have looked at me with contempt. She would have looked at any of our men with contempt—except, possibly, Trainor.

I watched and listened to Trainor then, speaking with Bernard. Trainor was tall and broad-shouldered, his hair white, face browned by the sun, very lean and very muscular.

"Have you ever seen any wild animals as far north as the cape?" Bernard asked, sketching. His fingers were swift and sure: That characterized him all the way, actually. He was soft-looking, but he moved with a sureness always. A dilettante artist, photographer, in his mid-thirties, rich enough not to work. There had been a mild affair with Corrie, but nothing serious. I didn't know why he was here.

"Deer," Trainor said in answer to his question. "There's a lot of things up in the brush. Foxes, rabbits, muskrats, possum."

"Anything big? I heard that lions were let loose, or escaped around West Palm Beach. Did they live, multiply?"

"Can't say."

"Heard there were panthers."

"Can't say."

"How about Indians? You must know if any of them are left in the swamps." Bernard's pencil stopped, but he didn't look at Trainor.

"Could be. Don't go inland much. No way to get inland, hard going by boat, hyacinths, thick enough to walk on. Too much stuff in the water everywhere. St. John's River used to be open, but not now."

"How about fish then? See any porpoises?"

"They come and go. Don't stay around long. Hear they're thick down around South America and in the Caribbean. Might be."

I watched Bernard for a long time. What was he after? And Trainor? I had a feeling that the seven people who had come to the city had seven different reasons, and that mine was the only simple one. Orders. When you work for the government and an undersecretary says go, you go. Why were the others here?

In bed later, I couldn't sleep. The odors all came back in triple strength after dark. I could feel the mold growing around me, on me, in my bedroll. The humidity was a weight on my chest. I finally got up again, drenched with sweat, my bed soaked through, and I went back to the second floor where I interrupted Delia and Bernard in a quiet conversation. I got a beer and sat down near the window, my back to them both. After a moment Delia yawned and got up.

At the doorway she paused and said, "Why don't you take him?"

I looked at her then. Bernard made a snorting sound and didn't answer. I turned back to the window. The silence was coming in along with the night-time humidity, and I realized that I had chosen my room on the wrong side of the building. The night air blew from the land to the sea. There was a faint breeze at the window. The oil lamp was feeble against the pressure of the darkness beyond the netting.

"Night," Delia said at the door, and I looked at her again, nodded, and she started through, then stopped. A high, uncanny, inhuman scream sounded once, from a long way off. It echoed through the empty city. The silence that followed it made me understand that what I had thought to be quiet before had not been stillness. Now the silence was profound; no insect, no rustling, no whir of small wings, nothing. Then the night sounds began to return. The three of us had remained frozen; now Bernard moved. He turned to Delia.

"I knew it," he said. "I knew!"

She was very pale. "What was it?" she cried shrilly.

"Panther. Either in the city or awfully close."

Panther? It might have been. I had no idea what a panther sounded like. The others were coming down again, Evinson in the lead, Corrie and J.P. close behind him. Corrie looked less frightened than Delia, but rattled and pale.

"For heaven's sake, Bernard!" J.P. said. "Was that you?"

"Don't you know?" Corrie cried. At the same time Delia said, "It was a panther."

"No! Don't be a fool!" Corrie said.

Evinson interrupted them both. "Everyone, just be quiet. It was some sort of bird. We've seen birds for three days now. Some of them make cries like that."

"No bird ever made a sound like that," Corrie said. Her voice was too high and excited.

"It was a panther," Bernard repeated. "I heard one before. In Mexico I heard one just like that, twenty years ago. I've never forgotten." He nodded toward the net-covered window. "Out there. Maybe in one of the city parks. Think what it means, Evinson. I was right! Wild life out there. Naturalized, probably." He took a breath. His hands were trembling, and he spoke with an intensity that was almost embarrassing. Corrie shook her head stubbornly, but Bernard went on. "I'm going to find it. Tomor-

row. I'll take Sax with me, and our gear, and plan to stay out there
for a day or two. We'll see if we can find a trace of it, get a shot.
Proof of some kind."

Evinson started to protest. If it wasn't his plan, he hated it.
"We need Sax to find water for us," he said. "It's too dangerous.
We don't know what the beast is; it might attack at sight."

I was watching Bernard. His face tightened, became older,
harsher. He was going. "Drop it, Evinson," I said. "They know
about me. The only water I'll find is the river, which I already
stumbled across, remember. And Bernard is right. If there's
anything, we should go out and try to find it."

Evinson grumbled some more, but he couldn't really forbid it,
since this was what the expedition was all about. Besides, he knew
damn well there was no way on earth that he could enforce any
silly edict. Sulkily he left us to plan our foray.

*   *   *

It was impossible to tell how the waterways had been laid out in
many places. The water had spread, making marshes, and had
changed its course, sometimes flowing down streets, again vanishing entirely, leaving dry beds as devoid of life as the Martian
canals. Ruined concrete and sand lay there now. And the ruins
went on and on. No frame houses remained; they had caved in, or
had been blown down, or burned. A trailer court looked as if
someone had taken one corner of the area and lifted it, tipping
the chrome and gaudy colored cans to one side. Creepers and
shrubs were making a hill of greenery over them. We rowed and
carried the boat and our stuff all day, stopped for the storms, then
found shelter in a school building when it grew dark. The
mosquitoes were worse the farther we went; their whining
drowned out all other noises; we were both a mass of swollen bites
that itched without letup. We saw nothing bigger than a squirrel.
Bernard thought he glimpsed a manatee once, but it disappeared
in the water plants and didn't show again. I didn't see it. There
were many birds.

We were rowing late in the afternoon of the second day when
Bernard motioned me to stop. We drifted and I looked where he

pointed. On the bank was a great gray heron, its head stretched upward in a strange but curiously graceful position. Its wings were spread slightly, and it looked like nothing so much as a ballerina, poised, holding out her tutu. With painful slowness it lifted one leg and flexed its toes, then took a dainty, almost mincing step. Bernard pointed again, and I saw the second bird, in the same pose, silent, following a ritual that had been choreographed incalculable ages ago. We watched the dance of the birds in silence, until without warning Bernard shouted in a hoarse, strange voice, "Get out of here! You fucking birds! Get out of here!" He hit the water with his oar, making an explosive noise, and continued to scream at them as they lifted in panicked flight and vanished into the growth behind them, trailing their long legs, ungainly now and no longer beautiful.

"Bastard," I muttered at him and started to row again. We were out of synch for a long time as he chopped at the water ineffectually.

We watched the rain later, not talking. We hadn't talked since seeing the birds' courtship dance. I had a sunburn that was painful and peeling; I was tired, and hungry for some real food. "Tomorrow morning we start back," I said. I didn't look at him. We were in a small house while the rain and wind howled and pounded and turned the world gray. Lightning flashed and thunder rocked us almost simultaneously. The house shook and I tensed, ready to run. Bernard laughed. He waited for the wind to let up before he spoke.

"Sax, we have until the end of the week, and then back to Washington for you, back to New York for me. When do you think you'll ever get out of the city again?"

"If I get back to it, what makes you think I'll ever want out again?"

"You will. This trip will haunt you. You'll begin to think of those parakeets, the terns wheeling and diving for fish. You'll dream of swimming in clean water. You'll dream of the trees and the skies and the waves on the beach. And no matter how much you want to get it back, there won't be any way at all."

"There's a way if you want it bad enough."

"No way." He shook his head. "I tried. For years I tried. No way. Unless you're willing to walk crosscountry, and take the risks. No one ever makes it to anywhere, you know."

I knew he was right. In Health and Education you learn about things like public transportation: there isn't any. You learn about travel: there isn't any, not that's safe. The people who know how to salvage and make-do get more and more desperate for parts to use, more and more deadly in the ways they get those parts. Also, travel permits were about as plentiful as unicorns.

"You wanted to go back to Mexico?" I asked.

"Yeah. For twenty years I wanted to go back. The women there are different."

"You were younger. They were younger."

"No, it isn't just that. They were different. Something in the air. You could feel it, sniff it, almost see it. The smells were . . ." He stood up suddenly. "Anyway, I tried to get back, and this is as close as I could get. Maybe I'll go ahead and walk after all." He faced the west where the sky had cleared and the low sun looked three times as big as it should have.

"Look, Bernard, I could quote you statistics; that's my job, you know. But I won't. Just take my word for it. That's what I'm good at. What I read, I remember. The birth rate has dropped to two per thousand there. As of six years ago. It might be lower now. They're having a hell of a time with communications. And they had plague."

"I don't believe that."

"What? The birth rate?"

"Plague." He looked at me with a strange smile.

I didn't know what he was driving at. I was the one with access to government records, while he was just a photographer. "Right," I said. "People just died of nothing."

"It's a lie, Sax! A goddamn fucking lie! No plague!" He stopped as suddenly as he had started, and sat down. "Forget it, Sax. Just forget it."

"If it wasn't the plague, what?"

"I said to let it drop."

"What was it, Bernard? You're crazy, you know that? You're talking crazy."

"Yeah, I'm crazy." He was looking westward again.

During the night I wakened to hear him walking back and forth. I hoped that if he decided to start that night, he'd leave me the canoe. I went back to sleep. He was still there in the morning.

"Look, Sax, you go back. I'll come along in a day or two."

"Bernard, you can't live off nothing. There won't be any food after tomorrow. We'll both go back, stock up, and come out again. I couldn't go off and leave you. How would you get back?"

"When I was a boy," he said, "my father and mother were rather famous photographers. They taught me. We traveled all over the world. Getting pictures of all the vanishing species, for one last glorious book." I nodded. They had produced two of the most beautiful books I had ever seen. "Then something happened," he said, after a slight hesitation. "You know all about that, I guess. Your department. They went away and left me in Mexico. I wasn't a kid, you see, but I'd always been with them. Then I wasn't with them anymore. No note. No letter. Nothing. They searched for them, of course. Rich gringos aren't—weren't—allowed to simply vanish. Nothing. Before that my father had taken me into the hills, for a hunt. This time with guns. We shot—God, we shot everything that moved! Deer. Rabbits. Birds. A couple of snakes. There was a troop of monkeys. I remember them most of all. Seven monkeys. He took the left side and I took the right and we wiped them out. Just like that. They shrieked and screamed and tried to run away, and tried to shield each other, and we got every last one. Then we went back to my mother and the next day they were gone. I was fifteen. I stayed there for five years. Me and the girls of Mexico. They sent me home just before the border was closed. All North Americans out. I got permission to go back to New York, and for seventeen years I never left again. Until now. I won't go back again, Sax."

He leaned over and picked up a rifle. He had had it with his photographic equipment. "I have ammunition. I've had it for years. I'm pretty good with it. I'd demonstrate, but I don't want to waste the shell. Now, you just pick up your gear, and toss it in the boat, and get the hell out of here."

I suddenly remembered watching television as a child, when they had programs that went on around the clock—stories, movies. A man with a rifle stalking a deer. That's all I could remember of that program, but it was very clear and I didn't want to go away and let Bernard be that man. I stared at the rifle until it began to rise and I was looking down the barrel of it.

"I'll kill you, Sax. I really will," he said, and I knew he would.

I turned and tossed my pack into the boat and then climbed in. "How will you get back, if you decide to come back?" I felt only bitterness. I was going back and he was going to be the man with the rifle.

"I'll find a way. If I'm not there by Friday, don't wait. Tell Evinson I said that, Sax."

"Bernard . . ." I let it hang there as I pushed off and started to paddle. There wasn't a thing that I could say to him.

I heard a shot about an hour later, then another in the afternoon, after that nothing. I got back to headquarters during the night. No one was up, so I raided the food and beer and went to bed. The next morning Evinson was livid with rage.

"He wouldn't have stayed like that! You left him! You did something to him, didn't you? You'll be tried, Sax. I'll see you in prison for this." Color flooded back into his face, leaving him looking as unnaturally flushed as he had been pale only a moment before. His hand trembled as he wiped his forehead, which was flaky with peeling skin.

"Sax is telling the truth," Delia said. She had circles under her eyes and seemed depressed. "Bernard wanted me to go away with him to hunt. I refused. He needed someone to help him get as far away as possible."

Evinson turned his back on her. "You'll go back for him," he said to me, snapping the words. I shook my head. "I'll report you, Sax. I don't believe a word of what you've said. I'll report you. You did something, didn't you? All his work for this project! You go get him!"

"Oh, shut up." I turned to Corrie. "Anything new while I was gone?"

She looked tired too. Evinson must have applied the whip. "Not much. We've decided to take back samples of everything. We can't do much with the equipment we brought. Just not enough time. Not enough of us for the work."

"If you knew your business you could do it!" Evinson said. "Incompetents! All of you! This is treason! You know that, don't you? You're sabotaging this project. You don't want me to prove my theory. Obstacles every step of the way. That's all you've been good for. And now this! I'm warning you, Sax, if you don't bring Bernard back today, I'll press charges against you." His voice had been high-pitched always, but it became shriller and shriller until he sounded like a hysterical woman.

I spun to face him. "What theory, you crazy old man? There is no theory! There are a hundred theories. You think those records weren't sifted a thousand times before they were abandoned? Everything there was microfilmed and studied again and again and again. You think you can poke about in this muck and filth and come up with something that hasn't been noted and discarded a dozen times? They don't give a damn about your theories, you bloody fool! They hope that Delia can come up with a radiation study they can use. That Bernard will find wild life, plant life that will prove the pollution has abated here. That J.P. will report the marine life has reestablished itself. Who do you think will even read your theories about what happened here? Who gives a damn? All they want now is to try to save the rest." I was out of breath and more furious than I had been in years. I wanted to kill the bastard, and it didn't help at all to realize that it was Bernard that I really wanted to strangle. The man with the gun. Evinson backed away from me, and for the first time I saw that one of his hands had been bandaged.

Corrie caught my glance and shrugged. "Something bit him. He thinks I should be able to analyze his blood and come up with everything from what did it to a foolproof antidote. In fact, we have no idea what bit him."

"Isn't Trainor any help with something like that?"

"He might be if he were around. We haven't seen him since the night we heard the scream."

Evinson flung down his plastic cup. It bounced from the table to the floor. He stamped out.

"It's bad," Corrie said. "He's feverish, and his hand is infected. I've done what I can. I just don't have anything to work with."

Delia picked up the cup and put it back on the table. "This whole thing is an abysmal failure," she said dully. "None of us is able to get any real work done. We don't know enough, or we don't have the right equipment, or enough manpower, or time. I don't even know why we're here."

"The Turkey Point plant?"

"I don't know a damn thing about it, except that it isn't hot. The people who built that plant knew more than we're being taught today." She bit her lip hard enough to leave marks on it. Her voice was steady when she went on. "It's like that in every field. We're losing everything that we had twenty-five years ago, thirty years ago. I'm one of the best, and I don't understand that plant."

I looked at Corrie and she nodded. "I haven't seen a transplant in my life. No one is doing them now. I read about dialysis, but no one knows how to do it. In my books there are techniques and procedures that are as alien as acupuncture. Evinson is furious with us, and with himself. He can't come up with anything that he couldn't have presented as theory without ever leaving the city. It's a failure, and he's afraid he'll be blamed personally."

We sat in silence for several minutes until J.P. entered. He looked completely normal. His bald head was very red; the rest of his skin had tanned to a deep brown. He looked like he was wearing a gaudy skullcap.

"You're back." Not a word about Bernard, or to ask what we had done, what we had seen. "Delia, you coming with me again today? I'd like to get started soon."

Delia laughed and stood up. "Sure, J.P. All the way." They left together.

"Is he getting anything done?"

"Who knows? He works sixteen hours a day doing something. I don't know what." Corrie drummed her fingers on the table, watching them. Then she said, "Was that a panther the other night, Davidson? Did you see a panther, or anything else?"

"Nothing. And I don't know what it was. I never heard a panther."

"I don't think it was. I think it was a human being."

"A woman?"

"Yes. In childbirth."

I stared at her until she met my gaze. She nodded. "I've heard it before. I am a doctor, you know. I specialized in obstetrics until the field became obsolete."

I found that I couldn't stop shaking my head. "You're as crazy as Bernard."

"No. That's what I came for, Davidson. There has to be life that's viable, out there in the Everglades. The Indians. They can stick it out, back in the swamps where they always lived. Probably nothing much has changed for them. Except that there's more game now. That has to be it."

"Have you talked to Evinson about this?"

"Yes, of course. He thinks it was Trainor who screamed. He thinks Trainor was killed by a snake, or something. After he got bitten himself, he became convinced of it."

"J.P.? Delia?"

"J.P. thinks it's a mystery. Since it has nothing to do with marine biology, he has no opinion, no interest. Delia thought Bernard was right, an animal, maybe a panther, maybe something else. She is afraid it's a mutated animal. She began to collect strange plants, and insects, things like that after you left. She even has a couple of fruit bats that she says are mutations."

I took a deep breath. "Corrie, why are we here? Why did the government send this expedition here?"

She shrugged. "What you told Evinson makes as much sense as anything else. The government didn't mount this expedition, you know. They simply permitted it. And sent an observer. It was Bernard's scheme from the start. He convinced Evinson that he would become famous through the proofs for his schoolboy theory. Bernard's money, Evinson's pull with those in power. And now we know why Bernard wanted to come. He's impotent, you know." She looked thoughtful, then smiled faintly at me. "A lot of impotent men feel the need to go out and shoot things, you know. And many, perhaps most men are impotent now, you know. Don't look like that. At least you're all right."

I backed away from that. "What about Evinson? Does he believe a leak or an explosion brought all this about?"

"Bernard planted that in his mind," she said. "He doesn't really believe it now. But it leaves him with no alternative theory to fall back on. You can't tell anything by looking at these rotten buildings."

I shook my head. "I know that was the popular explanation, but they did investigate, you know. Didn't he get to any of the old reports? Why did he buy that particular theory?"

"All those reports are absolutely meaningless. Each new administration doctors them to fit its current platforms and promises." She shrugged again. "That's propaganda from another source, right? So what did happen, according to the official reports?"

"Plague, brought in by Haitian smugglers. And the water was going bad, salt intrusion destroyed the whole system. Four years of drought had aggravated everything. Then the biggest hurricane of the century hit and that was just too bloody much. Thirty thousand deaths. They never recovered."

She was shaking her head now. "You have the chronology all mixed up. First the drop in population, the exodus, then the plague. It was like that everywhere. First the population began to sag, and in industrialized nations that spelled disaster. Then flu strains that no one had ever seen before, and plague. There weren't enough doctors; plants had closed down because of a labor shortage. There was no defense. In the ten years before the epidemics, the population had dropped by twenty percent."

I didn't believe her, and she must have known it from my expression. She stood up. "I don't know what's in the water, Sax. It's crawling with things that I can't identify, but we pretend that they belong and that they're benign. And God help us, we're the ones teaching the new generation. Let's swim."

Lying on my back under the broiling sun, I tried again to replay the scene with my boss. Nothing came of it. He hadn't told me why he was sending me to Miami. Report back. On what? Everything you see and hear, everything they all do. For the record. Period.

Miami hadn't been the first city to be evacuated. It had been the largest up to that time. Throughout the Midwest, the far west, one town, one city after another had been left to the winds and rains and the transients. No one had thought it strange enough to investigate. The people were going to the big cities where they could find work. The young refused to work the land. Or agribusiness had bought them out. No mystery. Then larger cities had been emptied. But that was because of epidemics: plague, flu, hepatitis. Or because of government policies: busing or open housing; or the loss of government contracts for defense work. Always a logical explanation. Then Miami. And the revelation that population zero had been reached and passed. But that had to be because of the plagues. Nothing else made any sense at all. I looked at Corrie resentfully. She was dozing after our swim. Her body was gold-brown now, with highlights of red on her shoulders, her nose, her thighs. It was too easy to reject the official reasons, especially if you weren't responsible for coming up with alternative explanations.

"I think they sent you because they thought you would come back," Corrie said, without opening her eyes. "I think that's it." She rolled on her side and looked at me.

"You know with Trainor gone, maybe none of us will get back," I said.

"If we hug the shore we should make it, except that we have no gas."

I looked blank, I suppose. She laughed. "No one told you? He took the gas when he left. Or the snake that killed him drank it. I think he found a boat that would get him to the Bahamas, and he went. I suppose that's why he came, to get enough gas to cruise the islands. That's why he insisted on getting down by sail, to save what gas Evinson had requisitioned for this trip. There's no one left on the islands, of course."

I had said it lightly, that we might not get back, but with no gas, it became a statement of fact. None of us could operate the sail, and the boat was too unwieldy to paddle. The first storm would capsize us, or we would run aground. "Didn't Trainor say anything about coming back?"

"He didn't even say anything about leaving." She closed her eyes and repeated, "There's no one there at all."

"Maybe," I said. But I didn't believe there was, either. Suddenly, looking at Corrie, I wanted her, and I reached for her arm. She drew away, startled. They said that sun-spot activity had caused a decrease in sexual activity. Sporadically, with some of us. I grabbed Corrie's arm hard and pulled her toward me. She didn't fight, but her face became strained, almost haggard.

"Wait until tomorrow, Davidson. Please. I'll ovulate tomorrow. Maybe you and I . . ." I saw the desperation then, and the fear—worse, terror. I saw the void in her eyes, pupils the size of pinpricks in the brilliant light, the irises the color of the endless water beyond us. I pushed her away and stood up.

Don't bring me your fear, I wanted to say. All my life I had been avoiding the fear and now she would thrust it upon me. I left her lying on the beach.

Evinson was sick that night. He vomited repeatedly, and toward dawn he became delirious.

J.P. and I took turns sitting with him, because the women weren't strong enough to restrain him when he began to thrash about. He flung Corrie against the wall before we realized his strength and his dementia.

"He's dying, isn't he?" J.P. said, looking at him coolly. He was making a study of death, I thought.

"I don't know."

"He's dying. It might take a while, but this is the start of it." He looked at me fixedly for a long time. "None of us is going back, Sax. You realize that, don't you?"

"I don't know about the rest of you, but I'm going back. You're all a bunch of creepies, crazy as bedbugs, all of you. But I'm going back!"

"Don't yell." His voice remained mild, neutral, an androgynous voice without overtones of anything human at all.

I stamped from the room to get a beer, and when I got back, J.P. was writing in his notebook. He didn't look up again. Evinson got much worse, louder, more violent, then his strength began to ebb and he subsided, moaning fitfully now and then, murmuring unintelligibly. Corrie checked him from time to time. She changed the dressing on his hand; it was swollen to twice its normal size, the swelling extending to his shoulder. She looked at him as dispassionately as J.P. did.

"A few more hours," she said. "Do you want me to stay up with you?"

"What for?" I asked coldly. "I must say you're taking this well."

"Don't be sarcastic. What good would it do if I put on an act and wept for him?"

"You might care because he's a man who didn't deserve to die in this stinking city."

She shrugged. "I'll go on to bed. Call me if there's any change." At the doorway she turned and said, "I'll weep for myself, maybe even for you, Sax, but not for him. He knew what this would be like. We all did, except possibly you."

"You won't have to waste any tears for me. Go on to bed." She left and I said to J.P., "You all hate him, don't you? Why?"

J.P. picked up his pen again, but he hesitated. "I hadn't thought of it as hating him," he said thoughtfully. "I just never wanted to be near him. He's been trying to climb onto the glory train for years. Special adviser to presidents about urban affairs, that sort of thing. Absolutely no good at it, but very good at politics. He made them all think there was still hope. He lied and knew he lied. They used to say those that can do; those that can't teach. Now the saying goes, those that can't become sociologists." He put his pen down again and began to worry at a hangnail. His hands were very long and narrow, brown, bony with prominent knuckles. "A real scientist despises the pseudo-scientist who passes. Something unclean about him, the fact that he could get permission for this when his part of it was certain to be negligible from the start."

"And yours was important from the start, I suppose?"

"For fifteen years I've wanted to get back into field research. Every year the funds dwindled more. People like me were put into classrooms, or let go. It really isn't fair to the students, you understand. I'm a rotten teacher. I hate them all without exception. I crammed and worked around the clock to get as good a background as I could, and when I was ready, I forced myself on Albert Lanier." He looked at me expectantly and I shook my head. Only later did I recall the name. Lanier had written many of the books on marine biology that were in the libraries. J.P. looked at me with contempt. "He was a great man and a greater scientist. During his last years when he was crippled with rheumatoid arthritis, I was his eyes, his legs, his hands. When he died all field research died with him. Until now."

"So you're qualified for this work."

"Yes, I'm qualified. More than that fool." He glanced at Evinson, who was breathing very shallowly. "More than anyone here. If only my work is made known, this farce will be worth ten of him, of all of you."

"If?"

"If. Would any one of my own students know what I'm doing? My own students!" He bit the hangnail and a spot of blood appeared on his thumb. He started to scribble again.

At daybreak Evinson's fever started to climb, and it rose steadily until noon. We kept him in wet sheets, we fanned him, Corrie gave him cool enemas. Nothing helped. He died at one-thirty. I was alone with him. Corrie and Delia were both asleep.

J.P. knew when he looked at my face. He nodded. I saw his pack then. "Where the hell are you going?"

"Down the coast. Maybe down the Keys, as far as I can get. I'd like to see if the coral is coming back again."

"We leave here Saturday morning at dawn. I don't give a damn who's here and who isn't. At dawn."

He smiled mockingly and shook his head. He didn't say good-bye to anyone, just heaved his pack onto his back and walked away.

I rummaged on the *Loretta* and found a long-handled, small-bladed shovel, and I buried Evinson high on the beach, above the high-water mark.

When I got back Corrie was up, eating a yellow fruit with a thick rind. I knocked it out of her hand reflexively. "Are you out of your mind! You know the local fruits might kill us." She had juice on her chin.

"I don't know anything anymore. That's a mango, and it's delicious. I've been eating the fruits for three days. A touch of diarrhea the first day, that's all." She spoke lightly, and didn't look at me. She began to cut another one.

"Evinson died. I buried him. J.P. left."

She didn't comment. The aromatic odor from the fruit seemed to fill the room. She handed me a slice and I threw it back at her.

Delia came down then looking better than she had in days. Her cheeks were pink and her eyes livelier than I had seen them. She looked at Corrie, and while she didn't smile, or do anything at all, I knew.

"Bitch," I said to Corrie bitterly. "Wait until tomorrow. Right. Bitch!"

"Take a walk, Sax," Delia said sharply.

"Let's not fight," Corrie said. "He's dead and J.P.'s gone." Delia shrugged and sat down at the table. Corrie handed her a piece of the mango. "Sax, you knew about me, about us. Whether or not you wanted to know, you did. Sometimes I tried to pretend that maybe I could conceive, but I won't. So forget it. What are you going to do?"

"Get the hell out of here. Go home."

"For what?" Delia asked. She tasted the slice of mango curiously, then bit into it. She frowned critically. "I like the oranges better."

"These grow on you," Corrie said. "I've developed an absolute craving for them in the past three days. You'll see."

"I don't know about you," I said furiously, "but I'm leaving Saturday. I have things to do that I like doing. I like to read. To see a show now and then. I have friends."

"Are you married? Do you live with a woman? Or a man?" Delia asked.

I looked at Corrie. "We're in trouble. It'll take the three of us to manage the boat to get back. We have to make plans."

"We aren't going back," Corrie said softly. "We're going to the Seminoles."

"Corrie, listen to me. I've been out farther than either of you. There's nothing. Ruins. Rot. Decay. No roads. Nothing. Even if they existed, you'd never find them."

"There's the remains of the road. Enough for us to follow west."

"Why didn't you try a little bribery with me?" I yelled at her. "Maybe I would have changed my mind and gone with you."

"I didn't want you, Sax. I didn't think the Seminoles would want to take in a white man."

I left them alone for the rest of the day. I checked the *Loretta* again, swam, fished, gloomed. That night I pretended that nothing had been said about Seminoles. We ate silently.

Outside was the blackness and the silence, and somewhere in the silence a scream waited. The silence seemed to be sifting in through the mosquito netting. The wind had stopped completely. The air was close and very hot inside the building. "I'm going out," I said as soon as I finished eating.

Delia's question played through my mind as I walked. Did I live with a woman? Or a man? I stopped at the edge of the water. There were no waves on the bay, no sound except a gentle water murmur. Of all the people I knew, I could think of only three that I would like to see again, two of them because I had lived with them in the past, and our relationships had been exciting, or at least not abrasive, while they had lasted. And when they were finished, the ending hadn't been shattering. Two women, both gone from my life completely. One man, a co-worker in my department. We did things together, bowled, swapped books, saw shows together. Not recently, I reminded myself. He had dropped out of sight.

A gust of wind shook me and I started back. A storm was coming up fast. The wind became erratic and strong, and as suddenly as the wind had started, the rain began. It was a deluge that blinded me, soaked me, and was ankle deep in the street almost instantly. Then, over the rain, I heard a roar that shook me through and through, that left me vibrating. A tornado, I knew, although I had never seen or heard one. The roar increased, like a plane bearing down on me. I threw myself flat, and the noise rocked the ground under me, and a building crashed to my left, then another, and another. It ended as abruptly as it had started.

I stumbled back to our building, shaking, chilled and very frightened. I was terrified that our building would be demolished, the women gone, dead, and that I would be alone with the silence and the black of the night.

Corrie opened the door on the first floor and I stumbled in. "Are you all right? It was a tornado, wasn't it?"

She and Delia were both afraid. That was reassuring. Maybe now they would be frightened enough to give up the nonsense about staying here. The storm abated and the silence returned. It didn't seem quite so ominous now.

"Corrie, don't you see how dangerous it would be to stay? There could be a hurricane. Storms every day. Come back with me."

"The cities will die, Sax. They'll run out of food. More epidemics. I can help the Seminoles."

* * *

Friday I got the *Loretta* ready for the return trip. I packed as much fruit as it would hold. Enough for three, I kept telling myself. Forbidden fruit. For three. I avoided Corrie and Delia as much as I could and they seemed to be keeping busy, but what they were doing I couldn't guess.

That night I came wide awake suddenly and sat up listening hard. Something had rattled or fallen. And now it was too quiet. It had been the outside door slamming, I realized, and jumped up from my bedroll and raced downstairs. No one was there, anywhere. They had left, taking with them Corrie's medical supplies, Delia's radiation kit, most of the food, most of the beer. I went outside, but it was hopeless. I hadn't expected this. I had thought they would try to talk me into going into the swamps with them, not that they would try it alone.

I cursed and threw things around, then another thought hit me. The *Loretta*! I ran to the dock in a frenzy of fear that they had scuttled her. But she was there, swaying and bobbing in the changing tide. I went aboard and decided not to leave her again. In the morning I saw that the sail was gone.

I stared at the mast and the empty deck. Why? Why for God's sake had they taken the sail?

They'll be back, I kept thinking all morning. And I'll kill them both. Gradually the thought changed. They would beg me to go with them inland, and I would say yes, and we would go into the first swamp and I would take their gear and leave them there. They would follow me out soon enough. They had needed the sail for a shelter, I thought dully. After noon I began to think that maybe I could go with them part of the way, just to help them out, prove to them that it was hopeless to go farther.

My fury returned, redoubled. All my life I had managed to live quietly, just doing my job, even though it was a stupid one, but getting paid and trying to live comfortably, keeping busy enough not to think. Keeping busy enough to keep the fear out. Because it was there all the time, pressing, just as the silence here pressed. It was a silent fear, but if it had had a voice, its voice would have been that scream we had heard. That was the voice of my fear. Loud, shrill, inhuman, hopeless. I felt clammy and chilled in the heat, and my stomach rejected the idea of food or drink.

Come back, I pleaded silently, willing the thought out, spreading the thought, trying to make contact with one of them. Come back for me. I'll go with you, do whatever you want to do. Please!

That passed. The storm came, and I shivered alone in the *Loretta* and listened to the wind and the pounding rain. I thought about my apartment, my work, the pamphlets I wrote. The last one I had worked on was titled: "Methods of Deep Ploughing of Alluvial Soils in Strip Farming in Order to Provide a Nutritionally Adequate Diet in a Meatless Society." Who was it for? Who would read past the title? No one, I answered. No one would read it. They were planning for a future that I couldn't even imagine. The silence was more profound than ever that evening. I sat on deck until I could bear the mosquitoes no longer. Below, it was sweltering, and the silence had followed me in. I would start back at first light, I decided. I would have to take a smaller boat. A flat-bottomed boat. I could row it up the waterway, stay out of the ocean. I could haul it where the water was too shallow or full of debris.

The silence pressed against me, equally on all sides, a force that I could feel now. I would need something for protection from the sun. And boiled water. The beer was nearly gone. They hadn't left me much food, either. I could do without food, but not without water and maps. Maybe I could make a small sail from discarded clothing. I planned and tried not to feel the silence. I lectured myself on synesthesia—I had done a pamphlet on the subject once. But the silence won. I began to run up the dock, screaming at Corrie and Delia, cursing them, screaming for them to come back. I stopped, exhausted finally, and the echo finished and the silence was back. I knew I wouldn't sleep; I built a fire and started to boil water.

I poured the water into the empty beer bottles and stacked them back in their original boxes. More water started to boil, and I dozed. In my near sleep, I heard the scream again. I jumped up shaking. It had been inhumanly high, piercing, with such agony and hopelessness that tears stood in my eyes. I had dreamed it, I told myself. And I couldn't be certain if I had or not.

Until dawn came I thought about the scream, and it seemed to me a thing uttered by no living throat. It had been my own scream, I thought, and I laughed out loud.

I loaded an aluminum rowboat the next day and rigged up a sail that might or might not fall apart when the wind blew. I made myself a poncho and a sun hat, and then, ready to go, I sat in the boat and watched some terns diving. They never had asked me what I had wanted to do, I thought bitterly. Not one of them had asked me what I would have liked to have done.

J.P. had complained about being forced into teaching, while I would have traded everything I had for the chance to write, to teach—but worthless things, like literature, art appreciation, composition. A pelican began to dive with the terns, and several gulls appeared. They followed the pelican down, and one sat on his head and tried to snatch the fish from his mouth.

I thought again of all the pamphlets I had written, all the thousands of pages I had read in order to condense them. All wasted because in reducing them to so little, too much had been left out. I started to row finally.

When I left the mouth of the bay, I turned the small boat southward. The sea was very blue, the swells long and peaceful. Cuba, I thought. That many people, some of them had to be left. And they would need help. So much had been lost already, and I had it, all those thousands of pages, hundreds of books, all up there in my head.

I saw again the undersecretary's white, dry, dead face, the hurt there, the fear. He hadn't expected me to come back at all, I realized. I wished I could tell Corrie.

The wind freshened. If not Cuba, then Central America, or even South America. I put up my little sail, and the wind caught it and puffed it, and I felt only a great contentment.

The Gahan Wilson Horror Movie Pocket Computer

Do you find yourself sitting blearily night after night before your sputtering television set, compulsively watching yet another inept vampire saga flicker on into the small hours, unable to turn the damned thing off, cursing feebly at the forced buffooneries of the cloddish, sleazily-shrouded master of ceremonies, grinding your teeth in embarrassment at permitting your mind to be fouled by the ads for Elvis Presley albums and truck driving academies, eating far more

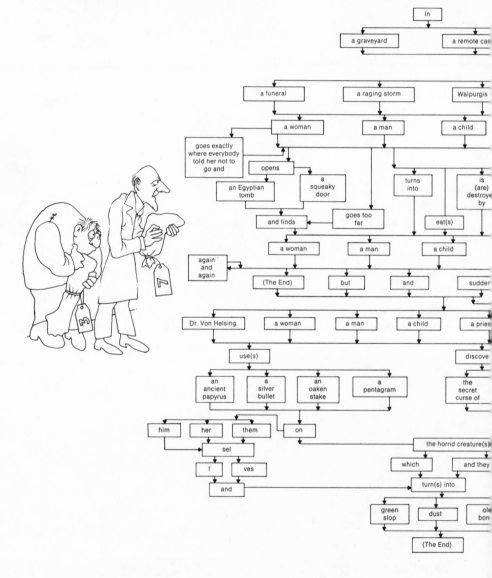

In

a graveyard — a remote cas[tle]

a funeral — a raging storm — Walpurgis[...]

a woman — a man — a child

goes exactly where everybody told her not to go and — opens — an Egyptian tomb — a squeaky door — turns into — is (are) destroye[d] by

and finds — goes too far — eat(s)

a woman — a man — a child

again and again — (The End) — but — and — sudden[ly]

Dr. Von Helsing — a woman — a man — a child — a pries[t]

use(s) — discove[rs]

an ancient papyrus — a silver bullet — an oaken stake — a pentagram — the secret curse of

him — her — them — on

sel — the horrid creature(s)

f — ves — which — and they

and — turn(s) into

green slop — dust — ol[d] bon[es]

(The End)

cashews than are good for you, and knowing all along that you fully intend to stay up for yet another ghastly film after this one has finally petered itself out? Then you, you poor bastard, are suffering from one of mankind's most debasing and humiliating afflictions— you are a horror movie addict.

There is no cure for this condition— I wish to God there were—but there *is* a way to divert the insatiable appetite for insulting drivel which plagues victims of this vile disease, and that is to carry at all times the Gahan Wilson Horror Movie Pocket Computer shown below. When, as usual, the pathetic wretch finds himself staring at some dreadful film about ambulatory mummies, all he need do is pull out the Computer, locate the position on it analogous to the dismal epic unfolding itself before him, and read through to any The End point he fancies. He will then find he can stand without aid, actually turn his set off, and go directly to bed. Thanks to the Gahan Wilson Horror Movie Pocket Computer, easily one of this century's greatest scientific and philanthropic achievements, he will have replaced hours of appalling bondage with one joyful glance at this wonderful device. □

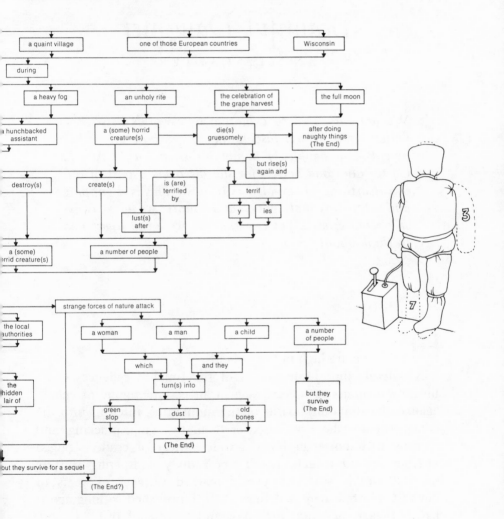

The Executioner's Beautiful Daughter

ANGELA CARTER

We are very used to exploring new worlds in science fiction. It is always fascinating to see how an author invents and peoples a planet far from Earth. Angela Carter does one better, for she discovers a part of our own Earth never revealed until now. This is a gripping and utterly fascinating look at a country we have always suspected existed, but one that we were too frightened to think about.

HERE, we are high in the uplands.

A baleful, almost-music, that of the tuneless cadences of an untutored orchestra repercussing in an ecstatic agony of echoes against the sounding boards of the mountains, lured us into the village square where we discover them twanging, plucking, and abusing with horsehair bows a wide variety of crude, stringed instruments. Our feet crunch upon dryly whispering shifting sawdust freshly scattered over impacted surfaces of years of sawdusts clotted, here and there, with blood shed so long ago it has, with age, acquired the color and texture of rust . . . sad, ominous stains, a threat, a menace, memorials of pain.

There is no brightness in the air. Today the sun will not irradiate the heroes of the dark spectacle to which accident and disharmony combined to invite us. Here, where the air is choked all day with diffuse moisture tremulously, endlessly on the point of becoming rain, light falls as if filtered through muslin so at all hours a crepuscular gloaming prevails; the sky looks as though it is about to weep and so, gloomily illuminated through unshed tears, the *tableau vivant* before us is suffused with the sepia tints of an old photograph and nothing within it moves. The intent immobility of the spectators, wholly absorbed as they are in the performance of their hieratic ritual, is scarcely that of living things and this *tableau vivant* might be better termed a *nature morte*, for the mirthless carnival is a celebration of a death. Their eyes, the whites of which are yellowish, are all fixed, as if attached by taut, invisible strings, upon a wooden block lacquered black with the spilt dews of a millennia of victims.

And now the rustic bandsmen suspend their unmelodious music. This death must be concluded in the most dramatic silence. The wild mountain-dwellers are gathered together to watch a public execution; that is the only entertainment the country offers.

Time, suspended like the rain, begins again in silence, slowly.

A heavy stillness ordering all his movements, the executioner himself adopts beside the block an offensively heroic pose, as if to do the thing with dignity were the only motive of the doing. He brings one booted foot to rest on the grim and sacrificial altar which is, to him, the canvas on which he exercises his art and proudly in his hand he bears his instrument, his axe.

The executioner stands more than six and a half feet high and he is broad to suit; the warped stumps of villagers gaze up at him with awe and fear. He is dressed always in mourning and always wears a curious mask. This mask is made of supple, close-fitting leather dyed an absolute black and it conceals his hair and the upper part of his face entirely except for two narrow slits through which issue the twin regards of eyes as inexpressive as though they were part of the mask. This mask reveals only his blunt-lipped, dark-red mouth and the grayish flesh which surrounds it. Laid out in such an unnerving fashion, these portions of his meat in no way fulfill the expectations we derive from our common knowledge of faces. They have a quality of obscene rawness as if, in some fashion, the lower face had been flayed. He, the butcher, might be displaying himself, as if he were his own meat.

Through the years, the close-fitting substance of the mask has become so entirely assimilated to the actual structure of his face that the face itself now seems to possess a parti-colored appearance, as if by nature dual; and this face no longer pertains to that which is human as if, when he first put on the mask, he blotted out his own, original face and so defaced himself forever. Because the hood of office renders the executioner an object. He has become an object who punishes. He is an object of fear. He is the image of retribution.

Nobody remembers why the mask was first devised or who devised it. Perhaps some tender-heart of antiquity adopted the concealing headgear in order to spare the one upon the block the sight of too human a face in the last moments of his agony; or else the origins of the article lie in a magical relation with the blackness of negation—if, that is, negation is black in color. Yet the executioner dare not take off the mask in case, in a random looking-glass or, accidentally mirrored in a pool of standing water, he surprised his own authentic face. For then he would die of fright.

The victim kneels. He is thin, pale, and graceful. He is twenty years old. The silent throng in the courtyard shudders in common anticipation; all their gnarled features twist in the same grin. No sound, almost no sound disturbs the moist air, only the ghost of a sound, a distant sobbing that might be the ululation of the wind amongst the scrubby pines. The victim kneels and lays his neck upon the block. Ponderously the executioner lifts his gleaming steel.

The axe falls. The flesh severs. The head rolls.

The cleft flesh spouts its fountains. The spectators shudder, groan and gasp. And now the string band starts to bow and saw again whilst a choir of stunted virgins, in the screeching wail that

passes for singing in these regions, intones a barbaric requiem
entitled: AWFUL WARNING OF THE SPECTACLE OF A DECAPITATION.

The executioner has beheaded his own son for committing the
crime of incest upon the body of his sister, the executioner's
beautiful daughter, on whose cheeks the only roses in these
highlands grow.

Gretchen no longer sleeps soundly. After the day his decapi-
tated head rolled in the bloody sawdust, her brother rode a bicycle
interminably through her dreams even though the poor child crept
out secretly, alone, to gather up the poignant, moist, bearded
strawberry, his surviving relic, and take it home to bury beside her
hen-coop before the dogs ate it. But no matter how hard she
scrubbed her little white apron against the scouring stones in the
river, she could not wash away the stains that haunted the weft
and warp of the fabric like pinkish phantoms of very precious
fruit. Every morning, when she goes out to collect ripe eggs for her
father's breakfast, she waters with felt but ineffectual tears the
disturbed earth where her brother's brains lie rotting, while the
indifferent hens peck and cluck about her feet.

This country is situated at such a high altitude water never
boils, no matter how deceptively it foams within the pan, so their
boiled eggs are always raw. The executioner insists his breakfast
omelette be prepared only from those eggs precisely on the point
of blossoming into chicks and, prompt at eight, consumes with
relish a yellow, feathered omelette subtly spiked with claw.
Gretchen, his tender-hearted daughter, often jumps and starts to
hear the thwarted cluck from a still gelid, scarcely calcified beak
about to be choked with sizzling butter, but her father, whose
word is law because he never doffs his leather mask, will eat no egg
that does not contain within it a nascent bird. That is his taste. In
this country, only the executioner may indulge his perversities.

High among the mountains, how wet and cold it is! Chill winds
blow soft drifts of rain across these almost perpendicular peaks;
the wolf-haunted forests of fir and pine that cloak the lower slopes
are groves fit only for the satanic cavortings of a universal Sabbath
and a haunting mist pervades the bleak, meager villages rooted so

far above quotidian skies a newcomer might not, at first, be able to breathe but only wheeze and choke in this thinnest of air. Newcomers, however, are less frequent apparitions than meteorites and thunderbolts; the villages breathe no welcome.

Even the walls of the rudely constructed houses exude suspicion. They are made from slabs of stone and do not have any windows to see out with. An inadequate orifice in the flat roof puffs out a few scant breaths of domestic smoke and penetration inside is effected only with the utmost difficulty through low, narrow doors, crevices in the granite, so each house presents to the eye as featureless a face as those of the Oriental demons whose anonymity was marred by no such commonplace a blemish as an eye, a nose, or a mouth. Inside these ugly, unaccommodating hutches, man and domestic beast—goat, ox, pig, dog—stake equal squatting rights to the smoky and disordered hearths, although the dogs often grow rabid and rush frothing through the rutted streets like streams in spate.

The inhabitants are a thick-set, sullen brood whose chronic malevolence stems from a variety of both environmental and constitutional causes. All share a general and unprepossessing cast of countenance. Their faces have the limp, flat, boneless aspect of the Eskimo and their eyes are opaque fissures since no eyelid hoods them, only the slack skin of the Mongolian fold. Their reptilian regards possess an intensity which is in no way intimate and their smiles are so peculiarly vicious it is all for the best they smile rarely. Their teeth rot young.

The men in particular are monstrously hirsute about both head and body. Their hair, a monotonous and uniform purplish black, grizzles, in age, to the tint of defunct ashes. Their womenfolk are built for durability rather than delight. Since all go always barefoot, the soles of their feet develop an intensifying consistency of horn from earliest childhood and the women, who perform all the tasks demanded by their primitive agriculture, sprout forearms the size and contour of vegetable marrows while their hands become pronouncedly scoop-shaped, until they resemble, in maturity, fat five-pronged forks.

All, without exception, are filthy and verminous. Their shaggy heads and rough garments are clogged with lice and quiver with fleas while their pubic areas throb and pulse with the blind convulsions of the crab. Impetigo, scabies, and the itch are too prevalent among them to be remarked upon and their feet start early to decompose between the toes. They suffer from chronic afflictions of the anus due to their barbarous diet—thin porridge; sour beer; meat scarcely seared by the cool fires of the highlands; acidulated cheese of goat swallowed to the flatulent accompaniment of barley bread. Such comestibles cannot but contribute effectively to those disorders that have established the general air of malign unease which is their most immediately distinctive characteristic.

In this museum of diseases, the pastel beauty of Gretchen, the executioner's daughter, is all the more remarkable. Her flaxen plaits bob above her breasts as she goes to pluck, from their nests, the budding eggs.

Their days are shrouded troughs of glum manual toil and their nights wet, freezing, black, palpitating clefts gravid with the grossest cravings, nights dedicated solely to the imaginings of unspeakable desires tortuously conceived in mortified sensibilities habitually gnawed to suppuration by the black rats of superstition whilst the needle teeth of frost corrode their bodies.

They would, if they could, act out entire Wagnerian cycles of operatic evil and gleefully transform their villages into stages upon which the authentic monstrosities of Grand Guignol might be acted out in every unspeakable detail. No hideous parody of the delights of the flesh would be alien to them . . . *did they but know how such things were, in fact, performed.*

They have an inexhaustible capacity for sin but are inexorably balked by ignorance. They do not know what they desire. So their lusts exist in an undefined limbo, forever *in potentia.*

They yearn passionately after the most deplorable depravity but possess not the concrete notion of so much as a simple fetish, their tormented flesh betrayed eternally by the poverty of their imaginations and the limitations of their vocabulary, for how may one transmit such things in a language composed only of brute grunts and squawks representing, for example, the state of the family pig in labor? And, since their vices are, in the literal sense of the word, unspeakable, their secret, furious desires remain ultimately mysterious even to themselves and are contained only in the realm of pure sensation, or feeling undefined as thought or action and hence unrestrained by definition. So their desires are infinite, although, in real terms, except in the form of a prickle of perturbation, these desires could hardly be said to exist.

Their lives are dominated by a folklore as picturesque as it is murderous. Rigid, hereditary castes of wizards, warlocks, shamans, and practitioners of the occult proliferate amongst these benighted mountain-dwellers and the apex of esoteric power lies, it would seem, in the person of the king himself. But this appearance is deceptive. This nominal ruler is in reality the poorest beggar in all his ragged kingdom. Heir of the barbarous, he is stripped of everything but the idea of an omnipotence which is sufficiently expressed by immobility.

All day long, ever since his accession, he depends by the right ankle from an iron ring set in the roof of a stone hut. A stout ribbon binds him to the ceiling and he is inadequately supported in a precarious but absolute position sanctioned by ritual and memory upon his left wrist, which is strapped in a similar fashion with ribbon to an iron ring cemented into the floor. He stays as still as if he had been dipped in a petrifying well and never speaks one single word because he has forgotten how.

They all believe implicitly they are damned. A folk-tale circulates among them, as follows: that the tribe was originally banished from a happier and more prosperous region to their present dreary habitation, a place fit only for continuous self-mortification, after they rendered themselves abhorrent to their former neighbors by the wholesale and enthusiastic practice of incest, son with father, father with daughter, etc.—every baroque variation possible upon the determinate quadrille of the nuclear family. In this country, incest is a capital crime; the punishment for incest is decapitation.

Daily their minds are terrified and enlightened by the continuous performances of apocalyptic dirges for fornicating siblings and only the executioner himself, because there is nobody to cut off his head, dare, in the immutable privacy of his leathern hood, upon his blood-bespattered block make love to his beautiful daughter.

Gretchen, the only flower of the mountains, tucks up her white apron and waltzing gingham skirts so they will not crease or soil but, even in the last extremity of the act, her father does not remove his mask for who would recognize him without it? The price he pays for his position is always to be locked in the solitary confinement of his power.

He perpetrates his inalienable right in the reeking courtyard upon the block where he struck off the head of his only son. That night, Gretchen discovered a snake in her sewing machine and, though she did not know what a bicycle was, upon a bicycle her brother wheeled and circled through her troubled dreams until the cock crowed and out she went for eggs.

Six Poems

It has been pointed out that this annual selection of poetry is the only continuing source of science-fiction poetry extant. This is a cheering thought, for there are few enough outlets for good poetry of any kind. As long as exceptional SF poetry is written we hope to always find a bit of space for it in this annual anthology.

After Weightlessness

LAWRENCE SAIL

Once, the random sweep of an arm sufficed
To disperse planets like seedballs, rearrange
A galaxy. There were whole systems, then,
Bent round my clever thumb: and I could utter
Stars by the thousand, or laughingly banish light-years
Within the compass of my own spread fingers.

Since then, how many vengeful atmospheres
Have crushed my joints! Each pebble that I lift
Here on Earth, bruises the skin with blood,
Leaving its dark ring. Wherever I look,
Rivers hurtle seawards, unbalanced trees
Topple, helpless, towards the hidden centre.

Within me, now, I feel the fatal mass
Of dreams grown heavy, each imagined order

Compacted, bearing me down through clay and water:
And when, with effort, I raise my face to the mirror,
Each day, with growing terror I confront
Someone else's definition of power.

A Picture by Klee

LAWRENCE SAIL

X-rayed against the double night
Of the cut moon and the dwarf sun,
The wire frames of your skeleton town
Might have been gutted by fire, or nudged
Askew by earthquake.

But over the leaning towers, bright flags
Semaphore their messages
Of occupation, refuse to submit
To natural disaster, or
Random history.

No town was ever so ruined, or sited
So far beyond the reach of weather,
The limits of naming: yet each step taken
Along its deserted streets, provokes
Familiar echoes.

For this is the fossil Troy, embedded
In all our minds: the child's first sketch
Of heaven, the old man's Holy City,
Clear as glass. The first and last
Possible settlement.

Backward, into Beasts Evolving

DICK ALLEN

Backward, into beasts evolving and headstrong,
like trochaic feet, our history flows—backward, backward.
The bioclocks pulsate and we seem evil-starred,
perhaps. Amoebas stretch out under microscopes and long
to break. Life pulls and darkens with the moon.
A tuber growing in a blackout jar predicts
the coming weather and prepares itself. I shall resume
my studies of Astrology. I shall transfix
myself upon the Future. I shall trust that there
are star-shaped plans, points flickering to Earth;
that we must be the struckdown of a brother race;
that in our isolation we must praise and care
and love, preserve historic consciousness. Henceforth
I shall remove the deathmask from Our Father's face.

Science Fiction Story

DUANE ACKERSON

The day the people left,
carrying boxes marked Fragile to other stars,
spaceships burning the sky and snowing
on the earth,
the animals began to grow.

At first, a little, a testing
of bone and muscle,
the first full thrust of bodies in eons.
They began to explore

their own scope:
The hawk gathered the sky under wing,
the rabbit beneath was a flurry in the snow,
his family making a blizzard of the land.
The whale took dominion of the sea,
shepherding fish in its mouth.

Coming to the city, the animals
were giants,
Macy's Day Balloons choking the sky,
breaking buildings like stalks
of coloured glass.

Below their feet, in the desert,
the power stations that sent up the rockets
crackled, and a Pandora's box
of yellow grasshoppers
snapped into the sky.

DNA

DUANE ACKERSON

The stones are learning.
You put one down in an empty place,
and soon you have a field of stones.

The stones are learning.
Leave a pile in an empty field,
and soon you have
an arch,
an obelisk,
a cathedral,
but never a tomb.

Meanwhile, domesticated animals
are collapsing into amoebae—
    farms look like jello factories.
The President and Miss Hollywood Bed
wake up the same morning
to discover they're The Blob.

What rude beast,
its limbs like a Stonehenge in motion,
is slouching toward us
to begin our sleep?

Eyes of a Woman—From a Portrait by Picasso

LISA CONESA

I miscalculated looking into her eyes.
They were of alien dimensions. Three open pupils
on the firmament of one face. As
if I were counting stars somewhere in contiguous skies
double images through reflecting smooth rivers
in a mirror where, as well as nimble fish
and golden sands, billowed the hair of the drowned.
                    With soundless motion?
Yes. And the sand was right at the bottom of
the galloping river. Over it the Seine
flows, combed by a flat little bark. A small
steamer and a swift yacht
with white wings of a dove instead of sails.
                    It was here
where the eyes really were. Triple brilliant
written on a face which I no longer remember.
Yet there was a face. Cut with lines
stiff but very human, plucked out of time
which was yet to come. Hence the excess of pupils

fixed biting like eyes of a snake
reflecting themselves.
                          —I don't know, I don't remember!
But I see those eyes, see them today, here
in the window of my house. Coming through the glass
through hair which time
unglues from my skull
through the body crevices
through the pith of spine.
Eyes of a woman from a portrait by Picasso—
my eyes.

Songs of War

KIT REED

*No one can accuse Kit Reed of being antifemlib—or
antifeminine. As wife, mother, and author she has
quietly succeeded in doing what many others are just
talking about. Now, with sweet piercing wit, she has
used the medium of science fiction to write the definitive
story of the feminine liberation movement. Or has she?*

FOR some weeks now a fire had burned day and night on a
hillside just beyond the town limits; standing at her kitchen sink,
Sally Hall could see the smoke rising over the trees. It curled
upward in promise, but she could not be sure what it promised,
and despite the fact that she was contented with her work and her
family, Sally found herself stirred by the bright autumn air, the
smoke emblem.

Nobody seemed to want to talk much about the fire, or what it
meant. Her husband, Zack, passed it off with a shrug, saying it was
probably just another commune. June Goodall, her neighbor, said
it was coming from Ellen Ferguson's place; she owned the land
and it was her business what she did with it. Sally said what if she
had been taken prisoner. Vic Goodall said not to be ridiculous; if
Ellen Ferguson wanted those people off her place, all she had to
do was call the police and get them off, and in the meantime, it
was nobody's business.

Still there was something commanding about the presence of the fire; the smoke rose steadily and could be seen for miles, and Sally, working at her drawing board, and a number of other women, going about their daily business, found themselves yearning after the smoke column with complex feelings. Some may have been recalling a primal past in which men conked large animals and dragged them into camp, and the only housework involved was a little gutting before they roasted the bloody chunks over the fire. The grease used to sink into the dirt, and afterward the diners, smeared with blood and fat, would roll around in a happy tangle. Other women were stirred by all the adventure tales they had stored up from childhood; people would run away without even bothering to pack or leave a note; they always found food one way or another, and they met new friends in the woods. Together they would tell stories over a campfire, and when they had eaten they would walk away from the bones to some high excitement that had nothing to do with the business of living from day to day. A few women, thinking of Castro and his happy guerrilla band, in the carefree, glamorous days before he came to power, were closer to the truth. Thinking wistfully of campfire camaraderie, of everybody marching together in a common cause, they were already dreaming of revolution.

* * *

Despite the haircut and the cheap suit supplied by the Acme Vacuum Cleaner Company, Andy Ellis was an underachiever college dropout who couldn't care less about vacuum cleaners. Until this week he had been a beautiful, carefree kid, and now, with a dying mother to support, with the wraiths of unpaid bills and unsold Marvelvacs trailing behind him like Marley's chains, he was still beautiful, which is why the women opened their doors to him.

He was supposed to say, "Good morning, I'm from the Acme Vacuum Cleaner Company and I'm here to clean your living room, no obligation, absolutely free of charge." Then, with the room clean and the Marvelsweep with twenty attachments and ten optional features spread all over the rug, he was supposed to make his pitch.

The first woman he called on said he did good work but her husband would have to decide, so Andy sighed and began collecting the Flutesnoot, the Miracle Whoosher, and all the other attachments and putting them back into the patented Bomb Bay Door.

"Well, thanks anyway . . ."

"Oh, thank *you*," she said. He was astounded to discover that she was unbuttoning him here and there.

"Does this mean you want the vacuum after all?"

She covered him with hungry kisses. "Shut up and deal."

At the next house, he began again. "Good morning, I'm from the Acme Vacuum Cleaner Company . . ."

"Never mind that. Come in."

At the third house, he and the lady of the house grappled in the midst of her unfinished novel, rolling here and there between the unfinished tapestry and the unfinished wire sculpture.

"If he would let me alone for a minute I would get some of these things done," she said. "All he ever thinks about is sex."

"If you don't like it, why are we doing this?"

"To get even," she said.

On his second day as a vacuum cleaner salesman, Andy changed his approach. Instead of going into his pitch, he would say, "Want to screw?" By the third day he had refined it to, "My place or yours?"

Friday his mother died, so he was able to turn in his Marvelvac, which he thought was just as well, because he was exhausted and depressed, and, for all his efforts, he had made only one tentative sale, which was contingent upon his picking up the payments in person every week for the next twelve years. Standing over his mother's coffin, he could not for the life of him understand what had happened to women—not good old Mom, who had more or less liked her family and at any rate had died uncomplaining—but the others, all the women in every condition in all the houses he had gone to this week. Why weren't any of them happy?

*   *   *

Up in the hills, sitting around the fire, the women in the vanguard were talking about just that: the vagaries of life, and woman's condition. They had to think it was only that. If they were going to go on, they would have to be able to decide the problem was X, whatever X was. It had to be something they could name, so that, together, they could do something about it.

They were of a mind to free themselves. One of the things was to free themselves of the necessity of being thought of as sexual objects, which turned out to mean only that certain obvious concessions, like lipstick and pretty clothes, had by ukase been done away with. Still, there were those who wore their khakis and bandoliers with a difference. Whether or not they shaved their legs and armpits, whether or not they smelled, the pretty ones were still pretty and the others were not; the ones with good bodies walked in an unconscious pride, and the others tried to ignore the differences and settled into their flesh, saying: Now, we are all equal.

There were great disputes as to what they were going to do, and which things they would do first. It was fairly well agreed that although the law said that they were equal, nothing much was changed. There was still the monthly bleeding; Dr. Ora Fessenden, the noted gynecologist, had shown them a trick which was supposed to take care of all that, but nothing short of surgery or menopause would halt the process altogether; what man had to undergo such indignities? There was still pregnancy, but the women all agreed they were on top of that problem. That left the rest: men still looked down on them, in part because in the main, women were shorter; they were more or less free to pursue their careers, assuming they could keep a baby sitter, but there were still midafternoon depressions, dishes, the wash; despite all the changes, life was much the same. More drastic action was needed.

They decided to form an army.

At the time, nobody was agreed on what they were going to do or how they would go about it, but they were all agreed that it was time for a change. Things could not go on as they were; life was often boring, and too hard.

* * *

She wrote a note:

Dear Ralph,

I am running away to realize my full potential. I know you have always said I could do anything I want, but what you meant was, I could do anything as long as it didn't mess you up, which is not exactly the same thing now, is it? Don't bother to look for me.

No longer yours,
Lory

Then she went to join the women in the hills.

* * *

I would like to go, Suellen thought, *but what if they wouldn't let me have my baby?*

* * *

Jolene's uncle in the country had always had a liver-colored setter named Fido. The name remained the same, and the dogs were more or less interchangeable. Jolene called all her lovers Mike, and because they were more or less interchangeable, eventually she tired of them and went to join the women in the hills.

* * *

"You're not going," Herb Chandler said.

Annie said, "I am."

He grabbed her as she reached the door. "The hell you are. I need you."

"You don't need me—you need a maid." She slapped the side of his head. "Now let me go."

"You're mine," he said, aiming a karate chop at her neck. She wriggled and he missed.

"Just like your ox and your ass, huh." She had gotten hold of a lamp, and she let him have it on top of the head.

"Ow," he said, and crumpled to the floor.

"Nobody owns me," she said, throwing the vase of flowers she kept on the side table, just for good measure. "I'll be back when it's over." Stepping over him, she went out the door.

*   *   *

After everybody left that morning, June mooned around the living room, picking up the scattered newspapers, collecting her and Vic's empty coffee cups and marching out to face the kitchen table, which looked the same way every morning at this time, glossy with spilled milk and clotted cereal, which meant that she had to go through the same motions every morning at this time, feeling more and more like that jerk, whatever his name was, who for eternity kept on pushing the same recalcitrant stone up the hill; he was never going to get it to the top because it kept falling back on him, and she was never going to get to the top, wherever that was, because there would always be the kitchen table, and the wash, and the crumbs on the rug, and besides she didn't know where the top was because she had gotten married right after Sweetbriar and the next minute, bang, there was the kitchen table, and, give or take a few babies, give or take a few stabs at night classes in something or other, that seemed to be her life. There it was in the morning, there it was again at noon, there it was at night; when people said, at parties, "What do you do?" she could only move her hands helplessly because there was no answer she could give that would please either herself or them. *I clean the kitchen table*, she thought, because there was no other way to describe it. Occasionally she thought about running away, but where would she go, and how would she live? Besides, she would miss Vic and the kids and her favorite chair in the television room. Sometimes she thought she might grab the milkman or the next delivery boy, but she knew she would be too embarrassed; either that or she would start laughing, or the delivery boy would, and even if they didn't, she would never be able to face Vic. She thought she had begun to disappear, like the television or the washing machine; after a while nobody would see her at all. They might complain if she wasn't working properly, but in the main she was just another household appliance, and so she mooned, wondering if this was all there was ever going to be: herself in the house, the kitchen table.

Then the notice came.

JOIN NOW

It was in the morning mail, hastily mimeographed and addressed to her by name. If she had been in a different mood she might have tossed it out with the rest of the junk mail, or called a few of her friends to see if they had gotten it too. As it was, she read it through, chewing over certain catchy phrases in this call to arms, surprised to find her blood quickening. Then she packed and wrote her note:

> Dear Vic,
> There are clean sheets on all the beds and three casseroles in the freezer and one in the oven. The veal one should do for two meals. I have done all the wash and a thorough vacuuming. If Sandy's cough doesn't get any better you should take her in to see Dr. Weixelbaum, and don't forget Jimmy is supposed to have his braces tightened on the 12th. Don't look for me.
> Love,
> June

Then she went to join the women in the hills.

*   *   *

Glenda Thompson taught psychology at the university; it was the semester break, and she thought she might go to the women's encampment in an open spirit of inquiry. If she liked what they were doing, she might chuck Richard, who was only an instructor while she was an assistant professor, and join them. To keep the appearance of objectivity, she would take notes.

Of course she was going to have to figure out what to do with the children while she was gone. No matter how many hours she and Richard taught, the children were her responsibility, and if they were both working in the house, she had to leave her

typewriter and shush the children because of the way R
when he was disturbed. None of the sitters she called cou
Mrs. Birdsall, their regular sitter, had taken off without
again, to see her son the freshman in Miami, and she exha
the list of student sitters without any luck. She thought briefl of
leaving them at Richard's office, but she couldn't trust him to
remember them at the end of the day. She reflected bitterly that
men who wanted to work just got up and went to the office. It had
never seemed fair.

"Oh hell," she said finally, and because it was easier, she packed
Tommy and Bobby and took them along.

✳   ✳   ✳

Marva and Patsy and Betts were sitting around in Marva's
room; it was two days before the junior prom and not one of them
had a date, or even a nibble; there weren't even any blind dates to
be had.

"I know what let's do," Marva said, "let's go up to Ferguson's
and join the women's army."

Betts said, "I didn't know they had an *army*."

"Nobody knows what they have up there," Patsy said.

They left a note so Marva's mother would be sure and call them
in case somebody asked for a date at the last minute and they got
invited to the prom after all.

✳   ✳   ✳

Sally felt a twinge of guilt when she opened the flier:

JOIN NOW

After she read it she went to the window and looked at the
smoke column in open disappointment: *Oh, so that's all it is.*
Yearning after it in the early autumn twilight, she had thought it
might represent something more: excitement, escape; but she
supposed she should have guessed. There was no great getaway,
just a bunch of people who needed more people to help. She knew
she probably ought to go up and help out for a while: she could

design posters and ads they could never afford if they went to a regular graphics studio. Still, all those women . . . She couldn't bring herself to make the first move.

"I'm not a joiner," she said aloud, but that wasn't really it. She had always worked at home; her studio took up one wing of the house and she made her own hours; when she tired of working she could pick at the breakfast dishes or take a nap on the lumpy couch at one end of the studio; when the kids came home she was always there; and besides, she didn't like going places without Zack.

Instead she used the flier to test her colors, dabbing blues here, greens there, until she had more or less forgotten the message and all the mimeographing was obscured by color.

*   *   *

At the camp, Dr. Ora Fessenden was leading an indoctrination program for new recruits. She herself was in the stirrups, lecturing coolly while everybody filed by.

One little girl, lifted up by her mother, began to whisper: "Ashphasphazzzzz-pzz."

The mother muttered, "Mumumumummmmmmmm . . ."

Ellen Ferguson, who was holding the light, turned it on the child for a moment. "Well, what does *she* want?"

"She wants to know what a man's looks like."

Dr. Ora Fessenden took hold, barking from the stirrups. "With luck, she'll never have to see."

"Right on," the butch sisters chorused, but the others began to look at one another in growing discomfiture, which as the weeks passed would ripen into alarm.

By the time she reached the camp, June was already worried about the casseroles she had left for Vic and the kids. Would the one she had left in the oven go bad at room temperature? Maybe she ought to call Vic and tell him to let it bubble for an extra half-hour just in case. Would Vic really keep an eye on Sandy, and if she got worse, would he get her to the doctor in time? What about Jimmy's braces? She almost turned back.

But she was already at the gate to Ellen Ferguson's farm, and she was surprised to see a hastily constructed guardhouse, with Ellen herself in khakis, standing with a carbine at the ready, and she said, "Don't shoot, Ellen, it's me."

"For God's sake, June, I'm not going to shoot you." Ellen pushed her glasses up on her forehead so she could look into June's face. "I never thought you'd have the guts."

"I guess I needed a change."

"Isn't it thrilling?"

"I feel funny without the children." June was trying to remember when she had last seen Ellen: over a bridge table? at Weight Watchers? "How did you get into this?"

"I needed something to live for," Ellen said.

By that time two other women with rifles had impounded her car, and then she was in a jeep bouncing up the dirt road to headquarters. The women behind the table all had on khakis, but they looked not at all alike in them. One was tall and tawny and called herself Sheena; there was a tough, funny-looking one named Rap, and the third was Margy, still redolent of the kitchen sink. Sheena made the welcoming speech, and then Rap took her particulars while Margy wrote everything down.

She lied a little about her weight, and was already on the defensive when Rap looked at her over her glasses, saying, "Occupation?"

"Uh, household manager."

"Oh shit, another housewife. Skills?"

"Well, I used to paint a little, and . . ."

Rap snorted.

"I'm pretty good at conversational French."

"Kitchen detail," Rap said to Margy, and Margy checked off a box and flipped over to the next sheet.

"But I'm tired of all that," June said.

Rap said, "Next."

*   *   *

Oh, it was good sitting around the campfire, swapping stories about the men at work and the men at home; every woman had a horror story, because even the men who claimed to be behind them weren't really behind them, they were paying lip service to avoid a higher price, and even the best among them would make those terrible verbal slips. It was good to talk to other women who were smarter than their husbands and having to pretend they weren't. It was good to be able to sprawl in front of the fire without having to think about Richard and what time he would be home. The kids were safely stashed down at the day-care compound, along with everybody else's kids, and for the first time in at least eight years Glenda could relax and think about herself. She listened drowsily to that night's speeches, three examples of wildly diverging cant, and she would have taken notes except that she was full, digesting a dinner she hadn't had to cook, and for almost the first time in eight years she wasn't going to have to go out to the kitchen and face the dishes.

*　　*　　*

Marva, Patsy and Betts took turns admiring each other in their new uniforms, and they sat at the edge of the group, hugging their knees and listening in growing excitement. Why, they didn't *have* to worry about what they looked like; that wasn't going to matter in the new scheme of things. It didn't *matter* whether or not they had dates. By the time the new order was established, they weren't even going to *want* dates. Although they would rather die than admit it, they all felt a little pang at this. Goodbye hope chest, goodbye wedding trip to Nassau and picture in the papers in the long white veil. Patsy, who wanted to be a corporation lawyer, thought: Why can't I have it *all?*

*　　*　　*

Now that his mother was dead and he didn't need to sell vacuum cleaners any more, Andy Ellis was thrown back on his own resources. He spent three hours in the shower and three days sleeping, and on the fourth day he emerged to find out his girl had left him for the koto player from across the hall. "Well, shit," he said, and wandered into the street.

He had only been asleep for three days, but everything was subtly different. The people in the corner market were mostly men, stocking up on TV dinners and chunky soups or else buying cooking wines and herbs, kidneys, beef liver and tripe. The usual girl was gone from the checkout counter, the butcher was running the register instead, and when Andy asked about it, Freddy the manager said, "She joined up."

"Are you kidding?"

"Some girl scout camp up at Ferguson's. The tails revolt."

Just then a jeep sped by in the street outside; there was a crash and they both hit the floor, rising to their elbows after the object that had shattered the front window did not explode. It was a rock with a note attached. Andy picked his way through the glass to retrieve it. It read:

WE WILL BURY YOU

"See?" Freddy said, ugly and vindictive. "See? See?"

*   *   *

The local hospital admitted several cases of temporary blindness in men who had been attacked by night with women's deodorant spray.

*   *   *

All over town the men whose wives remained lay next to them in growing unease. Although they all feigned sleep, they were aware that the stillness was too profound: the women were thinking.

*   *   *

The women trashed a porn movie house. Among them was the wife of the manager, who said, as she threw an open can of film over the balcony, watching it unroll, "I'm doing this for us."

*   *   *

So it had begun. For the time being, Rap and her cadre, who were in charge of the military operation, intended to satisfy themselves with guerrilla tactics; so far, nobody had been able to

link the sniping and matériel bombing with the women on the
hill, but they all knew it was only a matter of time before the first
police cruiser came up to Ellen Ferguson's gate with a search
warrant, and they were going to have to wage open war.

By this time one of the back pastures had been converted to a
rifle range, and even poor June had to spend at least one hour of
every day in practice. She began to take an embarrassing pleasure
in it, thinking, as she potted away:

*Aha, Vic, there's a nick in your scalp. Maybe you'll remember
what I look like next time you leave the house for the day.*

Okay, kids, I am not the maid.

*All right, Sally, you and your damn career. You're still only the
maid.*

Then, surprisingly: *This is for you, Sheena. How dare you go
around looking like that, when I have to look like this.*

This is for every rapist on the block.

By the time she fired her last shot her vision was blurred by
tears. *June, you are stupid, stupid; you always have been, and you
know perfectly well nothing is going to make any difference.*

Two places away, Glenda saw Richard's outline in the target.
She made a bull's-eye. *All right, damn you, pick up that toilet
brush.*

Going back to camp in the truck they all sang "Up Women"
and "The Internacionale," and June began to feel a little better.
It reminded her of the good old days at camp in middle
childhood, when girls and boys played together as if there weren't
any difference. She longed for that old androgynous body, the
time before sexual responsibility. Sitting next to her on the bench,
Glenda sang along, but her mind was at the university; she didn't
know what she was going to do if she got the Guggenheim because
Richard had applied without success for so long that he had given
up trying. What should she do, lie about it? It would be in all the
papers. She wondered how convincing she would be, saying, Shit,
honey, it doesn't mean anything. She would have to give up the
revolution and get back to her work; her book was only
half-written; she would have to go back to juggling kids and house
and work; it was going to be hard, hard. She decided finally that

she would let the Guggenheim Foundation make the decision for her. She would wait until late February and then write and tell Richard where to forward her mail.

Leading the song, Rap looked at her group. Even the softest ones had calluses now, but it was going to be some time before she made real fighters out of them. She wondered why women had all buried the instinct to kill. It was those damn babies, she decided: grunt, strain, pain, *Baby*. Hand a mother a gun and tell her to kill and she will say, *After I went to all that trouble?* Well, if you are going to make sacrifices, you are going to have to make sacrifices, she thought, and led them in a chorus of the battle anthem, watching to see just who did and who didn't throw herself into the last chorus, which ended: kill, kill, *kill*.

*   *   *

Sally was watching the smoke again. Zack said, "I wish you would come away from that window."

She kept looking for longer than he would have liked her to, and when she turned, she said, "Zack, why did you marry me?"

"Couldn't live without you."

"No, really."

"Because I wanted to love you and decorate you and take care of you for the rest of your life."

"Why me?"

"I thought we could be friends for a long time."

"I guess I didn't mean why did you marry *me*, I meant, why did you *marry* me?"

He looked into his palms. "I wanted you to take care of me too."

"Is that all?"

He could see she was serious, and because she was not going to let go, he thought for a minute and said at last, "Nobody wants to die alone."

*   *   *

Down the street, June Goodall's husband, Vic, had called every hospital in the county without results. The police had no reports of middle-aged housewives losing their memory in Sears or getting raped, robbed or poleaxed anywhere within the city limits. The police sergeant said, "Mr. Goodall, we've got more serious things on our minds. These bombings, for one thing, and the leaflets and the rip-offs. Do you know that women have been walking out of supermarkets with full shopping carts without paying a cent?" There seemed to be a thousand cases like June's, and if the department ever got a minute for them it would have to be first come first served.

So Vic languished in his darkening house. He had managed to get the kids off to school by himself the past couple of days. He gave them money for hot lunches, but they were running out of clean clothes and he could not bring himself to sort through those disgusting smelly things in the clothes hamper to run a load of wash. They had run through June's casseroles and they were going to have to start eating out; they would probably go to the Big Beef Plaza tonight, and have pizza tomorrow and chicken the next night and Chinese the next, and if June wasn't back by that time he didn't know what he was going to do because he was at his wits' end. The dishes were piling up in the kitchen and he couldn't understand why everything looked so grimy; he couldn't quite figure out why, but the toilet had begun to smell. One of these days he was going to have to try to get his mother over to clean things up a little. It was annoying, not having any clean underwear. He wished June would come back.

* * *

For the fifth straight day, Richard Thompson, Glenda's husband, opened *The French Chef* to a new recipe and prepared himself an exquisite dinner. Once it was finished he relaxed in the blissful silence. Now that Glenda was gone he was able to keep things the way he liked them; he didn't break his neck on Matchbox racers every time he went to put a little Vivaldi on the record player. It was refreshing not to have to meet Glenda's eyes, where, to his growing dissatisfaction, he perpetually measured himself. Without her demands, without the kids around to distract him, he would be able to finish his monograph on Lyly's

Euphues. He might even begin to write his book. Setting aside Glenda's half-finished manuscript with a certain satisfaction, he cleared a space for himself at the desk and tried to begin.

Castrated, he thought half an hour later. *Her and her damned career, she has castrated me.*

He went to the phone and began calling names on his secret list. For some reason most of them weren't home, but on the fifth call he came up with Jennifer, the biology major who wanted to write poetry, and within minutes the two of them were reaffirming his masculinity on the living-room rug, and if a few pages of Glenda's half-finished manuscript got mislaid in the tussle, who was there to protest? If she was going to be off there, farting around in the woods with all those women, she never would get it finished.

*   *   *

In the hills, the number of women had swelled, and it was apparent to Sheena, Ellen and Rap that it was time to stop hit-and-run terrorism and operate on a larger scale. They would mount a final recruiting campaign. Once that was completed, they would be ready to take their first objective. Sheena had decided the Sunnydell Shopping Center would be their base for a sweep of the entire country. They were fairly sure retaliation would be slow, and to impede it further, they had prepared an advertising campaign built on the slogan: YOU WOULDN'T SHOOT YOUR MOTHER, WOULD YOU? As soon as they could, they would co-opt some television equipment and make their first nationwide telecast from Sunnydell. Volunteers would flock in from fifty states, and in time the country would be theirs.

There was some difference of opinion as to what they were going to do with it. Rap was advocating a scorched-earth policy; the women would rise like phoenixes from the ashes and build a new nation from the rubble, more or less alone. Sheena raised the idea of an auxiliary made up of male sympathizers. The women would rule, but with men at hand. Margy secretly felt that both Rap and Sheena were too militant; she didn't want things to be completely different, only a little better. Ellen Ferguson wanted to annex all the land surrounding her place. She envisioned it as the capital city of the new world. The butch sisters wanted special legislation that would outlaw contact, social or sexual, with men, with, perhaps, special provisions for social meetings with their gay brethren. Certain of the straight sisters were made uncomfortable by their association with the butch sisters and wished there were some way the battle could progress without them. At least half of these women wanted their men back, once victory was assured, and the other half were looking into ways of perpetuating the race by means of parthenogenesis, or, at worst, sperm banks and AI techniques. One highly vocal splinter group wanted mandatory sterilization for everybody, and a portion of the lunatic fringe was demanding transsexual operations. Because nobody could agree, the women decided for the time being to skip over the issues and concentrate on the war effort itself.

By this time, word had spread and the volunteers were coming in, so it was easy to ignore issues because logistics were more pressing. It was still warm enough for the extras to bunk in the fields, but winter was coming on and the women were going to have to manage food, shelters, and uniforms for an unpredictable number. There had been a temporary windfall when Rap's bunch had hijacked a couple of semis filled with frozen dinners and surplus clothes, but Rap and Sheena and the others could sense the hounds of hunger and need not far away, and so they worked feverishly to prepare for the invasion. Unless they could take the town by the end of the month, they were lost.

*   *   *

"We won't have to hurt our *fathers*, will we?" Although she was now an expert marksman and had been placed in charge of a platoon, Patsy was still not at ease with the cause.

Rap avoided her eyes. "Don't be ridiculous."

"I just couldn't do that to anybody I *loved*," Patsy said. She reassembled her rifle, driving the bolt into place with a click.

"Don't you worry about it," Rap said. "All you have to worry about is looking good when you lead that recruiting detail."

"Okay." Patsy tossed her hair. She knew how she and her platoon looked, charging into the wind; she could feel the whole wild group around her, on the run with their heads high and their bright hair streaming. *I wish the boys at school could see,* she thought, and turned away hastily before Rap could guess what she was thinking.

* * *

I wonder if any woman academic can be happy. Glenda was on latrine detail, and this always made her reflective. *Maybe if they marry garage mechanics.* In the old days there had been academic types: single, tweedy, sturdy in orthopedic shoes, but somewhere along the way these types had been supplanted by married women of every conceivable type, who pressed forward in wildly varied disciplines, having in common only the singular harried look which marked them all. The rubric was more or less set: if you were good, you always had to worry about whether you were shortchanging your family; if you weren't as good as he was, you would always have to wonder whether it was because of all the other duties: babies, meals, the house; if despite everything you turned out to be better than he was, then you had to decide whether to try to minimize it, or prepare yourself for the wise looks on the one side, on the other, his look of uncomprehending reproach. If you *were* better than he was, then why should you be wasting your time with *him?* She felt light-years removed from the time when girls used to be advised to let *him* win the tennis match; everybody played to win now, but she had the uncomfortable feeling that there might never be any real victories. Whether or not you won, there were too many impediments: if he had a job and you didn't, then tough; if you both had jobs but he didn't get tenure, then you had to quit and move with him to a new place. She poured Lysol into the last toilet and turned her back on it, thinking: *Maybe that's why those Hollywood marriages are always breaking up.*

* * *

Sally finished putting the children to bed and came back into the living room, where Zack was waiting for her on the couch. By this time she had heard the women's broadcasts, she was well

aware of what was going on at Ellen Ferguson's place and knew as
well that this was where June was, and June was so inept, so soft
and incapable that she really ought to be up there helping June,
helping *them;* it was a job that ought to be done, on what scale
she could not be sure, but the fire was warm and Zack was waiting;
he and the children, her career, were all more important than that
abstraction in the hills; she had negotiated her own peace—let
them take care of theirs. Settling in next to Zack, she thought: *I
don't love my little pink dishmop, I don't, but everybody has to
shovel* some *shit.* Then: *God help the sailors and poor fishermen
who have to be abroad on a night like this.*

✻   ✻   ✻

June had requisitioned a jeep and was on her way into town to
knock over the corner market, because food was already in short
supply. She had on the housedress she had worn when she
enlisted, and she would carry somebody's old pink coat over her
arm to hide the pistol and the grenade she would use to hold her
hostages at bay while the grocery boys filled up the jeep. She had
meant to go directly to her own corner market, thinking, among
other things, that the manager might recognize her and tell Vic,
after which, of course, he would track her back to the camp and
force her to come home to him and the children. Somehow or
other she went right by the market and ended up at the corner of
her street.

She knew she was making a mistake, but she parked and began
to prowl the neighborhood. The curtains in Sally's window were
drawn, but the light behind them gave out a rosy glow, which
called up in her longings that she could not have identified; they
had very little to do with her own home, or her life with Vic; they
dated, rather, from her childhood, when she had imagined
marriage, had prepared herself for it with an amorphous but
unshakable idea of what it would be like.

Vic had forgotten to put out the garbage; overflowing cans
crowded the back porch, and one of them was overturned.
Walking on self-conscious cat feet, June made her way up on the
porch and peered into the kitchen: just as she had suspected, a

mess. A portion of her was tempted to go in and do a swift, secret cleaning—*The phantom housewife strikes*—but the risk of being discovered was too great. Well, let him clean up his own damn messes from now on. She tiptoed back down the steps and went around the house, crunching through bushes to look into the living room. She had hoped to get a glimpse of the children, but they were already in bed. She thought about waking Juney with pebbles on her window, whispering: Don't worry, mother's all right. But she wasn't strong enough; if she saw the children she would never be able to walk away and return to camp. She assuaged herself by thinking she would come back for Juney and Victor Junior just as soon as victory was assured. The living room had an abandoned look, with dust visible and papers strewn, a chair overturned and Vic himself asleep on the couch, just another neglected object in this neglected house. Surprised at how little she felt, she shrugged and turned away. On her way back to the jeep she did stop to right the garbage can.

The holdup went off all right; she could hear distant sirens building behind her, but so far as she knew, she wasn't followed.

The worst thing turned out to be finding Rap, Sheena, and Ellen Ferguson gathered around the stove in the main cabin; they didn't hear her come in.

". . . so damn fat and soft," Rap was saying.

Sheena said, "You have to take your soldiers where you can find them."

Ellen said, "An army travels on its stomach."

"As soon as it's over we dump the housewives," Rap said. "Every single one."

June cleared her throat. "I've brought the food."

*　　*　　*

"Politics may make strange bedfellows," Glenda said, "but this is ridiculous."

"Have it your way," she said huffily—whoever she was—and left the way she had come in.

*　　*　　*

Patsy was in charge of the recruiting platoon, which visited the high school, and she thought the principal was really impressed when he saw that it was she. Her girls bound and gagged the faculty and held the boys at bay with M-1s, while she made her pitch. She was successful but drained when she finished, pale and exhausted, and while her girls were processing the recruits (all but one percent of the girl students, as it turned out) and waiting for the bus to take them all to camp, Patsy put Marva in charge and simply drifted away, surprised to find herself in front of the sweetie shop two blocks from school. The place was empty except for Andy Ellis, who had just begun work as a counter boy.

He brought her a double-dip milkshake and lingered.

She tried to wave him away with her rifle. "We don't have to pay."

"That isn't it." He yearned, drawn to her.

She couldn't help seeing how beautiful he was. "Bug off."

Andy said, "Beautiful."

She lifted her head, aglow. "Really?"

"No kidding. Give me a minute, I'm going to fall in love with you."

"You can't," she said, remembering her part in the eleventh-grade production of *Romeo and Juliet*. "I'm some kind of Montague."

"Okay, then, I'll be the Capulet."

"I . . ." Patsy leaned forward over the counter so they could kiss. She drew back at the sound of a distant shot. "I have to go."

"When can I see you?"

Patsy said, "I'll sneak out tonight."

Sheena was in charge of the recruiting detail that visited Sally's neighborhood. Although she had been an obscure first-year medical student when the upheaval started, she was emerging as the heroine of the revolution. The newspapers and television newscasters all knew who she was, and so Sally knew, and was undeniably flattered that she had come in person.

She and Sally met on a high level: if there was an aristocracy of achievement, then they spoke aristocrat to aristocrat. Sheena spoke of talent and obligation; she spoke of need and duty; she spoke of service. She said the women needed Sally's help, and when Sally said, Let them help themselves, she said: They can't. They were still arguing when the kids came home from school; they were still arguing when Zack came home. Sheena spoke of the common cause and a better world; she spoke once more of the relationship between gifts and service. Sally turned to Zack, murmuring, and he said: "If you think you have to do it, then I guess you'd better do it."

She said: "The sooner I go the sooner this thing will be over."

Zack said, "I hope you're right."

Sheena stood aside so they could make their goodbyes. Sally hugged the children, and when they begged to go with her she said, "It's no place for kids."

Climbing into the truck, she looked back at Zack and thought: *I could not love thee half so much loved I not honor more.* What she said was, "I must be out of my mind."

Zack stood in the street with his arms around the kids, saying, "She'll be back soon. Someday they'll come marching down our street."

In the truck, Sheena said, "Don't worry. When we occupy, we'll see that he gets a break."

They were going so fast now that there was no jumping off the truck; the other women at the camp seemed to be so grateful to see her that she knew there would be no jumping off the truck until it was over.

June whispered: "To be perfectly honest, I was beginning to have my doubts about the whole thing, but with *you* along . . ."

They made Sally a member of the council.

*   *   *

The next day the women took the Sunnydell Shopping Center, which included two supermarkets, a discount house, a fast-food place, and a cinema; they selected it because it was close to camp and they could change guard details with a minimum of difficulty. The markets would solve the food problem for the time being, at least.

In battle, they used M-1s, one submachine gun and a variety of sidearms and grenades. They took the place without firing a shot.

The truth was that until this moment, the men had not taken the revolution seriously.

The men had thought: After all, it's only women.

They had thought: Let them have their fun. We can stop this thing whenever we like.

They had thought: What difference does it make? They'll come crawling back to us.

In this first foray, the men, who were, after all, unarmed, fled in surprise. Because the women had not been able to agree upon policy, they let their vanquished enemy go; for the time being, they would take no prisoners.

*   *   *

They were sitting around the victory fire that night, already aware that it was chilly and when the flames burned down a bit they were going to have to go back inside. It was then, for the first time, that Sheena raised the question of allies.

She said, "Sooner or later we have to face facts. We can't make it alone."

Sally brightened, thinking of Zack: "I think you're right."

Rap leaned forward. "Are you *serious?*"

Sheena tossed her hair. "What's the matter with sympathetic men?"

"The only sympathetic man is a dead man," Rap said.

Sally rose. "Wait a minute . . ."

Ellen Ferguson pulled her down. "Relax. All she means is, at this stage we can't afford any risks. Infiltration. Spies."

Sheena said, "We could use a few men."

Sally heard herself, sotto voce: "You're not kidding."

Dr. Ora Fessenden rose, in stages. She said, with force, "Look here, Sheena, if you are going to take a stance, you are going to have to take a stance."

If she had been there, Patsy would have risen to speak in favor of a men's auxiliary. As it was, she had sneaked out to meet Andy. They were down in the shadow of the conquered shopping center, falling in love.

*   *   *

In the command shack, much later, Sheena paced moodily. "They aren't going to be satisfied with the shopping center for long."

Sally said, "I think things are going to get out of hand."

"They can't." Sheena kept on pacing. "We have too much to do."

"Your friend Rap and the doctor are out for blood. Lord knows how many of the others are going to go along." Sally sat at the desk, doodling on the roll sheet. "Maybe you ought to dump them."

"We need muscle, Sally."

Margy, who seemed to be dusting, said, "I go along with Sally."

"No." Lory was in the corner, transcribing Sheena's remarks of the evening. "Sheena's absolutely right."

*   *   *

It was morning, and Ellen Ferguson paced the perimeter of the camp. "We're going to need fortifications here, and more over here."

Glenda, who followed with the clipboard, said, "What are you expecting?"

"I don't know, but I want to be ready for it."

"Shouldn't we be concentrating on *offense*?"

"Not me," Ellen said, with her feet set wide in the dirt. "This is my place. This is where I make my stand."

*   *   *

"Allies. That woman is a marshmallow. *Allies*." Rap was still seething. "I think we ought to go ahead and make our play."

"We still need them," Dr. Ora Fessenden said. The two of them were squatting in the woods above the camp. "When we get strong enough, then . . ." She drew her finger across her throat. "Zzzzt."

"Dammit to hell, Ora." Rap was on her feet, punching a tree trunk. "If you're going to fight, you're going to have to kill."

"You know it and I know it," Dr. Ora Fessenden said. "Now try and tell that to the rest of the girls."

As she settled into the routine, Sally missed Zack more and more, and, partly because she missed him so much, she began making a few inquiries. The consensus was that women had to free themselves from every kind of dependence, both emotional and physical; sexual demands would be treated on the level of other bodily functions: any old toilet would do.

*   *   *

"Hello, Ralph?"

"Yes?"

"It's me, Lory. Listen, did you read about what we did?"

"About what *who* did?"

"Stop trying to pretend you don't know. Listen, Ralph, that was us that took over out at Sunnydell. *Me.*"

"You and what army?"

"The women's army. Oh, I see, you're being sarcastic. Well listen, Ralph, I said I was going to realize myself as a person and I have. I'm a sublieutenant now. A sublieutenant, imagine."

"What about your novel you were going to write about your rotten marriage?"

"Don't pick nits. I'm Sheena's secretary now. You were holding me back, Ralph; all those years you were dragging me down. Well, now I'm a free agent. Free."

"Terrific."

"Look, I have to go; we have uniform inspection now and worst luck, I drew KP."

*   *   *

"Listen," Rap was saying to a group of intent women, "you're going along minding your own business and *wham*, he swoops down like the wolf upon the fold. It's the ultimate weapon."

Dr. Ora Fessenden said bitterly, "And you just try and rape him back."

Margy said, "I thought men were, you know, supposed to protect women from all that."

Annie Chandler, who had emerged as one of the militants, threw her knife into a tree. "Try and convince them it ever happened. The cops say you must have led him on."

Dr. Ora Fessenden drew a picture of the woman as ruined city, with gestures.

"I don't know what I would do if one of them tried to . . ." Betts said to Patsy. "What would you do?"

Oh Andy. Patsy said, "I don't know."

"There's only one thing *to* do," Rap said, with force. "Shoot on sight."

*   *   *

It was hard to say what their expectations had been after this first victory. There were probably almost as many expectations as there were women. A certain segment of the group was disappointed because Vic/Richard/Tom-Dick-Harry had not come crawling up the hill, crying, My God how I have misused you. Come home and everything will be different. Rap and the others would have wished for more carnage, and as the days passed the thirst for blood heaped dust in their mouths; Sheena was secretly disappointed that there had not been wider coverage of the battle in the press and on nationwide TV. The mood in the camp after that first victory was one of anticlimax, indefinable but growing discontent.

*   *   *

Petty fights broke out in the rank-and-file.

*   *   *

There arose, around this time, some differences between the rank-and-file women, some of whom had children, and the Mothers' Escadrille, an elite corps of women who saw themselves as professional mothers. As a group, they looked down on people like Glenda, who sent their children off to the day-care compound. The Mothers' Escadrille would admit, when pressed, that their goal in banding together was the eventual elimination of the role of the man in the family, for man, with his incessant demands, interfered with the primary function of the mother. Still, they had to admit that, since they had no other profession, they were going to have to be assured some kind of financial support in the ultimate scheme of things. They also wanted more respect from the other women, who seemed to look down on them because they lacked technical or professional skills, and so they conducted their allotted duties in a growing atmosphere of hostility.

It was after a heated discussion with one of the mothers that Glenda, suffering guilt pangs and feelings of inadequacy, went down to the day-care compound to see her own children. She picked them out at once, playing in the middle of a tangle of preschoolers, but she saw with a pang that Bobby was reluctant to leave the group to come and talk to her, and even after she said, "It's Mommy," it took Tommy a measurable number of seconds before he recognized her.

The price, she thought in some bitterness. *I hope in the end it turns out to be worth the price.*

*   *   *

Betts had tried running across the field both with and without her bra, and except for the time when she wrapped herself in the Ace bandage, she definitely bounced. At the moment nobody in the camp was agreed as to whether it was a good or a bad thing to bounce; it was either another one of those things the world at large was going to have to, by God, learn to ignore, or else it was a sign of weakness. Either way, it was uncomfortable, but so was the Ace bandage uncomfortable.

*   *   *

Sally was drawn toward home, but at the same time, looking around at the disparate women and their growing discontentment, she knew she ought to stay on until the revolution had put itself in order. The women were unable to agree what the next step would be, or to consolidate their gains, and so she met late into the night with Sheena, and walked around among the others. She had the feeling she could help, that whatever her own circumstance, the others were so patently miserable that she must help.

"Listen," said Zack, when Sally called him to explain, "it's no picnic being a guy, either."

* * *

The fear of rape had become epidemic. Perhaps because there had been no overt assault on the women's camp, no army battalions, not even any police cruisers, the women expected more subtle and more brutal retaliation. The older women were outraged because some of the younger women said what difference did it make? If you were going to make it, what did the circumstances matter? Still, the women talked about it around the campfire, and at last it was agreed that regardless of individual reactions, for ideological reasons it was important that it be made impossible; the propaganda value to the enemy would be too great, and so, at Rap's suggestion, each woman was instructed to carry her handweapon at all times and to shoot first and ask questions later.

* * *

Patsy and Andy Ellis were finding more and more ways to be together, but no matter how much they were together, it didn't seem to be enough. Since Andy's hair was long, they thought briefly of disguising him as a woman and getting him into camp, but a number of things—whiskers, figure, musculature—would give him away, and Patsy decided it would be too dangerous.

"Look, I'm in love with you," Andy said. "Why don't you run away?"

"Oh, I couldn't do that," Patsy said, trying to hide herself in his arms. "And besides . . ."

He hid his face in her hair. "Besides nothing."

"No, really. Besides. Everybody has guns now, everybody has different feelings, but they all hate deserters. We have a new policy."

"They'd never find us."

She looked into Andy's face. "Don't you want to hear about the new policy?"

"Okay, what?"

"About deserters." She spelled it out, more than a little surprised at how far she had come. "It's hunt down and shave and kill."

"They wouldn't really do that."

"We had the first one last night, this poor old lady, about forty. She got homesick for her family and tried to run away."

Andy was still amused. "They shaved all her hair off."

"That wasn't all," Patsy said. "When they got finished they really did it. Firing squad, the works."

*   *   *

Although June would not have been sensitive to it, there were diverging feelings in the camp about who did what, and what there was to do. All she knew was she was sick and tired of working in the day-care compound and when she went to Sheena and complained, Sheena, with exquisite sensitivity, put her in charge of the detail that guarded the shopping center. It was a temporary assignment, but it gave June a chance to put on a cartridge belt and all the other paraphernalia of victory, so she cut an impressive figure for Vic when he came along.

"It's me, honey, don't you know me?"

"Go away," she said with some satisfaction. "No civilians allowed."

"Oh for God's sake."

To their mutual astonishment, she raised her rifle. "Bug off, fella."

"You don't really think you can get away with this."

"Bug off or I'll shoot."

"We're just letting you do this, to get it out of your system." Vic moved as if to relieve her of the rifle. "If it makes you feel a little better . . ."

"This is your last warning."

"Listen," Vic said, a study in male outrage, "one step too far, and, *tschoom*, federal troops."

She fired a warning shot, so he left.

*   *   *

Glenda was a little sensitive about the fact that various husbands had found ways to smuggle in messages; some had even come looking for their wives, but not Richard. One poor bastard had been shot when he came in too close to the fire; they heard an outcry and a thrashing in the bushes, but when they looked for him the next morning there was no body, so he must have dragged himself away. There had been notes in food consignments, and one husband had hired a skywriter, but so far she had had neither word nor sign from Richard, and she wasn't altogether convinced she cared. He seemed to have drifted off into time past along with her job, her students, and her book. Once her greatest hope had been to read her first chapter at the national psychological conference; now she wondered whether there would even be any more conferences. If she and the others were successful, that would break down, along with a number of other things. Still, in the end she would have her definitive work on the women's revolution, but so far the day-to-day talks had been so engrossing that she hadn't had a minute to begin. Right now, there was too much to do.

*   *   *

They made their first nationwide telecast from a specially erected podium in front of the captured shopping center. For various complicated reasons the leaders made Sally speak first, and, as they had anticipated, she espoused the moderate view: this was a matter of service; women were going to have to give up a few things to help better the lot of their sisters. Once the job was done, everything would be improved, but not really different.

Sheena came next, throwing back her bright hair and issuing the call to arms. The mail she drew would include several spirited letters from male volunteers who were already in love with her and would follow her anywhere; because the women had pledged never to take allies, these letters would be destroyed before they ever reached her.

Dr. Ora Fessenden was all threats, fire, and brimstone. Rap took up where she left off.

"We're going to fight until there's not a man left standing . . ."

Annie Chandler yelled, "Right on."

Margy was trying to speak: ". . . just a few concessions . . ."

Rap's eyes glittered. "Only sisters, and you guys . . ."

Ellen Ferguson said, "Up, women, out of slavery."

Rap's voice rose. "You guys are going to burn."

Sally was saying, "Reason with you . . ."

Rap hissed: "Bury you."

It was hard to say which parts of these messages reached the viewing public, as the women all interrupted and overrode each other, and the cameramen concentrated on Sheena, who was to become the sign and symbol of the revolution. None of the women on the platform seemed to be listening to any of the others, which may have been just as well; the only reason they had been able to come this far together was because nobody ever did.

*   *   *

The letters began to come:

> "Dear Sheena, I would like to join, but I already have nine children and now I am pregnant again . . ."
>
> "Dear Sheena, I am a wife and mother but I will throw it all over in an instant if you will only glance my way . . ."
>
> "Dear Sheena, our group has occupied the town hall in Gillespie, Indiana, but we are running out of ammo and the water supply is low. Several of the women have been stricken with plague, and we are running out of food . . ."
>
> "First I made him lick my boots and then I killed him but now I have this terrible problem with the body, the kids don't want me to get rid of him . . ."
>
> "Who do you think you are running this war when you don't even know what you are doing, what you have to do is kill every

last damn one of them and the ones you don't kill you had better cut off their Things. . . ."

"Sheena, baby, if you will only give up this half-assed revolution you and I can make beautiful music together. I have signed this letter Maud to escape the censors but if you look underneath the stamp you can see who I really am."

*　　*　　*

The volunteers were arriving in dozens. The first thing was that there was not housing for all of them; there was no equipment, and so the women in charge had to cut off enlistments at a certain point and send the others back to make war in their own home towns.

The second thing was that, with the increase in numbers, there was an increasing bitterness about the chores. Nobody wanted to do them; in secret truth nobody ever had, but so far the volunteers had all borne it, up to a point, because they sincerely believed that in the new order there would be no chores. Now they understood that the more people there were banded together, the more chores there would be. Laundry and garbage were piling up. At some point around the time of the occupation of the shopping center, the women had begun to understand that no matter what they accomplished, there would always be ugly things to do: the chores; and now, because there seemed to be so *much* work, there were terrible disagreements as to who was supposed to do what, and as a consequence they had all more or less stopped doing any of it.

*　　*　　*

Meals around the camp were catch as catch can.

*　　*　　*

The time was approaching when nobody in the camp would have clean underwear.

*　　*　　*

The latrines were unspeakable.

*   *   *

The children were getting out of hand; some of them were forming packs and making raids of their own, so that the quartermaster never had any clear idea of what she would find in the storehouse. Most of the women in the detail who had been put in charge of the day-care compound were fed up.

*   *   *

By this time Sheena was a national figure; her picture was on the cover of both news magazines in the same week and there were nationally distributed lines of sweatshirts and tooth glasses bearing her picture and her name. She received love mail and hate mail in such quantity that Lory, who had joined the women to realize her potential as an individual, had to give up her other duties to concentrate on Sheena's mail. She would have to admit that it was better than KP, and besides, if Sheena went on to better things, maybe she would get to go along.

*   *   *

The air of dissatisfaction grew. Nobody agreed any more, not even all those who had agreed to agree for the sake of the cause. Fights broke out like flash fires; some women were given to sulks and inexplicable silences, others to blows and helpless tears quickly forgotten. On advice from Sally, Sheena called a council to try to bring everybody together, but it got off on the wrong foot.

Dr. Ora Fessenden said, "Are we going to sit around on our butts, or what?"

Sheena said, "National opinion is running in our favor. We have to consolidate our gains."

Rap said, "Gains hell. What kind of war is this? Where are the scalps?"

Sheena drew herself up. "We are not Amazons."

Rap said, "That's a crock of shit," and she and Dr. Ora Fessenden stamped out.

*   *   *

"Rape," Rap screamed, running from the far left to the far right and then making a complete circuit of the clearing. "Rape," she shouted, taking careful note of who came running and who didn't. "Raaaaaaaape."

Dr. Ora Fessenden rushed to her side, the figure of outraged womanhood. They both watched until a suitable number of women had assembled, and then she said, in stentorian tones, "We cannot let this go unavenged."

* * *

"My God," Sheena said, looking at the blackened object in Rap's hand. "What are you doing with that thing?"

Blood-smeared and grinning, Rap said, "When you're trying to make a point, you have to go ahead and make your point." She thrust her trophy into Sheena's face.

Sheena averted her eyes quickly; she thought it was an ear. "That's supposed to be a *rhetorical* point."

"Listen, baby, this world doesn't give marks for good conduct."

Sheena stiffened. "You keep your girls in line or you're finished."

Rap was smoldering; she pushed her face up to Sheena's, saying, "You can't do without us and you know it."

"If we have to, we'll learn."

"Aieee." One of Rap's cadre had taken the trophy from her and tied it on a string; now she ran through the camp, swinging it around her head, and dozens of throats opened to echo her shout. "Aiiiieeeee . . ."

* * *

Patsy and Andy were together in the bushes near the camp; proximity to danger made their pleasure more intense. Andy said: "Leave with me."

She said, "I can't. I told you what they do to deserters."

"They'll never catch us."

"You don't know these women," Patsy said. "Look, Andy, you'd better go."

"Just a minute more." Andy buried his face in her hair. "Just a little minute more."

*   *   *

"Rape," Rap shouted again, running through the clearing with her voice raised like a trumpet. "*Raaaaaaaape.*"

Although she knew it was a mistake, Sally had sneaked away to see Zack and the children. The camp seemed strangely deserted, and nobody was there to sign out the jeep she took. She had an uncanny intimation of trouble at a great distance, but she shook it off and drove to her house. She would have expected barricades and guards: state of war, but the streets were virtually empty and she reached her neighborhood without trouble.

Zack and the children embraced her and wanted to know when she was coming home.

"Soon, I think. They're all frightened of us now."

Zack said, "I'm not so sure."

"There doesn't seem to be any resistance."

"Oh," he said, "they've decided to let you have the town."

"What did I tell you?"

"Sop," he said. "You can have anything you want. Up to a point."

Sally was thinking of Rap and Dr. Ora Fessenden. "What if we take more?"

"Wipeout," Zack said. "You'll see."

"Oh Lord," she said, vaulting into the jeep. "Maybe it'll be over sooner than I thought."

She was already too late. She saw the flames shooting skyward as she came out the drive.

"It's Flowermont."

Because she had to make sure, she wrenched the jeep in that direction and rode to the garden apartments; smoke filled the streets for blocks around.

Looking at the devastation, Sally was reminded of Indian massacres in the movies of her childhood: the smoking ruins, the carnage, the moans of the single survivor who would bubble out his story in her arms. She could not be sure about the bodies: whether there were any, whether there were as many as she thought; but she was sure those were charred corpses in the rubble. Rap and Dr. Ora Fessenden had devised a flag and hoisted it from a tree: the symbol of the women's movement, altered to suit their mood—the crudely executed fist reduced to clenched bones and surrounded by flames. The single survivor died before he could bubble out his story in her arms.

*   *   *

In the camp, Rap and Dr. Ora Fessenden had a victory celebration around the fire. They had taken unspeakable trophies in their raid and could not understand why many of the women refused to wear them.

*   *   *

Patsy and Andy, in the bushes, watched with growing alarm. Even from their safe distance, Andy was fairly sure he saw what he thought he saw, and he whispered, "Look, we've got to get out of here."

"Not now," Patsy said, pulling him closer. "Tonight. The patrols."

*   *   *

By now the little girls had been brought up from the day-care compound and had joined the dance, their fat cheeks smeared with blood. Rap's women were in heated discussion with the Mothers' Escadrille about the disposition of the boy children: would they be destroyed or reared as slaves? While they were talking, one of the mothers who had never felt at home in any faction sneaked down to the compound and freed the lot of them. Now she was running around in helpless tears, flapping her arms and sobbing broken messages, but no matter what she said to the children, she couldn't seem to get any of them to flee.

Sheena and her lieutenant, Margy, and Lory, her secretary, came out of the command shack at the same moment Sally arrived in camp; she rushed to join them, and together they extracted Rap and Dr. Ora Fessenden from the dance for a meeting of the council.

When they entered the shack, Ellen Ferguson hung up the phone in clattering haste and turned to confront them with a confusing mixture of expressions; Sally thought the foremost one was probably guilt.

Sally waited until they were all silent and then said, "The place is surrounded. They let me through to bring the message. They have tanks."

Ellen Ferguson said, "They just delivered their ultimatum. Stop the raids and pull back to camp or they'll have bombers level this place."

"Pull back, hell," Rap said.

Dr. Ora Fessenden shook a bloody fist. "We'll show them."

"We'll fight to the death."

Ellen said, quietly, "I've already agreed."

*　　*　　*

Down at the main gate, Marva, who was on guard duty, leaned across the barbed wire to talk to the captain of the tank detail. She thought he was kind of cute.

"Don't anybody panic," Rap was saying. "We can handle this thing. We can fight them off."

"We can fight them in the hedgerows," Dr. Ora Fessenden said in rising tones. "We can fight them in the ditches, we can hit them with everything we've got . . ."

"Not from here you can't."

"We can burn and bomb and kill and . . . What did you say?"

"I said, not from here." Because they were all staring, Ellen Ferguson covered quickly, saying, "I mean, if I'm going to be of any value to the movement, I have to have this place in good condition."

Sheena said, quietly, "That's not what you mean."

Ellen was near tears. "All right, dammit, this place is all I have."

*　　*　　*

"My God," Annie Chandler shrieked. "Rape." She parted the bushes to reveal Patsy and Andy, who hugged each other in silence. "Rape," Annie screamed, and everybody who could hear above the din came running. "Kill the bastard, rape, rape, rape."

Patsy rose to her feet and drew Andy up with her, shouting to make herself heard. "I said, it isn't rape."

*   *   *

Rap and Dr. Ora Fessenden were advancing on Ellen Ferguson. "You're not going to compromise us. We'll kill you first."

"Oh," Ellen said, backing away, "that's another thing. They wanted the two of you. I had to promise we'd send you out."

The two women plunged, and then retreated, mute with fury. Ellen had produced a gun from her desk drawer, and now she had them covered.

"Son of a bitch," Rap said. "Son of a bitch."

*   *   *

"Kill them."
"Burn them."
"Hurt them."
"Make an example of them."
"I love you, Patsy."
"Oh, Andy, I love you."

*   *   *

Sally said softly, "So it's all over."

"Only parts of it," Ellen said. "It will never really be over as long as there are women left to fight. We'll be better off without these two and their cannibals; we can retrench and make a new start."

"I guess this is as good a time as any." Sheena got to her feet. "I might as well tell you, I'm splitting."

They turned to face her, Ellen being careful to keep the gun on Dr. Ora Fessenden and Rap.

"You're what?"

"I can do a hell of a lot more good on my new show. Prime time, nightly, nationwide TV."

Rap snarled. "The hell you say."

"Look, Rap, I'll interview you."

"Stuff it."

"Think what I can do for the movement; I can reach sixty million people; you'll see."

Ellen Ferguson said, with some satisfaction, "That's not really what you mean."

"Maybe it isn't. It's been you, you, you all this time." Sheena picked up her clipboard, her notebooks and papers; Lory and Margy both moved as if to follow her, but she rebuffed them with a single sweep of her arm. "Well, it's high time I started thinking about me."

                    *   *   *

Outside, the women had raised a stake, and now Patsy and Andy were lashed to it, standing back to back.

                    *   *   *

In the shack, Rap and Dr. Ora Fessenden had turned as one and advanced on Ellen Ferguson, pushing the gun aside.

The good doctor said, "I knew you wouldn't have the guts to shoot. You never had any guts."

Ellen cried out, "Sheena, help me."

But Sheena was already in the doorway, and she hesitated for only a moment, saying, "Listen, it's *sauve qui peut* in this day and time, sweetie, and the sooner you realize it the better."

Rap finished pushing Ellen down and took the gun. She stood over her victim for a minute, grinning. "In the battle of the sexes, there are no allies." Then she put a bullet through Ellen's favorite moosehead so Ellen would have something to remember her by.

                    *   *   *

The women had collected twigs and were just about to set fire to Patsy and Andy when Sheena came out, closely followed by Dr. Ora Fessenden and a warlike Rap.

Everybody started shouting at once, and in the imbroglio that followed, Patsy and Andy escaped. They would surface years later, in a small town in Minnesota, with an ecologically alarming number of children; they would both be able to pursue their chosen careers in the law because they worked hand in hand to take care of all the children and the house, and they would love each other until they died.

* * *

Ellen Ferguson sat with her elbows on her knees and her head drooping, saying, "I can't believe it's all over, after I worked so hard, I gave so much. . . ."

Sally said, "It isn't over. Remember what you said: as long as there are women, there will be a fight."

"But we've lost our leaders."

"You could . . ."

"No, I couldn't."

"Don't worry, there are plenty of others."

As Sally spoke, the door opened and Glenda stepped in to take Sheena's place.

* * *

When the melee in the clearing was over, Dr. Ora Fessenden and Rap had escaped with their followers. They knew the lay of the land and so they were able to elude the troop concentration which surrounded the camp, and began to lay plans to regroup and fight another day.

* * *

A number of women, disgusted by the orgy of violence, chose to pack their things and go. The Mothers' Escadrille deserted en masse, taking their children and a few children who didn't even belong to them.

* * *

Ellen said, "You're going to have to go down there and parley. I'm not used to talking to men."

And so Sally found herself going down to the gate to conduct negotiations.

She said, "The two you wanted got away. The rest of them—I mean us—are acting in good faith." She lifted her chin. "If you want to go ahead and bomb anyway, you'll have to go ahead and bomb."

The captain lifted her and set her on the hood of the jeep. He was grinning. "Shit, little lady, we just wanted to throw a scare into you."

"You don't understand." She wanted to get down off the hood, but he had propped his arms on either side of her. She knew she ought to be furious, but instead she kept thinking how much she missed Zack. Speaking with as much dignity as she could under the circumstances, she outlined the women's complaints; she already knew it was hopeless to list them as demands.

"Don't you worry about a thing, honey." He lifted her down and gave her a slap on the rump to speed her on her way. "Everything is going to be real different from now on."

"I bet."

Coming back up the hill to camp, she saw how sad everything looked, and she could not for the life of her decide whether it was because the women who had been gathered here had been inadequate to the cause or whether it was, rather, that the cause itself had been insufficiently identified; she suspected that they had come up against the human condition, failed to recognize it, and so tried to attack a single part, which seemed to involve attacking the only allies they would ever have. As for the specific campaign, as far as she could tell, it was possible to change some of the surface or superficial details, but once that was done, things were still going to be more or less the way they were, and all the best will in the world would not make any real difference.

*   *   *

In the clearing, Lory stood at Glenda's elbow. "Of course you're going to need a lieutenant."

Glenda said, "I guess so."

*   *   *

Ellen Ferguson was brooding over a row of birches that had been trashed during the struggle. If she could stake them back up in time, they might reroot.

June said, "Okay, I'm going to be mess sergeant."

Margy said, "The hell you will," and pushed her in the face.

*   *   *

Glenda said thoughtfully, "Maybe we could mount a Lysistrata campaign."

Lory snorted. "If their wives won't do it, there are plenty of girls who will."

*   *   *

Zack sent a message:

WE HAVE TO HELP EACH OTHER.

Sally sent back:

I KNOW.

*   *   *

Before she went home, Sally had to say goodbye to Ellen Ferguson.

Ellen's huge, homely face sagged. "Not you too."

Sally looked at the desultory groups policing the wreckage, at the separate councils convening in every corner. "I don't know why I came. I guess I thought we could really *do* something."

Ellen made a half-turn, taking in the command shack, the compound, the women who remained. "Isn't this enough?"

"I have to get on with my *life*."

Ellen said, "This is mine."

*   *   *

"Oh, Vic, I've been so stupid." June was sobbing in Vic's arms. She was also lying in her teeth, but she didn't care; she was sick of the revolution, and she was going to have to go through this formula before Vic would allow her to resume her place at his kitchen sink. The work was still boring and stupid, but at least there was less of it than there had been at camp; her bed was softer, and since it was coming on winter, she was grateful for the storm sashes, which Vic put up every November, and the warmth of the oil burner, which he took apart and cleaned with his own hands every fall.

*   *   *

Sally found her house in good order, thanks to Zack, but there was several weeks' work piled up in her studio, and she had lost a couple of commissions. She opened her drawer to discover, with a smile, that Zack had washed at least one load of underwear with something red.

"I think we do better together," Zack said.

Sally said, "We always have."

*   *   *

In the wake of fraternization with the military guard detail, Marva discovered she was pregnant. She knew what Dr. Ora Fessenden said she was supposed to do, but she didn't think she wanted to.

*   *   *

As weeks passed, the women continued to drift away. "It's nice here and all," Betts said apologetically, "but there's a certain *je ne sais quoi* missing; I don't know what it is, but I'm going back in there and see if I can find it."

Glenda said, "Yeah, well. So long as there is a yang, I guess there is going to have to be a yin."

"Don't you mean, so long as there is a yin, there is going to have to be a yang?"

Glenda looked in the general direction of town, knowing there was nothing there for her to go back to. "I don't know what I mean anymore."

*   *   *

Activity and numbers at the camp had decreased to the point where federal troops could be withdrawn. They were needed, as it turned out, to deal with wildcat raids in another part of the state. Those who had been on the scene came back with reports of incredible viciousness.

*   *   *

Standing at their windows in the town, the women could look up to the hills and see the campfire still burning, but as the months wore on, fewer and fewer of them looked, and the column of smoke diminished in size because the remaining women were running out of volunteers whose turn it was to feed the fire.

*   *   *

Now that it was over, things went on more or less as they had before.

Time Deer

CRAIG STRETE

*If Kit Reed speaks for an oppressed portion of the
American population, Craig Strete is the very clear voice
of another group far more terribly put upon. He is editor
of the world's first and only magazine of American
Indian SF, Red Planet Earth. Reading his journal is a lot
like putting your finger into an electric socket. You may
know intellectually the continuing evils being worked
upon the original Americans; Strete and his fellow
Indians make you feel it. Of all the stories in the first
issues, published for the first time this year, "Time Deer"
is the most outstanding.*

THE old man watched the boy. The boy watched the deer. The
deer was watched by all and the Great Being above.

The old man remembered when he was a young boy and his
father showed him a motorcycle thing on a parking lot.

The young boy remembered his second wife with some regret,
not looking forward to the coming of his first wife.

Tuesday morning the Monday-morning traffic jam was three
days old and the old man sat on the hood of a stalled car and
watched the boy. The boy watched the deer. The deer was
watched by all and the Great Being above.

The young boy resisted when his son, at the insistence of that white bitch of a wife he had married, had tried to put him in a rest home for the elderly. Now he watched a deer beside the highway. And was watched in turn.

The old man was on the way to somewhere. He was going someplace, someplace important, he forgot just where. He knew he was going.

The deer had relatives waiting for her, grass waiting for her, seasons being patient on her account. As much as she wanted to please the boy by letting him look at her, she had to go. She apologized with a shake of her head.

The old man watched the deer going. He knew she had someplace to go, someplace important. He did not know where she was going but he knew why.

The old man was going to be late. He could have walked. He was only going across the road. He was going across the road to get to the other side. He was going to be late for his own funeral. The old man was going someplace. He couldn't remember where.

＊   ＊   ＊

"Did you make him wear the watch? If he's wearing the watch he should—"

"He's an old man, honey! You know how his mind wanders," said Frank Strong Bull.

"Dr. Amber is waiting! Does he think we can afford to pay for every appointment he misses?" snarled Sheila, running her fingers through the tangled ends of her hair. "Doesn't he ever get anywhere on time?"

"He lives by Indian time. Being late is just something you must expect from—" he began, trying to explain.

She cut him off.

"Indian this and Indian that! I'm so sick of your god damn excuses I could vomit!"

"But—"

"Let's just forget it. We don't have time to argue about it. We have to be at the doctor's office in twenty minutes. If we leave now we can just beat the rush-hour traffic. I just hope your father's there when we get there."

"Don't worry. He'll be there," said Frank, looking doubtful.

*   *   *

But the deer could not leave and stay gone. She went a little way and then she turned and came back to where the boy watched her. And the old man was strangely moved because he knew the deer had come back because the boy knew how to look at the deer.

And the boy was happy because the deer chose to favor him. And he saw the deer for what she was. Great and golden and quick in her beauty.

And the deer knew that the boy thought her beautiful. For it was the purpose of the deer in this world on that morning to be beautiful for a young boy to look at.

And the old man who was going someplace was grateful to the deer and almost envious of the boy. But he was one with the boy who was one with the deer and they were all one with the Great Being above. So there was no envy, just the great longing of age for youth.

*   *   *

"That son of a bitch!" growled Frank Strong Bull. "The bastard cut me off." He yanked the gear shift out of fourth and slammed it into third. The tach needle shot into the red and the mustang backed off, just missing the foreign car that had swerved in front of it.

"Oh Christ! We'll be late!" moaned Sheila, turning in the car seat to look out the back window. "Maybe you can get into the express lane."

"Are you kidding? With this traffic!"

He had both hands on the wheel like a weapon. He lifted his right hand and slammed it on the gear shift. The gears ground, caught hold, and the mustang shot ahead. Yanking the wheel to the left, he cut in front of a truck, which hit its brakes, missing the mustang by inches. He buried the gas pedal and the car responded. He pulled up level with the sports car that had cut him off. He honked and made an obscene gesture as he passed. Sheila squealed with delight. "Go! Go!" she exclaimed.

* * *

The old man had taken liberties in his life. He'd had things to remember and things he wanted to forget. Twice he had married. The first time. He hated the first time. He'd been blinded by her looks and his hands got the better of him. He had not known his own heart, and not knowing, he had let his body decide. It was something he would always regret.

That summer he was an eagle. Free. Mating in the air. Never touching down. Never looking back. That summer. His hands that touched her were wings. And he flew and the feathers covered the scars that grew where he touched her.

He was of the air and she was of the earth. She muddied his dreams. She had woman's body but lacked woman's spirit. A star is a stone to the blind. She saw him through crippled eyes. She possessed. He shared. There was no life between them. He saw the stars and counted them one by one into her hand, that gift that all lovers share. She saw stones. And she turned away.

He was free because he needed. She was a prisoner because she wanted. One day she was gone. And he folded his wings and the earth came rushing at him and he was an old man with a small son. And he lived in a cage and was three years dead. And his son was a small hope that melted. He was like her. He could see it in his son's eyes. It was something he would always regret.

But the deer, the young boy, these were things he would never regret.

* * *

Dr. Amber was hostile. "Damn it! I can't sign the commitment papers if I've never seen him!"

Sheila tried to smile pleasantly. "He'll show up. His hotel room is just across the street. Frank will find him. Don't worry."

"I have other patients! I can't be held up by some doddering old man!" snapped Dr. Amber.

"Just a few more minutes," pleaded Sheila.

"You'll have to pay for two visits. I can't run this place for free. Every minute I'm not working, I'm losing money!"

"We'll pay," said Sheila grimly. "We'll pay."

*   *   *

The world was big and the deer had to take her beauty through the world. She had been beautiful in one place for one boy on one morning of this world. It was time to be someplace else. The deer turned and fled into the woods, pushing her beauty before her into the world.

The young boy jumped to his feet. His heart racing, his feet pounding, he ran after her with the abandon of youth that is caring. He chased beauty through the world and disappeared from the old man's sight in the depths of the forest.

And the old man began dreaming that—

*   *   *

Frank Strong Bull's hand closed on his shoulder and his son shook him, none too gently.

The old man looked into the face of his son and did not like what he saw. He allowed himself to be led to the doctor's office.

"Finally!" said Sheila. "Where the hell was he?"

Dr. Amber came into the room with a phony smile. "Ah! The elusive one appears! And how are we today?"

"We are fine," said the old man, bitterly. He pushed the outstretched stethoscope away from his chest.

"Feisty isn't he?" observed Dr. Amber.

"Let's just get this over with," said Sheila. "It's been drawn out long enough as it is."

"Not sick," said the old man. "You leave me alone." He made two fists and backed away from the doctor.

"How old is he?" asked Dr. Amber, looking at the old man's wrinkled face and white hair.

"Past eighty, at least," said his son. "The records aren't available and he can't remember himself."

"Over eighty, you say. Well, that's reason enough then," said Dr. Amber. "Let me give him a cursory examination, just a formality, and then I'll sign the commitment paper."

The old man unclenched his fists. He looked at his son. His eyes burned. He felt neither betrayed nor wronged. Only sorrow. He allowed one tear, only one tear to fall. It was for his son who could not meet his eyes.

And for the first time since his son had married her, his eyes fell upon his son's wife's eyes. She seemed to shrivel under his gaze, but she met his gaze and he read the dark things in her eyes.

They were insignificant, not truly a part of his life. He had seen the things of importance. He had watched the boy. The boy had watched the deer. And the deer had been watched by all and the Great Being above.

The old man backed away from them until his back was against a wall. He put his hand to his chest and smiled. He was dead before his body hit the floor.

*   *   *

"A massive heart attack," said Dr. Amber to the ambulance attendant. "I just signed the death certificate."

"They the relatives?" asked the attendant, jerking a thumb at the couple sitting silently in chairs by the wall.

Dr. Amber nodded.

The attendant approached them.

"It's better this way," said Sheila. "An old man like that, no reason to live, no—"

"Where you want I should take the body?" asked the attendant.

"Vale's Funeral Home," said Sheila.

Frank Strong Bull stared straight ahead. He heard nothing. His eyes were empty of things, light and dark.

"Where is it?" asked the attendant.

"Where is what?" asked Dr. Amber.

"The body? Where's the body?"

"It's in the next room. On the table," said Dr. Amber coming around his desk. He took the attendant's arm and led him away from the couple.

"I'll help you put it on the stretcher."

*   *   *

The old man who watched the deer. He had dreamed his second wife in his dream. He had dreamed that. But she had been real. She came when emptiness and bitterness had filled him. When the feathers of his youth had been torn from his wings and she filled him again with bright pieces of dreams. And for him, in that second half of his life, far from his son and that first one, he began again. Flying. Noticing the world. His eyes saw the green things, his lips tasted the sweet things and his old age was warm.

It was all bright and fast and moving, that second life of his, and they were childless and godless and were themselves children and gods instead. And they grew old in their bodies, but death seemed more like an old friend than an interruption. It was sleep. One night the fever took her. Peacefully. Took her while she slept, and he neither wept nor followed. For she had made him young again, and the young do not understand death.

*   *   *

"I'll help you put it on the stretcher."
They opened the door.

*   *   *

And the old man watched the boy and did not understand death. And the young boy watched the deer and understood beauty. And the deer was watched by all and the Great Being above. And the boy saw the deer for what she was. And like her, he became great and golden and quick. And the old man began dreaming that—

*   *   *

Frank Strong Bull's hand closed on his shoulder and his son shook him, none too gently.

*   *   *

They opened the door. The body was gone.

* * *

The last time it was seen, the body was chasing a deer that pushed its beauty through the world, disappearing from an old man's sight into the depths of the forest.

A Typical Day

DORIS PISERCHIA

Without trying to sound too male chauvinist, it is a pleasure to find an excellent science-fiction story by a woman that, in addition, captures the essential female-ness of the author. Women do look at life in a manner different from that of testosterone-impassioned males, and this difference should be encouraged and enjoyed. In stories such as this one.

IT begins with me pulling away all the furniture Father shoved against the door the preceding night. He does it every night so he won't be able to get out and spill important secrets after he has had too much to drink.

Father is a boozehound. And a genius. And a tortured soul. That description would serve for just about any of the nuts who have ever given something to the world and have received stones in return. The world is good at shortchanging. It's ungrateful. Or maybe it's simply confused, like Father.

We live in a tower. It isn't ivory and it has no ivy growing on it. It's made of rough concrete blocks, is a hundred feet high and about seventy feet wide. Home.

Father hates the world.

Or himself. He loves me.

After putting the furniture back in place, I opened the door and

228

looked out. What was to see? Nothing. A hallway and the elevator
Father used once in a blue moon, when he took the jeep and went
over the hills into town to stock up on food or to replenish his
booze supply. It was a hick town. I suppose Father and I were
hicks.

The morning of my typical day didn't last long. I dusted the
living room. I ate corn flakes. I turned the gas on under the lab
beakers—same thing every time I got up. A humdrum existence,
Father said. Maybe so. It was all right with me.

Lunch? I thought about it, looked at the clock. No, it wasn't
time for lunch, which meant there was something I had forgotten
to do. Schedules, schedules, what the hell did I leave out?

Oh, yeah, I forgot to watch the races. Checked the clock.
Wrong. It wasn't time for the races. Hmmm. Oh, sure, I didn't
wash my face and brush my teeth.

Did that. All finished. The phone rang.

"Hello."

"Hello. Hello?"

"Hello."

"Is that you, Doctor Dakis?"

"No, it ain't."

"Doctor? This is the University calling. Will you speak louder,
please? I can't—"

"Every damned day of the week, you call. Same time, same
place. Every damned day we go through the same spiel. I'm here,
you're there, but there's simply no communicating between us. I
know you, Miss Fat Rearend. Father told me your name. Miss Fat
Rearend, will you please kiss my—"

"Hello. Doctor Dakis?"

She finally gave up and hung up.

"Get the hell off the phone!" Father roared from his bedroom.

"I'm off."

He didn't come out, turned over so hard the bed whacked the
floor. In another minute I heard him snoring.

It started raining. I hung out the window in the north side of
the tower and watched the silver needles fall from the sky. God, I
loved rain. I spat down the tower, watched it mingle with the

clean washing from heaven, saw it disappear, wished the world would renew its acquaintance with Father so his misery would go away like my spit. I'm eight years old.

The phone rang.

"Hello."

"Doctor Dakis?"

"Hi, Miss Fat Rearend. No, we ain't got no eggs for you today. And we ain't got no sperm, neither."

"Doctor Dakis?"

I screamed in her ear and she hung up.

"Get the hell off the phone!" Father roared from his bedroom. He turned over and went back to sleep.

*　　*　　*

He got up at noon and we had lunch together.

"Make me eat it," he said to me. His head dangled over his plate as if it had a broken connection.

I spooned some egg into his mouth. He grabbed his cup of coffee and gulped. I stuffed toast through his teeth. Again he gulped coffee. I held a strip of bacon and he nibbled that.

I made him eat two eggs, three strips of bacon and two slices of toast. After he finished he wiped his mouth, belched, looked sick, got up and stumbled into the bathroom.

"Get the hell out," he growled—slammed the door in my face.

A bell rang somewhere. I ran to the open window, looked down. A blue truck was parked in the front yard and the driver was pounding on the door.

"What you want?" I said.

He backed away from the door, looked up, saw me and waved an envelope.

"Can't you read?" I said. "Put it in the basket and I'll pull it up."

He kept waving the envelope. I hung on the windowsill and watched him grow agitated. Finally he saw the basket, threw the envelope into it, gave me a severe glare and took his truck away.

The cable was from Germany. This time the zoo offered fifty thousand for the aphrodisiac.

"Who have you been talking to?" I said to Father as he came out of the bathroom. "I thought you didn't want anybody to know about the aphrodisiac."

He kicked a clothes hamper out of his way and hunted on a bureau top for a comb. He combed his hair, his most beautiful feature. It was long and white and wavy. His skin was almost as white as his hair, which was why he made me coax him to eat. His health was poor. I think if it wasn't for me he would have been dead long ago.

He combed his hair and smacked his lips, rubbed them with a trembly hand, looked at me with big sorrowful eyes. What he wanted was a stiff belt. What he expected me to bring him was a beer. What I got for him, out of the bureau, was a box of chocolate-covered cherries. With a shrug he took two and ate them, took two more and shoved them in his shirt pocket. He ate them before he got out the door. I had the box ready when he turned back. He had half a dozen.

Fine. When he ate candy he didn't have beer, and when he had no beer he didn't follow it up with whisky. Today he would do some work. Marvelous, that candy. Me, too.

In the beginning, Father had no money and figured he would end on a farm, but he was too bright and went to school nights and eventually he got hooked on genetics. Or he hooked it. Everything he did was right. He took his Ph.D. and taught at the University. After a while he stopped teaching and did only research.

Sex wasn't something people did, according to Father. Sex was a phenomenon, like life. Gender wasn't sex. Sex was mating, but not the mating of male and female people. It was the mating of living organisms inside people. Father didn't have a better word for the two things that joined to make a baby. Or he didn't want to go to the bother of explaining it to me in technical terms. "Bugs" was good enough. A girl bug and a boy bug mated and the whys and wherefores were mysteries to nearly everybody except my dad. A girl bug was an ovum, or an egg, while a boy bug was a sperm, or a beak. Beaks pierced eggs and the rest was downhill coasting.

Bugs were too selective to suit most geneticists. Why did they

seem to want to mate only with their own species? Anyhow, once
a beak pierced an egg, the egg either died or accommodated the
invader. This was hazardous joining on the microscopic level.
Father never seemed to rise beyond this level as far as his personal
life was concerned. At least, I didn't think he was mating with
anyone. . . . How did I get on this subject?

Father became famous when he invented the racecourse. We
had one in the den. Plenty of people had them now.

It was a daily chore of mine to clean the racecourse after lunch.
I dismantled it, placed the parts in a tub of antiseptic solution and
left them for Father to put back together. The course was a
transparent tube with an incubator in its center and two little
bubbles on the ends. The whole thing was about twenty-four
inches long.

While he reassembled the parts, Father talked. "You take an
egg—you think she has no personality? That little girl is complete
within herself, eats, eliminates, breathes, moves—and damned if
she doesn't have a purpose. That's to mate—butter and bread to
her. She loves it. Another thing, she kills her lover when she's done
with him."

I knew all that. He had told me many times. I knew the sperm,
or beak, was suicidal and basically a rapist. He was sex-happy, had
nothing else on his mind. He would mate or die—in fact, he
would kill himself in the attempt rather than leave off. Father said
the beak screamed just before he died. Father was working on a
miniature amplifier to pick up their sounds. Anyhow, the beak was
stupid, or else he didn't expect to get eaten, just wanted what he
wanted and to hell with the consequences.

As for the egg, she had poor sensory equipment and recognized
only sperm from her own species. Father wanted to study this
phenomenon and find out why she would have nothing to do with
certain sperm. He thought maybe it was their smell, or something
simple like that. Often she turned down one of her own kind and
took a total stranger—of course, Father had given the stranger a
squirt of his invention so she would notice him. Or smell him. Or
whatever it was eggs did. It was best to talk about them as if they

were men and women, because, actually, the bugs were the only true sexes in the world. They were male or female and no maybes about it.

People were dumb. They thought they could jump in bed and that was all there was to it, but the bugs in their bodies were out to get together, and nothing short of disaster or bad breath or body odor or whatever could stop them. The bugs didn't care about population control—there was plenty of clean space in their worlds. People didn't realize there were life forms in their bodies that could destroy the planet.

"I'm a male chauvinist pig," said Father. "I admit it. That's what half the people in this world call me. What it means is that I'm like the bugs inside me. I want what I want when I want it. I have no consideration. It's the same with women. They're female chauvinist pigs. If they can't get what they want they have a fit. They're larger extensions of the bugs inside them. If we all came up from the slime, we couldn't have been very big in those wet days. Still, who won the climb up the evolutionary ladder? Whose environment is polluted, who's killing each other off, who hates each other?" Father tapped his fingers on the table top. "I keep asking myself the same damned question—which came first, the chicken or the egg?"

He stopped talking. He stared up at the ceiling perplexed, bruised of soul.

I stood looking at the racecourse. It was shaped like a female reproductive system. A sperm was ejected from a depository into one of the bubbles at the ends of the tube and an egg was ejected into the other bubble. Fluid carried them to the incubator where they were supposed to join. Sometimes they didn't. It depended upon how my dad was feeling. If he felt crabby or pensive, the sperm got a squirt of Dad's invention—the aphrodisiac—and the joining was frenzied. If he felt sad or apprehensive, the sperm got no treatment and the egg remained aloof and impenetrable.

Squirting an egg produced no reaction.

Father said the squirting muffled the sperm's undesirable qualities. What they were, he didn't know. He suspected the egg exuded a killer fluid that destroyed stranger sperm. He had better look, smell, taste or sound right or she would murder him before he did his duty.

*   *   *

The rendezvous in the incubator in Father's lab always involved an egg and a sperm from different species. Once, long before, I asked him why and he said, "Who wants to mate a duo of human bugs? I know fellows who do that all the time. Nate Farrell likes it. He's at the University. Teaches a couple of classes and spends his spare time complaining about the liberalized abortion laws. He claims the fetus is alive at conception. In the basement of his house he whiles away the time by creating human fetuses in a racecourse. He dumps them in the toilet when he's done."

I peered into the eyeplate fixed in the top of our racecourse. Automatic electronic microscopes tracked a tiger and a lion as they sped to the incubator. Of course they were really only bugs, but I knew where they had originated. Father always marked the depositories with dabs of dye. A yellow one was a tiger sperm, a pink one was a lion egg, et cetera. I had memorized them all.

The mating of tiger and lion bugs wasn't at all difficult, so I knew Father was feeling sad that day. Such a mating could have taken place in a zoo between two real animals. Racecourse mating between tiger and lion bugs occurred ninety-nine times out of a hundred. In a zoo, these animals rarely mated and getting a baby from them was more rare.

The course sat on a white table and was about at my chest level. I stood bent over the eyeplate and watched the race. The little tadpole and the larger ball fell into the incubator, spied one another, had a tussle. The tadpole stabbed with his nose, the ball squeezed him and gave him a thrill and then she opened and he fell in with a scream, after which she ate him. And I could have sworn I heard the scream.

The phone rang a moment later and Father stomped out of the lab. He never answered the phone, but he wouldn't get rid of it and I knew why. When it rang the outside world spoke—and Father needed to hear that sound.

I answered it. "Hello."

It was the same old thing. They couldn't hear me because of my speech impediment and all they wanted was to fleece my dad out of his formula. The University wanted him to come back to his professorship. Sometimes they offered him money for the formula, but not often, because they knew of the exorbitant offers he had received from abroad.

I thought he couldn't keep a secret, believed he had blabbed to someone in town during one of his drunken excursions. His explanation was that they had figured it out for themselves.

"They're idiots but they aren't morons," he said. "How can I send them a living dog-cat fetus in a box unless I know how to make the sperm bug acceptable? I tell them it was an accident. Sure. Then they beg me for more and I send them a sparrow-hamster fetus. It never ends. They bitch because the hybrids can't reproduce. Finally they conclude I'm doing something they can't do. Hell, I've always done that."

Either he wasn't telling me all of the truth or he had simply forgotten. The moochers might have guessed he knew how to make stranger-sperm acceptable, but it wasn't coincidence when they called the formula an aphrodisiac. Dad had called it that because it amused him to do so. The formula didn't heighten the bugs' desire to mate. That was already at fever pitch. Dad must have blabbed, probably to the bartender in town, a University fink planted there to pick up information.

＊　　＊　　＊

In the late afternoon Father took a nap and I read a book I had already read three times. It was about a distant-future Earth in which most life forms were integrated. The hero built a time-machine and traveled into the past to the twenty-first century when man was beginning to experiment with cross-breeding. The experimental subjects had survived mostly through the ignorance and errors of the experimenters. At first they were called freaks. They lived in communes and were subjected to persecutions. The hero of the book was so horrified by the hatred directed toward him by homo sapiens that he fled a few centuries into the future.

There he found the situation less violent but nevertheless distressing. The freaks were still a minority, but their customs and habits were threatening the overall structure of society. For instance, a morse (man-horse) married a mog (man-dog) and then they quarreled about the cuisine. Or a masnake married a mird and they quarreled about the sleeping and working hours. Within certain species it was customary for the male to care for the children—when they married more conventional strangers the loving couples had fights after the babies came. In the meantime homo sapiens—what was left of him—was desperately trying to preserve his own traditions. At the end of the book the hero became disgusted with humanity and its myriad shapes and philosophies. He went home to the future, smashed his time-machine, sank his roots twenty feet into the ground, veiled his face with his weeping hair so the women would leave him alone, and then he spent the next hundred years brooding.

I enjoyed reading the book again. It helped me to understand Father better. He wasn't like the men who made bombs or deadly bacteria—he was aware of his moral dilemma. Should he give the world the aphrodisiac or not? He drank because he was double-damned and he hated the world because it always peered over his shoulder.

I told him about the book while we ate supper.

"Talk!" he said, as he eyed his plate with revulsion. "Remember how you used to do it when you were small? Try to recreate those sounds."

I gabbed, chattered, ran at the mouth. I said there was always a hero somewhere, like in the book. If a holocaust was observed by a single objective eye, that holocaust hadn't occurred in vain. In other words, my dad should give up the aphrodisiac. The consequences would become mundane history. It wouldn't be the same as dumping a gallon of botulism in the East River. Fallout from a nuclear explosion was a compound fracture of the moral femur. Like a bomb, the aphrodisiac was a potential bonebreaker, but only because people were stiff-necked and unimaginative.

"That isn't the way to talk!" said Father. A piece of lettuce disappeared between his teeth. "You know damned well you're doing it all under your breath. Nobody can hear you. You have every right to talk out loud. Use your larynx and your mind and your desire—"

Spilling my milk, I said, "I will when you break all your bottles."

I understood. He worried about things like antiabortion groups. We all had a big wide wonderful planet in which to botch things up. Another word for world was trial-and-error.

"Don't cry," I said. "You're like everybody you loathe. I love you. You care."

"Come here."

I shook my head.

He ate a boiled potato. "Come here."

"It isn't time. We have our family relationship after supper— while we watch TV, when the tower is shut up like a grave and all the kibitzers out there have put you out of mind until another day."

*   *   *

Later we settled down in front of the TV and he held me in his lap.

"Whisper in my ear," he said. "As loud as you can. Break my eardrum."

I watched the cowboys shoot up the town. And in the meantime I smelled my father. The hair on his chest tickled my nose. He stroked my legs, my back, my hair, he pinched my cheek, pressed his nose against mine and we stared into each other's eyes until mine crossed.

He was clever, but he gave me his mind when he fathered me, lent me too much of his savvy. He stroked me to draw me to him, desired for us to have a meeting of souls.

"I won't say I can't," I said. "I'll say I won't. Does that make sense?"

"Don't let them hurt you. You can be anything you want."

"I don't want to be anything. I just want to be."

He took my chin between his big hands. "Say, 'ah.' "

"Ah."

"Not just with your mouth. Make the world hear."

"Ah."

"See my tears? Do you enjoy breaking your old dad's heart?"

"You're a souse."

"Say something to me out loud. Scream at me."

"You ought to use a little soap and water to clean your ears. They're like caves of dirty gold."

He squeezed me until my ribs crunched. I howled, but soundlessly.

"One day we'll leave this goddamned tower," he said. "You think about that. We'll walk down the main street of New York City. Hand in hand. When they all come out and say, 'Doctor Dakis, you and your child are welcome in this world,' that's the day I'll hand them the aphrodisiac."

He believed I was suffering. I was. Said I, "On the day you break your bottles—that's the day I'll walk out of here with you. I'll go on TV, if you like. I'll yell through a microphone. Everybody from Guam to the Virgin Islands will hear me. Except we'll have to come back here to the tower every night. It isn't me who prevents my talking out loud. I do it for you. They don't hurt me that much. But you hurt me, all the days of my life. I won't talk because you drink. You drink because you're jealous."

I laid my head on his shoulder.

"Don't do that," he said.

Couldn't be helped. Getting sleepy. Thumb in mouth. Suck, suck, it helped me to fantasize. Suck, suck.

Father tried to hold me back. "I'll snuggle you all night, I'll keep you warm, I'll comfort you. Stay with me."

Suck, suck. I dreamed—halfway here, halfway in another world. One was as bad or as good as the other since both were safely remote. I soared in luxurious comfort. Away in the distance Father called to me. I knew why. He was an almost perfect person. His one fault was that he was intolerant.

Someone called, and this time it was another. The voice was my imagination, or at least I thought it was. I never really asked.

Father held me fast. I yanked away. I left him to his bottles that waited for him everywhere in the tower. Father, I can't help this thing. Maybe we both have a bridge to cross. Perhaps someday I'll stay with you at night, you'll break your bottles, we'll go outside again, I'll talk your head off, we'll grow up together. I love you.

I opened the door at the end of the hall and closed it behind me. The big room was dark and silent, but not totally silent. The snakes in their cages watched me, warned me not to touch their screens. The guinea pigs thought it might be morning and whistled for breakfast, the dogs whimpered as nightmares threatened, the baboon cursed me for trailing my hand across his bars.

Stopping beside the last cage, I took off my clothes, opened the door, quietly slipped inside and walked to the cot in the corner. Her arms lifted and I fell into them as a sinner enters heaven: with exhausted happiness. Deep into her hairy bosom I nestled. We kissed, kissed, kissed. She licked my face, fumbled over my hairless body for nonexistent fleas. Carefully she squeezed, lest she destroy me. I lay with my cheek against my mother's breast, felt her powerful arms tighten around me and I let the world go to hell while I slept.

Programmed Love Story

IAN WATSON

How well Ian Watson lifts the curtain of the future and gives us a glimpse of some interesting computer programs never considered before. How well he also looks into the human heart.

O NCE upon a time in the year Two Thousand there will be a hostess in the Queen Bee cabaret in Tokyo, called Kei. Her marriage to a young businessman has turned out sadly. He has quarreled with her. And why? Because he is convinced she has the wrong personality. She is pretty, yes. She is graceful and tactful, yes. They make love with all the proficiency and enthusiasm that Dr. Sha Kokken has prescribed. But as his business prospects grow he has grown superstitious—and the firm's astrology computer has lately whispered in his ear that she is wrong for him. That they should have taken more heed of their horoscopes (which modern science, increasingly conscious of the existence of patterns in the universe, has validated by the year Two Thousand) and less of romantic love. That her palm print is incompatible with his—a fact that he never noticed while they were courting and holding hands. That her grace and softness will hold him back, for what the firm needs during the coming millennium is tough aggressive managers for overseas, with tough aggressive wives to goad them on. So he has grown bitter toward her, reproaching her for her tender and yielding (though amorous) nature, exhorting her day by day to reform her personality, to change herself—though into what she has to change herself he has never quite made up his mind. And this has gone on until one sad day, simply because she loves him and would not stand in his way, she has left him.

Once upon a time in the year Two Thousand there will be a woman called Kei who works as a cabaret hostess to support herself, though even in the year Two Thousand the pay at the Queen Bee is not so good considering the nature of the services demanded. . . .

Only a stone's throw away from Nihonbashi Bridge which travelers used to set off from in the old days in palanquins borne by high-stepping servants on their way to Kyoto, which modern man sets off from in neon-striped taxis with automatic doors on the fifty-seven stages of extravagance known as the Ginza; only a stone's throw away from where the metal dragons of the bridge rear their heads (though only just) between the lanes of the overhead expressway—is the Queen Bee's extensive, if shabby, facade. By the year Two Thousand the Queen Bee has done her damnedest to keep up with the times.

Kei's pliant yielding nature—if it did not seem to qualify her very well for life with her husband the Almost Twenty-First Century Businessman—did uniquely qualify her for work at the Queen Bee.

Today when a customer walks into that cabaret, he is handed a computer sheet showing twenty situations—modest traditional bride, brisk nurse tending the wounded war hero, sailor-suited schoolgirl presenting an apple to the teacher, fat nude trussed up lightly so that her flesh bulges over the ropes like the Michelin tire man . . . he marks the four scenes he likes best, in order of preference; the computer locates her closest to his heart among the hundred hostesses. . . .

By the year Two Thousand the Queen Bee has installed a far more sophisticated computer of the SWARM variety—a Suggestibility Wizard & Rapport Machine. As soon as the customer (honored guest, as they say) has chosen the face he fancies from the catalogue of a hundred pretty faces, and the personality type he yearns for from the pack of a hundred situation cards—take note that a hundred pretty faces multiplied by a hundred personalities will give him the choice of ten thousand women— the owner of the pretty face is summoned to the changing room. Suppose that the pretty face is Kei's; she will need all her pliant yielding nature then, for only a genuine yielding nature can accept the Suggestibility Wizard & Rapport Machine's imprinting of a fresh personality upon it without giving signs of a schizophrenia distressing to an honored guest. . . .

Once upon a time in the year Two Thousand there will be a hostess called Kei upon whose brain a Suggestibility Wizard & Rapport Machine imposes a fresh personality nightly—which is to say up until two in the morning when the Queen Bee shuts up shop and a hundred hostesses, passing through the front door onto the Ginza, pass through an erasure field too and find themselves out there among the neon lights, dehypnotized, with memories of being other people, so many miniskirted high-heeled swamis dreaming of reincarnation. . . .

Once upon a time in the year Two Thousand a pliant gentle personality will be prior essential for any girl who wants to be a Queen Bee hostess and adopt personalities which are not hers, personalities that need not themselves be particularly pliant or gentle. . . . (For does not Situation Card 64 depict a leather-clad lady whipping her escort with a riding crop?)

Once upon a time in the year Two Thousand there will be a rising young businessman called Kenzo whose status with the firm ensures his section chief taking him along precisely once a month to some cabaret or other to entertain clients into the wee hours of the morning, all expenses paid. . . .

Thus one evening in the year Two Thousand this Kenzo will walk into the Queen Bee along with his section chief and a client from Kyoto and be handed a catalogue of a hundred pretty faces, among which he is mildly surprised to find his wife Kei. Now whether it was Kenzo's reluctance to watch his wife entertaining strangers . . . or whether he had decided to play a practical joke upon her (his bitterness not having entirely abated yet), he chose this particular face from among the hundred to be his hostess; and from the pack of cards selected number 78—Strength in High Places, the Imperial Concubine.

The transistor hidden in her brassiere gave a beep summoning Kei to the changing room, where she submitted herself obediently to the Suggestibility Wizard & Rapport Machine, emerging a few moments later with arrogance and precision, cruel, bent on power, mind hatching devious plots, mostly centered on the swift rise to a position of eminence of her new protégé, whom she would shortly meet, cajole, mold and entice. For her the whiskies she pressed on her victim at 100 New Yen a shot were transactions of great significance; the colored water she drank herself (at 100 New Yen a shot) a clever way of evading the poisoner's art.

Once upon a time in the year Two Thousand a rising businessman will summon his lost wife before him in the image of the Imperial Concubine—and she will cajole him, mold him, entice him, under the envious eyes of his Section Chief, till he sighs, "What such a woman could do for me!" and falls helplessly in love with her. . . .

Long after midnight, when the Section Chief has paid Queen Bee for their night's entertainment and Kenzo is traveling home in a neon taxi with stereo chansons playing softly, he still loves her helplessly and thinks about her; for poetic justice cuts both ways. . . .

The next night on his own he made his way back to the Queen Bee, pointed at that pretty face in the catalogue, asked for personality number 78.

Sitting opposite the Imperial Concubine, watching with dismay how fast she drained the glasses of colored water, Kenzo cried out at last:

"Do you know who I am, Kei?"

And she smiled the Austere Perfection Smile appropriate to the castration ceremonies of court eunuchs; and nodded.

"Do you know I am your husband?"

"Husband?" She laughed lightly, a laugh appropriate to an enemy's execution reported earnestly by a doting prince.

"With you by my side—*this* you—I could climb so high. . . ."

The prospect of power . . . she leaned forward.

"Shall I inform you how to twist that Section Chief of yours round your little finger? Did you take note which girl he chose? What she represented?"

Shamed, he shook his head.

"You should have noticed—for that was the key to his soul."

"I was too busy noticing you, my darling wife."

"Nonsense! I am an Imperial Concubine—you know we can never be wed. We can only meet in safety as conspirators."

Once upon a time in the year Two Thousand there will be a rising young businessman who conceives an obsession for the Imperial Concubine of the Queen Bee, to whom he was once married, and woos her a second time, spending all his salary, then all his savings, on glasses of whisky-colored water, and little dishes of rice crackers . . . and still her heart—in that incarnation—is chiseled out of ice. . . .

And early every morning at two o'clock after his fruitless visits she walks out, dehypnotized, onto the Ginza, weeping at the Imperial Concubine's inability to thaw, and yield. . . .

In the year Two Thousand, on the Ginza, once upon a time there will be a benighted businessman who has gone so deep into debt that he embezzles thousands of New Yen from his firm to pay the Queen Bee, till his Section Chief discovers and fires him; who goes with his last pocketful of change to spend it on colored water and rice crackers for an Imperial Concubine he is sure is at last on the very point of yielding. . . .

Once upon a time on the Ginza there will be a tender yielding hostess, Kei by name, who submits to a Suggestibility Wizard & Rapport Machine nightly, till one night she submits to it no more . . . who elopes from the Queen Bee forever with her protégé, passing through an erasure field as she leaves the door, to become . . .

"Oh Kenzo!"

"Oh Kei!"

. . . the tough hard wife of a ruined ex-businessman, with whom she walks along the Ginza through the neon forest—for they can't afford a taxi fare—till at last they come to Shimbashi

Station where the shoeshine people have left their equipment out overnight—who would steal shoeshine equipment?

In the year Two Thousand there will be a tough handsome couple shining people's shoes in the early morning as the trains rattle overhead and the neon taxis swing past. You can still see this couple, older now and beginning to suffer from chest trouble from the exhaust fumes, shining and repairing shoes on the street by Shimbashi Station through the night. If you look for them carefully. Once upon a time in the future.

This story is brought to you by a Suggestibility Wizard & Rapport Machine programmed to print out stories about itself suitable for junior high schools during the slack periods of the day, by courtesy of the management, Queen Bee Cabaret, Tokyo, tax-deductible for educational purposes.

We do not sell merchandise; we sell human nature.

Afterword:
The Galaxy Begins at Home
BRIAN W. ALDISS

WHEN Editor Harrison conceived the idea of committing me to this yearly Afterword, I intended to keep my eyes firmly on science fiction and to avoid commenting on the state of the world at large. But reality keeps breaking in.

This year, I will concentrate on some really excellent books, novels, and nonfiction, which have appeared over the last few months. Since SF in its upper registers lays claim to dealing with matters that concern us all, it nevertheless seems absurd not to mention the power crisis afflicting the world. This dramatic turn in mundane affairs has resulted in part from increasing unity and political awareness in the Arab states. The Arab states have exercised their powers only moderately, not halting the flow of oil but merely refusing to increase production, since the stuff is of more value to them lying in rock strata underground than as slowly diminishing cash in the bank. The result of this moderation is to bring progress grinding to a halt, or at least changing into lower gear, in a crisis that SF failed to predict.*

* * *

Much of the SF that earlier generations of SF writers created— let our John W. Campbells and Robert Heinleins stand as representative—has as one of its basic premises the idea that western technological culture will extend itself forever to the stars. This assumption largely lies unexamined—and is difficult to

* Though there is a novel called *Barefoot in the Head* (1969) which shows what happened when the Arab World wrecked the West, using LSD rather than oil as a weapon.

examine, since the underlying motivation is emotional rather than rational. Now we can see more clearly that the assumption is part of a general optimism and opportunism in our culture, and a comforting one at that. Nobody likes to think that they or, by extension, their family, their nation, or their civilization, will pass away. Galactic empires discount death.

But the galaxy begins at home, and really challenging SF goes much further than comfort. Discomfiture is more essentially its business. Olaf Stapledon's two great works, *Last and First Men* and *Star-Maker*, are demonstrations on the largest scale of how individuals, societies, whole species, must eventually pass. Stapledon dedicated his atheism to rewriting Ecclesiastes: " 'Vanity of vanities,' saith the preacher. 'All is vanity.' "

Discomfiture has now come among us in real life, although mainly with a whisper that things may be worse yet. The global climate also seems to be ganging up on us. What appear to be rapid shifts in weather patterns are creating a series of bad harvests which, linked with enormously increased costs of fertilizers and pesticides (no longer cheap since oil prices spiraled), mean an almost immediate increase in world hunger, malnutrition, and famine.

In the circumstances, it is natural enough to take a wry look, not so much at technology, as at society. Technology is still capable of getting us out of many an awful mess (even if it got us there in the first place), but the people who control technology are not up to the job; and those are people chosen by our society— though you may not think that "chosen" is the right word either. But however you cut it, the time is more than ripe for a look at the nature of society.

You hoped I would get back to science fiction, and so I have. For the four novels I most enjoyed this year are all, in different ways, devoted to examining our society or producing fresh variants of it that increase our perception of the old one. There is nothing new in this procedure, but these novels do their job extremely well. After one or two years of disappointing books, this year has yielded a magnificent crop.

First shall be Ursula Le Guin's *The Dispossessed*, which says a great deal about human societies while relating the story of Shevek, a man divided between two worlds.

The two worlds are Urras and its satellite, Annares. Just as Annares is not the Moon under another name, so Urras is not the Earth; parallels are not drawn, analogies are. Urras is Earthlike, and several of its nations flourish under a mild form of capitalism.

*   *   *

Attention focuses mainly on Annares, the moon. Annares is a sparse place, only marginally habitable; but a colony has survived there for one hundred and seventy years. The colony maintains a proud independence from Urras, and there are few contacts between the two worlds. Both the survival and the independence of the colony are due to their political belief, Odonism, a blend of nonauthoritarian communism and sheer anarchy which propelled them from their mother world in the first place. Odonism also fosters male-female equality. Names of everyone in the colony are chosen by computer, consist of six letters, and have no gender connotations. While this is an intriguing idea for a political tract, it proves slightly defeating in a novel, since it plasters everyone with a flavorless label until the novelist can remove that first impression of blankness.

Odonism is presented in such a way that the reader accepts it as an admirable system for the semisterile conditions on Annares. One of the delights of the book is to see the system working, notably when under strain during a famine and everyone chips in to help everyone else.

I'm not sure how scientific is the concept of a planet with flora but not fauna; but the scenario is dramatically right for Annares. No birds sing there. When Shevek gets to Urras, he is delighted to hear birds singing. He rejoices in the bounty of nature on the mother planet.

His pleasure fades as he comes to understand the workings of Urras' political systems more clearly and to see that even he is being corrupted by them. Then the birds sing a different tune; what he hears them chirping is "This is my propertee-tee." More and more, Shevek becomes disgusted with himself and the system.

At this point in the novel, a softer intellect than Le Guin's would turn back and show us how the Annarean culture was the preferable one, for all its austerities. Instead, we see through Shevek how Odonism on Annares is weakening and giving way to a more fear-oriented society, where people do what they should because they dread puritanical public opinion. This turning point of disillusion is nicely judged.

The advance to this kind of level of political thinking from the old one (one recalls the implausibly kidnapped politician in Heinlein's *Double Star*) is considerable. Le Guin is much to be congratulated on encompassing two somewhat polar qualities, strong-mindedness and delicacy.

Despite all of which, I found *The Dispossessed* a novel more to admire than actually enjoy. Theory directs characters rather than emerging from them. The result is formidable, yes, memorable, yes, but just a touch arid.

Philip K. Dick's latest novel is far from arid. *Flow My Tears, the Policeman Said* has a new warmth to its portrayal of the central characters—Jason Taverner, the media star who suddenly finds himself in a bleak world that has no place for him; General Buckman, the police chief who believes in the rules and cheats to maintain them, and to maintain himself in a position of power to maintain them; and the women close to the two men: the waiflike Kathy, who does a good job of forging; the simple potter, Mary Ann Dominic; the amorous and weary Ruth Rae; and especially Alys Buckman, the tormented sister and lover of Felix Buckman.

There is an ample cast in *Flow My Tears*, but it is smaller than usual in a Dick novel, its personae less eccentric for eccentricity's sake—which perhaps leaves more room for warmth of portrayal.

Thank heaven, the book marks no radical change from the Dick we know and love. We get, for instance, Cheerful Charlie, the talking toy, and the rare one-dollar stamp that is prized by collectors—Dick always shows a mixture of envy and contempt for collectors, one of whom is here represented as collecting old TV commericals, specializing in plugs for Alka-Seltzer. And of course that old question of what is real, what fake, turns up, worked to potent effect right into the heart of the plot.

What is not radically changed is certainly deepened and developed. The real/fake question is not confined to objects or sensational reversals of life (as in such striking Dick novels as *Martian Time-Slip* and *The Three Stigmata of Palmer Eldrich*, where characters find they are trapped in other people's hallucinations); here the question becomes part of the very life-style of the characters involved.

There is no finer character in any Dick novel than Buckman, the tortured cop. As usual with Dick's heroes, he is a fixer; he supports the status quo against worse things. Things fall apart, the center will not hold—but Dick's guys often die in the attempt to defy such deterioration. Buckman is a deeply flawed man, who fakes for what he conceives to be the general good. He pretends to be a "seven," a genetic mutation that would confer real advantages to him were he one; but the mere pretense of being one confers a genuine advantage when dealing with Taverner, who is a "six."

More subtly, the real/fake question is used to its most telling effect in a touching passage where Buckman, deeply grieved by the news of his sister's death, is persuaded by a henchman, Herb, to fake the reasons for her death to further his own survival. "It froze his blood to find himself thinking of such matters already." But he quickly sketches out a series of credible lies. "I must turn a terrible personal tragedy into an advantage, Buckman realized. Capitalize on the accidental death of my own sister."

Flow My Tears is entertaining and exciting. It is grounded in a highly charged view of contemporary American society, but theory never overrides Dick's power to portray people, incidents, and pictures.

At one point, Taverner thinks, "Betrayal was an everyday event; a refusal to betray, as in his case, was miraculous. . . . We have a betrayal state, he realized. When I was a celebrity I was exempt. Now I'm like everyone else: I now have to face what they've always faced." The novel vividly embodies this concept of corrupt society.

We rejoice that we have writers of the caliber of Le Guin and Dick in our midst. Both have a great range of material and a bold command of it; Le Guin at least is not at the height of her powers. Incidentally, a special issue of *Science Fiction Studies*, published by Indiana State University and editors R. D. Mullen and Darko Suvin, devotes itself to the work of these two authors. Good timing, gentlemen.

So, more briefly, to another pair of novels. Both are by well-known names and seem to me excellent in themselves, as well as an advance in the art of their authors.

Robert Silverberg's *Born with the Dead* (actually three novellas) marks fully the emergence of the new Silverberg, who now lives easily inside the different person he has become. One felt in some previous novels that he was slightly straining for effect or, where not that, deliberately refusing to employ an SF concept fully, in case he might appear to be slipping back into the old Galactic Silverberg (such refusals flaw the otherwise remarkable performance of *Dying Inside*).

In *Born with the Dead*, Silverberg gives us an alternate society which lives within an ordinary terrestrial society: the society of the dead. The dead are revived and live their own lives, often in their own cities, the very names of which have a certain chill—Zion Cold Town, San Diego Cold Town. Jorge Klein's wife is now one of the deads. He pursues her; she is not interested.

"For nine years it had been Jorge and Sybille, Sybille and Jorge. I and thou forming *we*, above all *we*, a transcendental *we*. He had loved her with almost painful intensity. . . . She was a part of him, he of her, and until the moment of her unexpected death he had assumed it would be like that forever."

Now Sybille walks the Earth again, goes hunting with friends in Zanzibar, and will not bother with Jorge. Because Silverberg abstains from producing some plausible account of the actual process whereby deads are revived from total death—and Gavin Watson has recently been offering us ways of concocting such an account—the metaphorical value of the situation comes over to us as well as the purely science-fictional value. This is an enrichment of the order of Dick's and Le Guin's. Jorge has his special fictional problems; he stands also for any man who has lost his wife, whether from death, dereliction, or adultery.

My fourth and last novel may seem a lesser one than the three preceding. Nevertheless, it is always a cause for cheering when an old hand at turning out standard material quietly injects something else and thereby excels himself. This is what James White has done in *The Dream Millennium*.

White likes to get himself out to the galaxy, and here he is again, in one of those giant spaceships making their way from Earth to a colony world with the colonists frozen below hatches. It's a slow ship, and will take a thousand years to reach its destination; during which time, two crew members are roused from cryogenic sleep every century to check that all systems are still go.

The sleepers in their caskets are plagued by bad dreams, shot through with death. Circumstances become bad enough to threaten the success of the mission.

All this is good standard SF fodder, soporific rather than enlivening. And matters are not helped by what seems like palpable neglect of all those interesting contemporary theories of sleep and dream, which might well have been extrapolated a little to enrich the story.

Yet there is much in *The Dream Millennium* to get excited about. White makes it clear from the start that the society being left behind on Earth is a loathsome and depressing one, where the law rests mainly with block-by-block vigilante groups. Society is decaying and the great ship, its off-spawning, also decays. While the colonists and crew lie unaging, the ship slips into senility. White makes of it a beautifully haunted place, still thundering through galactic space with its backup systems on the blink, just like the systems it left behind.

James White lives in Andersonstown, Belfast, Northern Ireland. He knows what he is talking about. His flashbacks to Earth have a gritty gray reality that commands conviction.

As an aside, I reflected again as I closed the novel on the appropriateness of SF as a medium for comment on our present. It would be difficult for White or anyone else to draw a picture of life in Belfast today, producing it as a realistic novel. But as SF, one can be oblique, one need produce only the commanding effects, and throw away the detail. White has certainly produced some commanding effects.

*   *   *

To my mind, these four novels alone, each with its marked individual qualities, each delineating an aspect of society, are enough to make this a vintage year.

I might point out that 1974 was also rounded off by the publication (in the U.S.) of compiler Donald Tuck's *Encyclopaedia of Science Fiction and Fantasy,* or at least of Volume I of this large work. Congratulations to Tuck and Advent, Chicago, who have published so many useful books for science-fiction readers.

In the U.K., editor Anthony Frewin has just published a seductive book entitled *One Hundred Years of Science Fiction Illustration.* It, together with the French-published *Hier, L'An 2000,* edited by Jacques Sadoul, at last presents the general reader with some notion of the wealth of science-fiction illustration which has accumulated unknown to all but devotees. As SF itself has won a wider public, thanks to the perseverance of a handful of authors, so we may hope that the merits of artists like Frank R. Paul, Dold, Rogers, Schneeman, and many others will finally be recognized by the world at large.